What Reviewers

"Readers who see ....g from a mystery format will find *Johnson Road* is more aptly described as a story incorporating the undertones of a murder mystery with the psychological depth typical of many a novel. For this reason, it's a recommendation for both novel readers and mystery fans - and the latter audience should be prepared for far more than the usual 'whodunnit'." (5 Stars) *Diane Donavan, Senior Reviewer, Midwest Book Reviews*

"I just didn't want to stop until I'd read the whole thing. Recommend the book to those that enjoy a good thriller that is dark and unpredictable." (5 stars) *C. Middleton, Goodreads*

"You have small town Americana, weird occurrences, disappearances, abduction, mysteries, deaths... nothing is as it seems and the events are crazy terrible." (5 stars) *J. Brewster, Indie Book Reviewers*

"I didn't expect to be so sucked into this world that Mr. Spriggs created as I was. ...there is so much mystery and intrigue that you can't help but want to keep reading more and more." (4-5 stars) *B. Maxwell, Goodreads*

"Johnson Road is one of the most creepy, original, and well-crafted novels I've read in a long time! Can see fans of Steven King loving this one." (4 stars) *A. Johnson, Shelfari*

What Reviewers Are Saying...

"...you won't want to stop reading until you've finished it all!! Crazy, twisted, thriller that will appeal to fans of the genre." (4 stars) *T. Parks, Indie Book Reviewers*

"Johnson Road is one of the most original and just flat out interesting mystery/thriller suspense novels I've ever read. ...a great book that will stay with me for a long time." (4 stars) *S. Decker, Shelfari*

This book is dedicated to

Wayne Joseph Cowan
July 23, 1963 – January 30, 2012

I miss you every day.

Soon the child learns that there are strangers,

and ceases to be a child.

Max Müller

Prologue
April 24, 1963: 4:17 pm

Something was wrong. He couldn't explain it. He couldn't point it out, but he could feel it in his gut. The local authorities were gathered near their haphazardly-parked squad cars, looking official and concerned, but Robert knew this was all for show. The detective realized that none of the local deputies or state troopers suspected foul play. He was doubtful that any of them would know what to do about it if they were wrong. Sure, they all wanted to do their job, but they just weren't equipped or trained to do it effectively. All the same, the men needed their positions and their paychecks. Robert understood how they felt. He'd been there once himself.

There wasn't much difference between the deputies and the state troopers. On the outside, you could tell them apart. The troopers had that air of experience and 'gravitas' that they'd worked hard to acquire and even harder to exhibit, and, of course, those hats. Their presence that day ensured the sheriff's deputies maintained a degree of professional decorum. Monkey see, monkey do, Robert mused.

Detective Robert Stallworth had worked hard to get where he was, but it wasn't just hard work that had made him successful – it was instinct. He didn't know why he had those gut feelings that served him so well, but he knew not to ignore them. His gut was screaming at him now, and he wasn't about to let it go.

Poking around in the dirt on the ground with his boot, Robert detected what he thought was a slight difference in texture in the shaded spot under the big oak halfway down the ravine. When his men saw him crouching down, they knew what was coming next.

"Get the shovels. We'll dig here," Robert shouted.

The troopers were already on their way, knowing the detective's MO and reputation for finding dead things. The local deputies' initial reaction was familiar to Robert – something between incomprehension and disbelief; like a herd of cows seeing a running tractor for the first time. Taking their cue from the state troopers, the deputies quickly followed suit, trying to assume a show of competency, despite the obvious reluctance of the local sheriff.

"Now now, Detective, just what do you expect to find?" bellowed Sheriff Clifford Gaskin, a good ole boy who wasn't about to let these outsiders disrespect his position.

Robert ignored the sheriff's question as he stared at the ground beneath his feet, trying to mentally size up the exact parameters of the imminent dig. The troopers returned with the shovels, and started to dig.

Sheriff Gaskin started to repeat his question, but thought twice about it. He didn't want to be shown up in front of his boys in the event something important was unearthed, so he decided it wasn't in his best interest to voice any more opposition at this point. After a couple of seconds, the sheriff climbed down to where the men were gathering to get a closer look.

"Don't just stand there, boys, dig in," he instructed his two closest deputies, with a grandiose show of authority.

Clifford hadn't become sheriff by accident, nor by hard work, but by the hard work of others and enough sense to tag along. He was hedging his bets. If there was success – he would share in the praise. If there wasn't – he'd already stated his doubts. No one could claim he wasn't a team player.

As the shovels tore deeper and deeper into the mud, with nothing coming up but dirt and roots, it appeared as though Sheriff Gaskin had been right all along. As each scoop was torn from the ground with no results, the men began to hesitate, but Detective Stallworth's gaze never wavered. Given his Zen-like focus, there was no misunderstanding. The digging wasn't over.

When it seemed that even the detective might abandon the quest, a slight discoloration appeared in the deeper soil. It looked as if some sort of white powder had been mixed in with the dark, moist earth. Observing the sudden find, everyone present thought the same thing – quicklime.

Minutes later, a white rounded object became visible against the black muck. The men set their shovels aside and brushed gently through the soil until the object unearthed. A hush enveloped the group as they gazed down into the dank hole and its grisly contents.

The deputies looked at the state troopers, who looked toward the detective. Robert's eyes met the sheriff's for a moment, and the two men let out a faint sigh in unison before returning their attention to the sight at their feet.

The men silently stared at the macabre item. Each man present would feel the sting of guilt as the terrible vision disturbed his slumber in the years that followed – the haunting image of a human skull, gazing unseeing into the empty sky, seeking justice long denied.

Chapter One
Sixteen years earlier

The property was secluded. Consisting of a few acres reaching out from Riverside Highway, the land eventually dropped into a steep ravine with a small stream at the bottom. Forested mostly with oak and pine, with a few birch and pecan trees thrown in for good measure, the land was unremarkable with one exception – it was cheap. Purvis Johnson didn't have much in the way of wealth; no cash on hand, savings in the bank, or even gainful employment – just the land.

Since his time in the service, Purvis was unable to motivate himself long enough to sustain even a modest income. His meager disability payments were only minimally improved by sporadic paychecks, too few and far between to allow anything in the way of savings. Luckily, he'd managed to hold on to what little he had inherited from his late mother's estate, although that wouldn't stretch very far. He'd used most of the money to purchase the land. There wasn't much left over for the construction of a house, but he managed to scrape together enough to build himself a modest abode. It was a cottage with just enough space for a quiet man whose only desire was for solitude. As it turned out, solitude is never truly desirable for any length of time, and even harder to maintain.

The house, which could be described more accurately as a shack, was almost invisible from the highway. It was in a constant state of disrepair since the construction was never completed. A small dirt road served as a driveway back to the end of the property. If not for the mailbox at the entrance to the road, most motorists would pass by without ever knowing there was anything hidden amongst the shadows. Even the locals seemed unaware of the house's presence, or of its inhabitant.

Purvis was as motivated in fixing up his surroundings as he was in living life in general. Sometimes he wondered if he'd always lacked motivation, but he seemed to remember a time when he had looked forward to his future with anticipation. He admitted to himself that he was never particularly ambitious, but, at least at one time, he had hopes and dreams. He wished he could remember what they were.

Purvis knew when his attitude had changed, although he couldn't pinpoint an exact moment or event that precipitated it. He only knew that it was when he died, at least on the inside. He vaguely remembered the boredom and the constant underlying fear interrupted by moments of sheer terror that he'd experienced during the war. He never recollected more than small flashes, and didn't want to. The nightmares came regularly, but he repressed most of his daytime memories. In the process, he repressed most of his life.

He had enlisted with patriotic fervor when he came of age. Corporal Johnson had served admirably under the worst of conditions, but became a casualty of the madness of war. The ghost of Purvis Johnson had returned home from the war in the shape of a man with the name of a boy who had disappeared amongst the nameless corpses in a far-away place with an unpronounceable name – a place more commonly known as hell.

He may have felt like a ghost, but there came a time when he could no longer deny that he was a man. Despite his need for seclusion, the undeniable force of human nature drove him to seek the company of others. He found himself lingering a little longer at the local market when shopping for his groceries and other supplies. His nods to the other shoppers grew into greetings, and soon he began to engage in occasional meaningless conversation about the weather. Before long, he was making sporadic visits to Lil' Ray's, the local watering hole, and nursing a drink or two in the company of others. Not one for conversation, he generally sat by himself, though he sometimes graduated to muttering a word or two to one of the barstool jockeys who sat near him.

Lil' Ray's was a hangout where locals could come for beer, music, and bait, providing that they weren't too particular about the quality of any of it. Located a few miles up the road from Purvis's house, this long-standing establishment resembled the hundreds of little honky-tonks and highway bars found throughout the South. Cracked and dry-rotted floorboards, cheap wooden siding walls in need of paint, and neon beer signs gave the dingy room the ambiance of an abandoned country hangout in long need of demolition.

The proud proprietor of this fine establishment could never be described as being 'little', nor was he named Ray. In fact, the morbidly obese bearded gentleman went by the name of Bubba. Fat Bubba's seemed a little clichéd even for this backwoods address. Lil' Ray's was the moniker of the bar long before Bubba ever set foot in the door, so the name stuck, along with the décor.

The jukebox, which worked sporadically at best, sported an array of country songs even the eldest customers could recognize. The cigarette machine sitting in the corner was equally antiquated; the freshness of its contents always questionable. A lone pool table stood along the back wall, drink stains and cigarette burns attesting to its misuse. No one could remember the last time bait was actually purchased at Lil' Ray's.

Lil' Ray's maintained its backwoods theme for the benefit of what could best be described as its trailer-park clientele. Once the final ingredient, the bar's personnel, was added to the mix, only then was the desired ambiance obtained. There was, of course, Bubba, who tended bar or barked orders at the staff when he wasn't distracted by his buddies or the endless loop of whatever sporting event was playing on the television above the cooler.

Sweeping the floors, cleaning the bathrooms, and tending to the odd general repairs fell to Danny Boy. Danny Boy was fifty-seven, though most thought him to be well into his eighties. A life of menial labor, hard drinking, chain-smoking, and bad luck had taken its toll on Danny, and it showed. Standing just under six feet, he looked shorter, given the hunched over posture he exhibited. Always on the thin side, his lack of an adequate diet, along with a life-long relationship with beer and hard liquor, contributed to his malnourished appearance. A cigarette was always hanging from his lips; the smoke obstructing his already poor vision could explain his lack of thoroughness in his janitorial duties.

The truth, however, was that Danny had never put much value in a job well done. He figured he'd gotten this far without expending any real effort, so there wasn't any incentive to change now. Danny's hearing was quite acute, although he did suffer from a serious case of selective hearing loss. Most people contributed his hearing problems to his suspected old age and poor health, and Danny Boy was more than happy to play the part.

The 'belle of the ball' at Lil' Ray's was Susan Brennan, better known as Sweet Sue. Officially the barmaid, Sue did everything that needed doing; including tending the bar, bussing the tables, and making small talk that kept the regulars relaxed.

Born and raised in the area, her story was known by all. Sue had married Jimmy Magee, her high school sweetheart, and soon gave birth to a son. Unfortunately, not long after her child's birth, Sue felt the sting of abandonment and faced the trials and tribulations of single motherhood. It seemed her sweetheart turned husband turned ex-husband had managed to not-so-secretly juggle more than one woman in his life, and Jimmy Magee had elected to run off with the woman in his life that he wasn't married to and with whom he didn't have children.

Sue felt that she should've known better all along. When she looked back at their marriage, she had to admit that the relationship was lacking in almost every category. Still, she was shocked when Jimmy didn't return home from a beer-run one afternoon. She reported him missing to the sheriff's office the next day, but when she saw their hesitant reactions, her heart sank. Once a call or two was made to confirm the obvious, Sue became the second to last person in the county to know the truth. It fell to her to inform the last person – her son. Sue broke the bad news to little Jimmy later that night, which proved to be a difficult task and one she remained bitter about for years.

After a few short-term relationships, painful broken promises, and downgrades in her standard of living, Sweet Sue learned how to fend for herself and provide for her son. She secured a position at Lil' Ray's, and she soon discovered how to handle the countless come-ons by its customers. Experience taught her to navigate that fine line between flirtation and rejection, and Sue handled it like a pro. She had to; after all, a good portion of her income came from tips.

When the weight of loneliness bore down on her, she gave in to an occasional intimate encounter. Managing such encounters wasn't always easy, or without drama. By now, Sue had learned to keep enough distance so there wasn't too much turf to transverse when it was time to retreat.

Her latest partner was Harry Lejuine, an electrician who sometimes frequented Lil' Ray's for an after-work beer or two. Although he'd been coming in off and on for years, Harry hadn't made many overt moves toward the barmaid beyond a little light flirtation. This was mostly because he had a wife and three children at home, eagerly awaiting his arrival from work.

Sue would never have considered giving a married man the time of day, much less sharing her bed with one, until one night in June. Harry came in for his usual after-work refreshments, but, this time, he stayed way past happy hour and drank a couple of long-necks over his limit. As his brain cells swam in the ever-increasing pool of fermented barley and hops, Harry's newly enhanced visual acuity allowed him to see Sweet Sue in a new light.

Harry grew bolder as the evening advanced, and he poured on the charm. At least, that's how he saw it. Sue could see where this was headed early on, and she reminded Harry of the late hour and his responsibilities at home, thinking that would be that. Harry then informed her that his wife had taken the kids to Arkansas to visit her father, who was gravely ill. It was a shame that he wasn't able to go with them, he explained somberly, since he didn't think his father-in-law's prognosis looked good, but he had obligations and responsibilities that required his presence at home. Harry explained his unfortunate situation with as much sincerity as he could muster.

Sue just bit her tongue to keep from appropriately responding to such obvious nonsense.

As the night wore on, Sue admitted that the idea of Harry's warm body in her bed sounded preferable to sleeping alone. At the end of her shift, she volunteered to be the designated driver and ferry the drunken Harry home. The two of them enjoyed their intimate encounter that night without any expectations or empty promises about the future.

Since then, they'd managed a discreet hook-up now and then, although not often enough to cure her loneliness or his horniness. The only thing it did accomplish was providing Sue with a small amount of pleasure, followed by a larger amount of guilt. Still, Sue rationalized, it kept her out of trouble.

As Sue and Harry's rendezvous became more infrequent, she admitted to herself that she should pursue a more stable and legitimate relationship. After all, she had her son to look after as well as herself, and she wasn't getting any younger. Sue was aware that she wasn't getting any richer either and that scraping by from week-to-week to provide shelter and food was taking its toll. Her survival instincts kicked in, and she found herself sizing up her customers, mentally noting their attributes and drawbacks.

It was about this time that a quiet loner, who drifted in from time to time, caught her eye. He wasn't much to look at and didn't appear to have much in the way of wealth, but he seemed nice enough, and, most importantly, he wasn't married. Purvis, or something like that, was his name. Weird name, she thought, but it was better than Bubba or anyone named Magee.

Over the next few months, Sweet Sue chatted with Purvis, and he reciprocated. Gradually coming out of his shell, Purvis found himself at ease with Sue. It wasn't long before the conversations moved from general topics to more personal matters.

Although Purvis was by nature a quiet and reserved man, he began to open up and show a more personable side of himself. Pretty soon, he became more gregarious with everyone. He found himself socializing with the rest of the crowd at the bar.

Sue noticed this change, and she was pleased that she could be a positive influence on someone to whom she was attracted. She admitted that Purvis was having an effect on her as well. She began to feel more content and less desperate. Sue hadn't felt this way for a long time. He had ignited a spark in her and left her wanting more.

No one could say for sure when the chatting became flirting, or when they became more than friends. There had been no official dates. All the same, they found themselves on the fringe of a relationship, with the progression toward intimacy all but inevitable.

Purvis was as unmotivated and nonaggressive in regard to Sue as he was with life in general, and she could see a push was in order to get things moving to the next level. Before long, that push was provided by outward circumstances neither one of them could foresee.

It was two weeks before Christmas when Sue came into the bar, visibly upset.

"I'm losing my apartment," she muttered, trying to hold back tears.

"What?" asked Purvis.

"My landlord, Mark, decided to sell the apartment building I live in. I have to be out by the end of the month. What am I going to do?" She broke down in tears, "I have nowhere to go. What about Jimmy? This is the worst Christmas ever!"

"It's going to be okay. I'm sure something will work out."

"Yeah, I know. I just don't want to do this all over again."

She looked down, her shoulders drooping, a tissue clutched tightly in her hand as she sighed and choked back the tears. Purvis felt his stomach turn, but he didn't know what to say. He knew he had to say something, do something; he just didn't know what. The silence grew, and he could feel a distance between them creeping in – a distance he didn't like.

"Do what all over again?" he managed to ask.

Sue looked at Purvis, and their eyes met for a moment before she dropped her gaze.

In a flat voice, she answered, "Move in with a guy I used to date – Tommy. He offered us a place to stay until I get on my feet again, but I never thought it would come to this. If I stay there, I....," her voice trailed off.

She didn't need to finish; Purvis knew what it meant. He felt his insides burning, his heart racing, but he managed to hide his feelings. He was used to bottling up his emotions. Purvis remained silent, allowing Sue to continue, all the while, his mind was racing, considering his next move.

"I have no money, no savings. I have nowhere else to go," she sobbed. "What am I going to do?"

Her tears fell from her closed eyes and rolled down her cheeks. Purvis sat unmoving, frozen in his indecisiveness. He knew things were bound to come to this one day. All the same, he was unprepared. Did he really want to be alone anymore? He knew he didn't. How could he allow Sue to go off with Tommy now? It would eat at him forever. Purvis knew he would have to do something, but he hated it when he had to act. Those were the moments in his past that led to the nightmares later.

"You and Jimmy could stay with me," Purvis feebly replied.

Sue sat quiet for a moment; then she looked into Purvis's eyes.

"Thanks for your offer, but we both know you don't want that. I know you're just trying to be nice and all, but I have a six year old boy at home. We're a handful, even for a nice guy like you. I can't do this to you. Don't worry, I'll be okay."

Purvis would have none of it. It may have taken him awhile to stand up to the plate, but, as slow as he was to get there, he was even slower to step back.

"I'm not worried, and you'll be okay because you'll be with me," he said emphatically. "You'll both be with me. I have a house, a small house I admit, but my own house. I have a good bit of land around it, and there's plenty of room for a growing boy."

He took her hands in his, and looked into her eyes. Sue could see he wasn't going to take no for an answer, and her heart began to beat loudly in her chest. A minute ago, she'd felt as bad as she'd ever felt since her ex-husband went out for beer and didn't come back. Now, she was happier than she'd been in a long time.

She took a deep breath, told herself not to get her hopes up, but, for reasons she couldn't comprehend, it felt different this time. It felt like this time she might finally have found a home for herself and her son.

It didn't take long after Sue and Jimmy moved in with Purvis until it became obvious that they were there to stay. Purvis didn't mind one bit. The platonic friendship they shared quickly became an intimate one, to their mutual delight. Purvis joked that now he knew why they called her 'Sweet' Sue; she slyly winked back with a naughty look and replied that things could always get sweeter.

It was the first time in a long time either one of them could say they were happy, and it showed. He gave her a silver necklace with a heart-shaped locket attached – an inexpensive token of his affection for her. Sue placed a tiny picture of little Jimmy inside the locket, and it never left its place around her neck.

After awhile, Sue cut back her hours at work and Purvis was almost never to be found at Lil' Ray's. The nights Sue would work, he was at home, spending time with her son. The Sundays spent over beer and football at Lil' Ray's were replaced by weekly visits to the First Baptist Church over on Rattlesnake Ridge. Along with their new found social respectability came the time to make their living situation legitimate.

The wedding was held on a muggy Saturday afternoon in May. With only a few fellow parishioners and Pastor Greg's sizable brood in attendance, the happy couple exchanged vows in a quiet ceremony, with little Jimmy bearing the rings.

Not much money was left over for a honeymoon, so Mr. and Mrs. Johnson accepted the pastor's wife's offer to watch over Jimmy on their wedding night so the newlyweds could be alone. They had a big house anyhow, the pastor's wife explained, and, with six children already, one more wouldn't be a problem.

One night alone in their tiny shack at the end of that dirt road was all that the couple had to start their lives together. It would have to do. With all of the anticipation of a wedding night and the effort in arranging a sleep-over for Jimmy, they were bound to be a little disappointed. Not that their wedding night was terrible, but once the initial excitement had worn off, neither one could claim that the experience was extraordinary.

Purvis put about as much effort into their sex life as he did everything else, and his lack of enthusiasm didn't sit well with Sue. His endless tossing and turning, with his occasional screaming outburst in his sleep, didn't help, either. The result was that they were both tired during the daytime, and they almost dreaded nighttime. Still, they both were better off than they had been. Purvis had a family; Sue and little Jimmy had a home.

As time wore on, little Jimmy grew to be not so little, and the quaint cottage they all shared seemed to get smaller by the day. The once grateful Sue became increasingly irritated by Purvis's lack of motivation and ambition, and her inability to change his ways amplified her frustration over the situation, and it began to show.

As the years passed, the region around their homestead began to grow. New neighborhoods, new businesses, and new opportunities arose. As Sue saw it, the problem was that Purvis refused to grow at all. He seemed incapable of pursuing any means of gainful employment, and as their house dwindled in living space, their bills and property taxes escalated. Something had to give.

Their once-civil discussions concerning the household budget developed into heated arguments, with no hope of resolution. Fortunately, a reprieve presented itself with a knock on the door. A local homebuilder was interested in buying their land. The company had been purchasing properties around the area and dividing them up into individual home sites. Once the lots were divided up, they would contract to build the homes, thus, creating subdivisions, neighborhoods, and a sizable profit.

Unfortunately for Sue and the builder, Purvis exhibited little interest in the idea of selling his land. He exclaimed that he would rather die in his little shack than part ways with it, and she knew he wouldn't budge. Finally, when faced with losing it to the Internal Revenue Service, Purvis relented – with one stipulation. He would agree to sell most of his property, but retain a half-acre plot on which his house stood. He would sell the remaining acres to the developer to build a subdivision.

Before long, that long dirt driveway stretching from Riverside Highway to Purvis's house became a smooth paved road called Johnson Road. On either side of the road, the land was subdivided and became single-family dwellings and homes for new inhabitants.

This was the American dream, now available to the working class. Dreams come in all forms, interpreted solely by the individual dreamer. For some, however, dreams become nightmares.

*

April 24, 1963: 3:32 pm

Sheriff Gaskin was drifting off to sleep when his head quickly popped up. His police cruiser was parked in front of Lil' Ray's, just off the highway where the oncoming traffic wouldn't see him until it was too late. This was his favorite stake-out spot on the odd times he could get away from the station by himself and away from being harassed by the endless stream of nonsense that came with his job.

Besides having a prime view of vehicles that were almost always speeding down the highway, his vantage point afforded him the opportunity to disrupt the schedules of the bar's clientele. To the sheriff's amusement, the local alcoholics were virtually trapped inside of the run-down honky-tonk as long as he was parked outside. Clifford had no sympathy. As far as the sheriff was concerned, they had no business getting trashed in the middle of the day, only to go barreling down the road three-sheets-to-the-wind, endangering the lives of everyone they passed.

There was a time when Clifford was cognizant of the fact that he possessed a little bit of a mean streak. However, after spending several years as sheriff, he'd lost almost all sense of self-awareness. He'd always been a bully with a power trip, but as sheriff, he felt his actions were completely justified. After all, he was the good guy, or, at least, that's what he told himself.

The big man shifted his weight and stretched to wake himself up. It would be embarrassing if anyone caught him napping in such a public place. It was extremely doubtful that anyone would ever mention such an occurrence to his face, much less confront him with it, but the sheriff knew that small talk and gossip behind his back would erode much of the intimidation he mistook for respect that he'd worked hard over the years to foster.

Glancing over at Lil' Ray's, he observed Danny Boy working around the side of the run-down establishment. The old yokel was haphazardly spraying down some grungy bar mats with a garden hose and, in the process, making a complete mess. The ridiculous sight reminded Clifford of a scene from a Charlie Chaplin silent movie; that is, if Chaplin had been mentally retarded.

"Moron," he muttered to himself with a chuckle.

Suddenly, a convoy of state troopers streamed down the highway in front of the sheriff's car, and they were moving with a purpose. Three, four, five official cruisers blew past him. There were no lights flashing or sirens blaring, although clearly they were going somewhere on official business. He bolted straight up in his seat, caught totally by surprise. The sheriff had heard no calls on his police radio that would explain this unexpected event.

"What the hell?" he spit out with indignation.

This was his county, Goddamn it, and he expected, no – demanded – respect. Whatever those troopers were up to was as much his business as it was theirs, if not more. He reckoned he would just have to remind them of that in person, so he threw his cruiser in drive and hit the gas. Clifford snatched up the receiver of the police radio as he raced out of the parking lot, his tires flinging shells and dust into the air.

"Mabel, Gaskin here. Ten-twenty: Moving south down Riverside just past Ray's. Give me some company down here ASAP. Ten-ninety-eight: Johnson Road."

Clifford was calling up his minions; he wasn't about to be outnumbered by the troopers on his own turf. Whatever was up, he and his boys weren't about to take a back seat to those glory hounds.

Chapter Two

Jake and Mary Bickman had only been married a short time, just over two years, but they'd already been together much too long. To those who barely knew them, the couple appeared to be a happy pair and attentive to each other's needs. The few people who knew them well didn't share this illusion. There was little doubt that trouble was ever present and danger always lurking beneath the surface.

Mary thought Jake was insecure, way too jealous, and extremely possessive. She felt smothered and scared. He watched her every move. Even the smallest subtle impropriety, whether real or imagined, would result in an outpouring of abuse, usually verbal, although occasionally physical. Mary learned quickly to hide the bruises, either with heavy makeup or reports of migraines or other maladies that would confine her indoors for days. Over time, she adjusted and evolved, yet the endless minefield that she had to navigate was ever present. She was tired, worn out, and longing for more – or less, as it were.

As far as Jake was concerned, he was the martyr. He worked long and hard to provide for their growing family. What little appreciation he received for his troubles was given with, what he considered to be, a lack of enthusiasm. Jake felt pressured to do better, bring home more, and remain upwardly mobile, or he would lose it all.

It may not have ever been spoken, but he could feel it in his bones that his wife could not be trusted. She would leave him if she had a better offer, he reasoned. He knew he had to come down a little hard to keep things in order, but he deemed it necessary for the sake of his family.

Jack was their first child, born just long enough after the nuptials to keep the whispers to a minimum. Frank came along the next year, raising a few unspoken questions in Jake's mind that had lingered ever since. As much as he tried to put his suspicions out of his mind, he couldn't shake his doubts. Jake found himself repeatedly doing the math in his head, but the results were always inconclusive. The seeds of doubt had been sown, and no matter how much he tried to set aside his suspicions, those seeds had sprung roots.

Even though Jake's doubts about his younger son's parentage often haunted him, it was the one question he never voiced aloud. He tried to think of anyone who could be a possible alternative as his son's father, but always came up empty. Still, he had to stop himself from examining the boy's features a little too closely from time to time, and he tried to not let his doubts affect his behavior toward the child.

The Bickmans lived in a trailer owned by one of Jake's uncles, not far from the body shop where he worked. The rent was cheap, but the place was small, and the couple agreed that it was time to take that first step into home ownership. Jake had been working hard and Mary had put away as much as she could manage from their meager earnings to make a down payment on the American dream.

New housing developments were sprouting up overnight in a frenzied attempt to cash in on the rising tide of a strong middle class. With all of the incentives and discounts being offered by the fierce competition amongst builders and mortgage brokers, the time to make their first purchase was at hand.

Mary and Jake began shopping around town, eyeing all of the available real estate. At first, they looked at a few older properties, but most were in need of a lot of repair. They widened their search to include some of the new developments, although most of these were out of the range of their meager budget.

As the couple looked farther and farther from their current home, they became discouraged. It seemed that nothing was quite what they were looking for, and every time they returned from their search to face their current residence, the more they hated it. It hadn't been too long ago that they'd been happy to move there, happy they had a place to themselves. Now, all they saw was a run-down mobile home on somebody else's land.

It seemed like a long shot the day they ventured out past the old fire station and drove what felt like twenty miles down Riverside Highway to meet their realtor, Barney. Barney Spencer was an up and coming real estate agent, short on experience, but full of ambition and drive. He wanted badly to succeed in business and have a job he could be proud of. He wore a tie, and that alone gave him a sense of accomplishment. He was a businessman, and to Barney, that was like being a doctor, lawyer, or senator. The memory of his childhood and the thought of his young family having to live in the same manner that he'd once lived made Barney sick to his stomach.

He'd been raised the son of a sharecropper. He had seven brothers and sisters, at least counting the ones who made it past infancy. His father was barely literate, and this embarrassed Barney his whole life. He felt he was destined for more, and he sought every opportunity to run as far away from his roots as he could. He understood too well what true poverty meant, and he had no intention of ever going back.

The Bickmans agreed to meet Barney at the new property. Barney was desperate to make the sale; the Bickmans were desperate to find a home. The entire endeavor almost didn't happen because Jake and Mary initially passed up the little road and drove miles farther from their intended destination.

As Barney waited at the new showing, he started to think they weren't coming at all. He had shown at least a dozen houses to the couple, and nothing was ever right. The agent could sense their frustration, and was afraid that soon they'd move on without him.

He needed this sale, needed the commission, and was running out of options for the buyers. He'd put a lot of time and energy in this house search, and the prospect of failure at this point motivated him to push his options. He exhaled a sigh of relief when he saw the Bickman's Oldsmobile turn into Johnson Road and coast to a slow stop in front of him. Barney flicked his cigarette onto the fresh pavement, ground the butt with the heel of his Florsheim Oxfords, steadied his nerves, and pasted his practiced smile on his face.

"Good afternoon," he cheerfully exclaimed as he approached the couple.

He offered Jake a firm, businessman handshake, briefly nodded to Mary, and then quickly returned his gaze to Jake. Barney sensed early on Jake's possessiveness of Mary and her barely concealed trepidation whenever he paid any attention to her, so he tried his best to navigate that tightrope. To Barney, it was all about the sale, and he didn't want to blow it by doing anything stupid, even if stupid meant merely acknowledging the woman's presence.

"We passed this place right up," explained Jake, nodding his head toward the newly constructed house. "It's a lot farther out here than I thought it would be."

"I guess it all depends on where you're coming from and where you're going. If you move here, everything else will seem far away," Barney replied, trying his best to downplay the remoteness of the new subdivision.

Jake remained silent, letting Barney know that his argument hadn't been very effective and trying to maintain the leverage he felt he had in a potential deal. Mary shifted her stance slightly, doing her best to appear aloof and neutral, although inwardly she was excited at the idea of inspecting the new house.

"Well, we drove all the way out here. We might as well have a look-see," Jake eventually muttered.

The three nodded in silent agreement, then made their way up the freshly paved walkway toward the newly-constructed house.

"This house was just completed a week ago, according to the builder," Barney informed the couple. "I talked to him yesterday and he said that he doesn't expect it to be vacant for very long."

The realtor let that sink in while he fiddled for the keys to the front door.

"How many houses are they building on this street?" Jake asked, glancing down the small road.

There were two other dwellings nearing completion, one on the same side of the street, two lots down from the one they were looking at, and the other one across the street. Three slabs had already been poured and at least a half dozen other lots had been staked out.

"I'm not rightly sure, but I doubt any more than ten or twelve," answered Barney, looking up and down the road. "It's just the one street right here, so there aren't too many that can fit. The good thing is that they will all be new homes, built for growing families. A great place to raise kids without worrying about crime or the wrong kind of people living next to you."

In the South, everyone understood what that meant, and no elaboration or further comment was necessary.

"Who lives in that odd shack down there?" Mary inquired, pointing to a small dilapidated cottage hidden in the overgrowth at the end of the road. "It looks like it's facing the wrong way."

"I'm sure that was here before the road," Barney replied. "The bulldozers must have missed it, behind all of those trees. I doubt it will be here long."

He turned the key in the lock, opened the front door, and moved the couple inside as rapidly as he could before any further uncomfortable questions could arise.

The house was everything Jake and Mary were looking for. The exterior colors glimmered brightly against the newly planted green sod. The freshly painted interior smelled like heaven to the couple who'd been living in the tiny, aged, and moldy trailer for two years. This house had three bedrooms, two bathrooms, a nice kitchen and dining area, a living room, and even a decent sized back yard. The pair could envision their growing family enjoying life in that house just as they'd always imagined.

The Bickmans tried their best to hold their excitement in check. Things never really worked out well for them, and neither one of them wanted to get their hopes up. The boom was sure to fall, and their anticipated disappointment began to grow inside of them both.

"What's the asking price?" Jake cautiously asked.

"Not as much as you'd think, considering the new construction and generous amenities." Barney began his spiel. "It's listed at ten thousand, but that's with very little in the way of a down payment. If you can manage a better down payment, I'm sure we can use that as leverage to negotiate a better price and, more importantly, a lower monthly note."

The couple looked at each other hesitantly. The asking price was more than they could safely afford, given their meager budget, but not by much.

"I don't think we can manage much more in the way of a down payment," replied Jake. "It's a little more than we were expecting to pay."

"Well, if you really like it, maybe you should take a day or two to think about it. I'm not sure how long this particular property will be available, but more houses will be built, and, of course, there are older houses around. It may take awhile, but I'm sure something will come up. In the meantime, you might be able to save more money for a bigger down payment, which will help you find a home with a smaller mortgage."

Barney knew he had them on the hook by the look in their eyes. It might take a small adjustment to their current budget, but he was sure they would qualify for a loan and he could make the sale go through. Once they set foot back in their old, dingy trailer, they'd be begging him to show them another house like this one.

"I'll tell you what, if y'all really like this house, and are prepared to move on it quickly, I'm sure I could probably get the builder to come down a little bit on the price. I doubt if he'll reduce it much without a better down payment, but if we make a reasonable offer, I think he'll accept it. He's going to make plenty off of the rest of these houses, and the sooner nice families like yours move into the neighborhood, the better those houses will look."

The couple stared at each other in silence, trying to read the other's thoughts while, at the same time, figuring out the complicated math of their budget in their heads.

"If y'all want, I can step outside and have a smoke to give you two a chance to talk about it in private," he offered. "Go ahead, walk around the house some more and decide if this is really what the two of you are looking for."

By the time the heel of Barney's Oxfords extinguished the last sparks of his Marlboro, the Bickmans were on their way to buying their first home, and he was on his way to making another sale. There were a few more hurdles to overcome and more bargaining and maneuvering as there always is with the purchase of a home, but it wouldn't be long before Barney was picking up the For Sale sign and Jake and Mary were putting down roots.

Not counting the oddly misplaced shack that the Johnsons called home, the Bickman's home was the first house occupied on Johnson Road. In no time, more houses were built, more people moved in, and the new subdivision off of Riverside Highway became what the builder, realtors, and mortgage companies advertised – the perfect place to raise a family.

*

April 24, 1963: 3:05 pm

Robert was missing something, but he couldn't figure out what it was. His gut-feelings were usually more focused, enabling him to act upon them decisively. The problem this time was that his intuition lacked direction. The detective couldn't pinpoint when exactly the gnawing in his stomach had begun. It had started gradually as a nagging feeling that he'd forgotten something. When the feeling wouldn't go away, he started to think that whatever it was he'd forgotten might be something important. Unfortunately, he couldn't remember what it was.

As he drove his unmarked cruiser through the narrow streets of Old Town, his mind reviewed the events of the past couple of weeks, hoping that something would jog his memory. Old Town was just that, the oldest part of their little community, and was centered round a town square, which could best be described as a small green area surrounded by mom-and-pop stores that had been there forever. There was a hardware store, drug store, soda-shop, second-hand furniture store, and diner where Robert ate lunch most days, but not today. His memory lapse seemed to have taken away his appetite.

Sitting at a red light at the corner of Fourth and Pine Streets, waiting for the light to change, he ran through a list of places he'd been to recently and the people he'd spoken with, hoping to jog his memory, but to no avail. The sharp burst of a car horn behind him brought him back to the present. Noticing that the light had changed, he took a left turn and drove slowly down the road, trying to concentrate more on his driving.

When his car approached the school zone near Oakdale Elementary School, he found himself caught up in the slow moving traffic that always occurred around dismissal time. Between the school buses coming and going, the parents that chose to pick up their children themselves, and the walkers and bike-riders making their way slowly down the sidewalks, there was no way to get around the delay. Robert didn't mind today. It gave him more time to probe his memory for that missing piece that had him so frustrated.

He glanced at an old woman who was scolding an unfortunate boy for some unknown transgression. The boy's face looked like a mixture of 'oh shit' and 'I really don't care' thought Robert, and he couldn't help but crack a smile. He'd been one of those boys himself when he was that age. He was relieved when the old woman turned away from the boy to attend to some other unpleasant task and the boy hurried away, happy to be free.

Out of his driver's side window, he noticed the crossing guard on the corner, keeping the children back on the sidewalk, so that the vehicular traffic could move. The guard was an older heavy-set man with a scruffy beard. Judging by appearances alone, he was probably the last person you would want in close proximity to your children, Robert mused. Actually, he thought, the guard vaguely resembled Sheriff Gaskin. The sheriff wasn't someone Robert figured you'd really want around your children either.. The detective chuckled at that thought as he waited for the children to cross the street.

An unexpected feeling suddenly arose inside him when he thought of the sheriff. Yes, that was it! Whatever was buried in his subconscious had something to do with the sheriff. As the children passed in front of his car, Robert's mind methodically examined the last few times he'd seen Sheriff Gaskin. Where had he met with Gaskin, and who else had been present? Was anything about the surroundings or environment slightly off? His mind quickly dissected each moment for any possible clue, his stomach now churning. Unfortunately, he came up with nothing.

The last of the walkers strolled past, with a few stragglers walking their bicycles finishing up the procession. For some reason, his eyes were drawn to a little girl as she reached the curb and mounted her small pink bicycle, ringing the little bell attached to the handlebar. The crossing guard was now waving for the cars to take their turn, but he just sat there.

The drivers in the cars behind him began blowing their horns in frustration, but, lost in thought, the detective didn't hear them. He watched the girl ride her bike down the street and out of view before he returned his attention to the road ahead and pressed on the accelerator.

Chapter Three

From the day she was born, Elizabeth Jenkins was the sparkle in her parent's eyes. With beautiful soft blonde hair and bright blue eyes, she never wanted for the attention and affection of others. Her pleasant demeanor and sweet nature made it easy for others to love her.

Even at a young age, Elizabeth displayed signs of a budding intellect. By the time she was able to speak in sentences, she had started to ask questions – a lot of questions. Her frequent inquiries didn't prove to be as much annoying as they were hard to answer. Innocently asked, many of the questions the precocious girl put forth bordered on the profound. There was the time in Sunday school when Elizabeth asked Pastor Greg's wife, Barbara, who made her, and the woman told her that God made her.

Elizabeth thought for a moment before countering with, "Who made God?"

Barbara could find no answer. She quickly changed the subject and moved on, but from time to time, she thought about that very question.

It was not surprising that Elizabeth would be cherished by her mother and father given the uncertainty of her conception and birth. Gladys and Thomas had tried everything they could to have a child.

Sex was never the problem. Thomas was more than ready, willing, and able to perform on any given occasion, and Gladys displayed no hesitation on her part. They were young, healthy, attractive, and in love. The couple had just assumed having children would happen sooner rather than later.

Their courtship was short; their engagement lasting just long enough to plan and arrange the wedding. What a beautiful wedding it turned out to be. Family and friends cheerfully celebrated the happy couple, toasts were made to their promising future, and all wished them the best of luck. Pictures were taken and they were sent on their way with hugs and kisses to the white sands of the Florida panhandle for their honeymoon.

After a week of sun, surf, sand, and sex, they returned home to begin their long, happy lives together. Starting a family and raising children was just assumed to be the next step.

Months went by, but no pregnancy. Gladys started keeping a fertility calendar. She began to study the relationship between ovulation and copulation and to plan their love making with scientific precision and discipline. As time went by without positive results, other variables were examined, such as sexual positions, lunar cycles, and dietary intake.

Thomas began to suspect that his wife was becoming a little obsessed with getting pregnant, but he didn't complain since he benefited happily from his wife's attention. He wasn't overly enthusiastic about the grapefruit juice his wife began to serve him with his biscuits and honey every morning, but it was a small price to pay for frequent sexual gratification.

Thomas never forgot the day he had to face the true depth of their problem. Arriving home one evening after work, he walked into a house of shadows. The sun had begun to set, but no lights illuminated their small cottage, no dinner was cooking in the kitchen, no sound of his wife's voice welcomed him home. Feeling disoriented and confused, he held his breath for a moment, before hearing the muffled sounds of quiet sobs and hushed whimpers.

Panic washed over him and his heart thumped loudly in his chest. He raced across the room, down the short hallway, and pushed open the door to the bathroom to find Gladys sitting on the cold tiles, leaning against the porcelain tub. She looked up at him, her eyes red and puffy, tears running down her cheeks. He dropped to his knees and took her into his arms.

"Oh, honey, baby, what's wrong?" he asked as his fingers gently brushed her matted hair away from her sad face.

"I'm so sorry," Gladys replied, choking back her tears.

"Sorry? Sorry for what?"

"I want to give you a baby so much. No matter what I do or how hard I try, nothing works."

She buried her face into his chest and sobbed as he held her in his arms. Thomas remained silent for a moment, his mind racing, and then he softly whispered into her ear, "Honey, maybe it has nothing to do with you. Maybe it's me." He finally spoke aloud the fear he'd been burying deep inside for so long.

What if it was him, he thought. He knew how much she wanted a child, wanted to be a mother. They'd talked about it for almost as long as they'd known each other. Her eyes sparkled like diamonds anytime the subject of babies came up. What if he was unable to give her one?

Thomas loved his wife with all of his heart. He wanted to be her husband and wanted her to be his wife, his friend, his girl forever. He wanted her to be the mother of his children. The thought that there might not be any children hadn't occurred to him until now.

More than anything in the world, he wanted his wife to be happy, and he knew that she would never be truly happy unless she became a mother one day. If it couldn't be with him, eventually, he reasoned, it would be with someone else.

That thought burned through his soul like acid. She was his girl; he was her man. What kind of a husband can't give his wife the one thing that makes a man a man? He could feel his insides twisting, the fire in his intestines somewhere between pain and panic. His wife's silence in response to his comment didn't make him feel any better.

Taking a deep breath, he offered, "Why don't we make an appointment with Dr. Benfield and see what we're up against?"

Truth be told, this wasn't the first time this course of action had occurred to Thomas. He'd hoped all along that things would just happen naturally and he wouldn't have to go through with it. His fear of what they might find out had kept him from contemplating this option, but the sudden realization of the consequences of his inaction forced his hand. His happiness, family, and future were on the line, and he was going to do anything he could to save them.

"Are you really willing to do that?" Gladys finally spoke up.

She'd been to see Dr. Benfield already and knew her fertility was not in question. Gladys was as afraid as her husband was of what they might find out about him, and what that would mean about their future.

Like most things in life, the answer that the anxious couple was seeking wasn't as easy to come by as they'd wished. Naturally, they were relieved when they found out that there was nothing physically wrong with either one of them that would prevent them from having children. Unfortunately, now that they'd eliminated all of the possibilities, they still weren't any closer to becoming parents.

"Don't worry. Relax. It will happen when it's right," Dr. Benfield assured them.

The couple didn't find any of Dr. Benfield's advice reassuring, and then it happened. For the first few weeks that Gladys was late, she kept it to herself, afraid that her hopes would be dashed. She finally confirmed her suspicions by a visit to the doctor's office. Dr. Benfield almost took credit for it himself and reminded her of his good advice with an "I told you so."

That night, Gladys prepared Thomas's favorite dinner in anticipation of the moment she could share the wonderful news. Thomas's face beamed with joy when he heard the words from his wife. He leaped from his chair and took her into his arms. He couldn't remember a moment in his life when he felt so full of happiness and love.

Thomas found he could focus on his career with new zeal. Motivated by a strong desire to provide for his lovely wife and the child she was carrying, he strove for perfection in his job at the bank. It did not go unnoticed by his superiors, and he was given more responsibility, accompanied by a much needed increase in salary. When the coveted position of Assistant Bank Manager in the neighboring county was offered to him, he jumped at the opportunity. Soon the couple was excited to be in search of a home closer to his new office.

In preparation for the move, Thomas made the acquaintance of another upwardly mobile, motivated professional – Barney Spencer. The real estate agent knew the area well and understood just what the couple was looking for. The newly constructed home at one hundred three Johnson Road was perfect. It had all the amenities that the family needed and wanted, and he was able to get them a great deal.

Even though Thomas had been working hard at the bank, and his new position as Assistant Bank Manager came with a decent increase in salary, the couple didn't have much in savings. A large down-payment was not something that Thomas could comfortably afford because he wasn't in a position to deplete their savings account. His job required him to be financially solvent, and, if he had any hopes of keeping his position or becoming a branch manager in the future, he would need to give a respectable account of his personal finances.

Fortunately, his role at the bank did mean he was somewhat savvy in the world of real estate loans, interest, and investments. He had a network of mortgage experts at his disposal, and Barney proved to be adept at bargaining with the developer. Only a small amount of haggling was required, and almost no down payment was needed. Within a few short weeks, the young couple found themselves the proud owners of a new home in a family-friendly neighborhood.

The move went without a hitch. In little over a weekend, they were sitting around their dinner table in their new kitchen, their faces beaming. That night as they lay together in their recently purchased king size bed, whispering to each other intimately, the two lovers talked for hours about their hopes, dreams, and future in their new home.

They imagined their children playing in the yard, having sleepovers with their little friends, and gathering under the Christmas tree waiting for Santa to arrive. One day, they told each other, they would even have grandchildren, who would come over on weekends and holidays to visit Grandpa and Grandma, who would spoil them and smother them with love. Happy days were ahead for the Jenkins; fond memories to be made in their new home.

Four months later, Thomas saw it all come crashing down when he got that terrible call. Panic coursed through his body as he rushed to the hospital to be by his wife's side. He heard the word – miscarriage – that awful, repulsive word that drilled a painful hole into his heart and threatened to create a deep chasm between the once happy couple.

They faced it bravely, but their words and actions felt hollow. Silence crept into their time together. Not the peaceful silence they had shared before that terrible day, but a silence born of grief and hopelessness. Days became weeks; weeks became months. Time drifted slowly by for the grieving couple, their new dream house now too big and too empty for just the two of them.

With time, things between them got better, although never as good as before. Some of the old doubts and fears that Thomas had bottled up so long ago had begun to claw their way into his thoughts. He imagined his life crumbling around him, stone by stone, while he stood frozen on the edge of an abyss.

One afternoon, he came home at the usual time and instantly sensed a change in his wife's demeanor. She was trying her hardest to act as if nothing was out of the ordinary, but he'd been with her long enough to know something was up.

"What's going on, honey? You're acting a little strange," he inquired.

"Nothing. I don't know what you mean."

He could tell she was holding back. Her eyes avoided his, and she bit her lower lip like she always did when she was trying to hide something.

"Come on," he urged. "You know you can't keep anything from me. I know you too well."

"I know you do," she replied sheepishly.

Gladys took a deep breath, before pausing for a moment. Thomas held his breath and braced himself for what she had to tell him, praying it wasn't something terrible.

"I'm pregnant!" she shouted out as she threw her arms around her husband's neck.

"You're.... pregnant? Pregnant?" Thomas kissed his wife and they held each other close, tears of joy running down both of their faces.

This time around they tried to remain calm and temper their expectations. Another disappointment would be too much for them to bear. The found that keeping their excitement in check was impossible as the months passed and the expectant date grew closer and closer. They both felt deep down inside that this was it. Gladys was going to be a mother; Thomas, a father.

At six thirty-seven in the morning on September twenty-fourth, nineteen hundred fifty-one, Elizabeth Mary Jenkins took her first breath and let out her first cry. The piercing wail of the newborn was the most beautiful sound that her mother and father had ever heard. Once she was gently wiped clean by the maternity nurse and presented to her mother's breast, tiny Elizabeth was wrapped in a deep immeasurable love that can only exist between a mother and child, and a bond was forever created in that moment that could never be broken.

As Elizabeth grew from a happy, beautiful baby into a lovely child, her parents doted on her, cherishing her every moment. Her first words, her first steps, her first laugh, her first everything became a reason for celebration. The couple now had their baby girl, their family was complete. The dream house they lived in no longer felt too big or too empty; it just felt like home.

*

April 24, 1963: 1:47 pm

"Sheriff, Mr. Peterson is looking for you again," Mabel hollered across the busy station house as Clifford passed through.

The sheriff ignored this information; he had more pressing issues to attend to at the moment.

"Johnnie, bring me a copy of the report we sent to State last Tuesday," Gaskin grunted as he marched into his office and dropped down into his chair.

"It's on your desk," the officer yelled back to the sheriff, never taking his eyes off one of the many reports he always seemed to be working on.

"Damn," muttered the sheriff.

His desk was like the Bermuda Triangle when it came to finding paperwork. No matter how recently he'd been working on something, or when he placed something neatly on top of it, the desk swallowed it whole. Nothing could ever be found without at least a twenty-minute search. The search itself was something to be avoided at all costs. It meant he would invariably find other reports or papers that would remind him of urgent matters that would now be long overdue. Sometimes, he really hated his job.

The phone rang and he glanced down at the annoying contraption. He ignored it for the moment as he rummaged through the various files and forms piled up in front of him. For once, his luck held and he found the prized paperwork with little effort. Clifford thumbed through the pages as he picked up the phone and placed it to his ear, more to shut the damned thing up than for any interest in who was on the other end or what new problem they were going to dump into his lap.

"Sheriff Gaskin here," he answered officially.

The irate voice on the other end belonged to George Peterson. Clifford had long tired of his endless whining, and almost at once began to ignore the caller and return to the report in front of him.

"Uh huh."

"Go on."

"I see."

The sheriff muttered occasionally, feigning interest, as Peterson explained his plight in great detail. If it had been any other caller, Clifford would have hung up long before, or set things straight using his well honed skills of intimidation and bullying, but George Peterson was a different breed. His family was as much royalty as one could imagine in the backwoods town of Hidden Springs. Hell, Clifford was sheriff of Peterson County, for Christ's sake. Sometimes, even Clifford had to act humble, and he hated every second of it.

As George berated the sheriff for his inaction and complained about his bumbling deputies, Gaskin tried to organize the information in the report in a more user-friendly way. What he really was looking for was documentation that proved his latest theory – any pertinent information that was at the disposal of the state authorities came from his office as the result of his hard work. He took out his red pen and began to circle, underline, and draw stars and arrows around anything that could provide the slightest proof. After a few minutes, he realized that there was silence coming from the other end of the phone.

"I see. Is that all?" he muttered quickly, hoping George had been too busy talking to notice that no one had been listening.

Another pause, then the sound of breathing told Gaskin that he wasn't so lucky.

"Is that all?" blasted George. "Have you even been listening to me? This is an outrage!"

"Now, now, hold on for a minute," replied the sheriff defensively. "I know you're upset. I promise that we'll do everything we can. Unfortunately, this is not the only thing our department has to deal with at the moment. I'll send an officer to your house as soon as I can to take down any and all information and have him report back to me. Once that happens, I'll personally direct an investigation into any complaints you may have and let you know what we come up with."

Clifford had recited the well-used monologue so frequently that he had it memorized. The trick was always to deliver it with enough freshness and sincerity that it would get him off the hook. He hoped that this would take care of the matter and he'd never have to deal with George personally until the problem was resolved.

Peterson was upset that his daughter was seeing the Johnson boy, who he thought was beneath her. Of course, George Peterson thought everyone was beneath him and his daughter, so the urgency of his concerns wasn't shared by anyone in the Sheriff's Department.

"When is your deputy coming? I don't have all day," George eventually replied, somewhat placated.

"I'll pass your call back to Mabel and she'll let you know."

"Don't make the mistake of ignoring this, Sheriff. My family has been running things in this county since before you were born. I shouldn't have to remind you that your job depends on getting results."

No one ever had to even remotely remind anyone that George Peterson's family was the most powerful in the county, thought Clifford, as he transferred the call back to Mabel. Damn, how he despised that little silver-spooned twerp.

Bringing his attention back to his original task of making sure he'd receive any and all credit that might be due him from the work of others, Clifford noticed a pattern. Detective Robert Stallworth's name was all over this report. Stallworth wanted to know this; he wanted to know that. Worse yet, he wanted the sheriff to do all of the legwork necessary to get the information. The whole process was exhausting, and more than a little annoying.

The sheriff would be required to question the fine citizens of Peterson County, only to hand over any information he got to the detective. Detective Stallworth would then thank him by interrogating him from twenty different angles, only to be upset when he couldn't answer most of the ridiculous questions the detective asked.

Stallworth was concerned about the most trivial, unimportant details, and he lacked any semblance of tact when trying to get those details. It was no wonder few of the people in the community would agree to answer the detective's questions. That left the sheriff with the impossible task of questioning a bunch of morons, who never seemed to know shit.

The irony of the situation, as Sheriff Gaskin saw it, was that this time it looked like someone else was trying to take credit for the work he actually did. Fuck that, he thought, as his red pen ran wild across the pages of the report.

Just then, the phone rang again, causing him to jump. He stared at the aggravating thing for a minute; then he hopped up from behind his desk and made his way out of the station. The ringing could be heard in the background as he started out the front door.

"I'm running out by Ray's to patrol the highway. Hold down the fort," he shouted to Mabel before the door closed behind him, eliminating any chance of him being kept in the office a moment longer.

Chapter Four

Peterson County was in the middle of nowhere. Throughout its history, the area had never been deemed important or relevant to anyone who wasn't stuck there. Consisting mostly of old cotton plantations, peanut farms, and pine forests, there was never a time when it was remotely considered possible that any industry would take root and prosper. No important crossroads, waterways, or metropolitan centers inhabited the county, and it looked doubtful that any ever would. Not one notable historical person of interest, who might give the outside world notice that the quiet rural area was on the map, hailed from the area. It was no wonder that the best person that anyone could come up with to bear the county's name was Colonel Franklin Peterson.

Colonel Peterson served as an infantry commander for the Confederate Army during the Civil War. He had fought and died bravely in the battle of

Fredericksburg on December thirteenth, eighteen hundred sixty-two. Survived by his widow, Mary Jean, and their seven children, his legacy in the region was maintained primarily by their relentless efforts. His plantation had comprised much of the usable land in the county at that time, and, although the main buildings had been completely destroyed during the war, land was always worth something.

His many children and their subsequent offspring multiplied in the years following the bloody conflict, and the land eventually was partitioned off and much of it sold. Even so, the advantage of having anything in an area where most had nothing enabled the vast Peterson clan to remain at the top of the food chain in local political and economic circles.

Because of their position in the community, the Petersons had been able to have the name of the county changed to Peterson County, the name of the county capital renamed Petersonville, the name of the park in the center of the capital's town square named Peterson Park, and a bronze statue of the dashing and valiant Colonel Peterson placed in the center.

The statue was a thing to behold. It featured the gallant Colonel Peterson mounted on his mighty steed, leading his battle-hardened troops into combat. Historians generally dissented about the validity of the monument, being that the Colonel was an infantry commander, who hadn't been riding on a horse the day he was decapitated by an errant cannonball fired by a Confederate artillery brigade. His 'battle-hardened troops' were ill-trained, poorly armed farmers at best, facing the first and last conflict in what, for most, proved to be their only battle and early demise. All the same, the statue of the soldier poised on his mighty stallion provided a favorite dumping ground for pigeons far and wide.

Like any large group of relatives, the venerated Peterson family had a few black sheep over the years. Always mindful of the importance of giving the impression of respectability, the Petersons never aired their dirty laundry for the public's consideration. By the mid-part of the twentieth century, only a few of the Petersons still retained any actual wealth, although almost nobody outside of the tightly-knit clan knew this. Most of the extended family members lived either rent free or only paid nominal rent to others in the family and lived on the few parcels of property still owned by relatives. Only two or three of the Peterson brood owned their property out-right. Most owed a considerable amount of money to the bank for the property they claimed. The effort it took to maintain an air of wealth didn't come cheap; the maintenance fees to belong to that exclusive club were slowly disqualifying the majority of its members.

Cheryl Bradford was the second child in the family that lived in the lower middle-class community of Oak Hill, thirty miles east of Petersonville. Her older brother was the pride and joy of her parents. He played third base on his high school baseball team and strong safety on the football team. He was the center of attention at family gatherings, and everyone knew his future was certain to be a bright one.

Cheryl couldn't stand him. He was stupid, mean, and a bully in her eyes, although everyone else who recognized the truth seemed to ignore the obvious. When she tried to broach the subject to her mother or little sister, she was chastised and accused of jealousy. She never entertained the thought of criticizing her brother in the presence of her father; after all, he was the tree from which the apple fell.

Highly religious and inflexibly pious, Luke Bradford thought of himself as the guardian of his family's morality. Brother Luke was the deacon of the local Pentecostal congregation and was held in high esteem throughout the vicinity for being such a devout and righteous Christian. To his eldest daughter, Cheryl, he was a cold, cruel, unforgiving, bitter man, devoid of compassion and love. She wisely kept these feelings to herself for fear of being punished for her wickedness, a punishment that would be severe by any measure.

The one instance when she had to admit in her heart she was guilty of the unforgivable mortal sin of jealousy was with her younger sister, Cindy. She truly loved Cindy, but Cheryl couldn't help but resent her sibling all the same. Cindy was beautiful; Cindy was well behaved; Cindy could get away with murder without any consequences from her strict father. Nothing Cindy did was ever wrong; nothing Cheryl did was ever right.

Cheryl knew this wasn't her sister's fault. Her sister lacked the cruel disposition possessed by both their father and brother, but knowing this didn't eliminate the feelings of injustice that angered her deep down inside. It was jealousy, plain and simple, and she knew it was wrong, knew it was a sin, and knew her father would disapprove. She hated her father, but longed for his approval more than anything else in the world.

It was that approval that spurred her on in her relationship with George Peterson. Naturally, she enjoyed getting attention from a boy for a change. She'd never been considered attractive, and had never gotten much notice from the few boys she came in contact with. It's not that she was unattractive, but between her strict, religious father, her brother the tyrant, and her beautiful younger sister, she had little hope of attracting a suitor. Then, George Peterson came along.

The two sat next to each other in civics class during their junior year at Robert E. Lee High School. Although they sat side by side for almost the entire year, they rarely acknowledged each other's presence. It wasn't unusual for Cheryl not to speak to George; she was always quiet and withdrawn, especially around boys. If George hadn't asked for help with his upcoming term paper near the end of the second semester, it's doubtful that the two would've spoken to each other at all.

Cheryl was introverted and bookish, but extremely bright. She excelled in her studies. The quiet girl never had many friends and was happy to help the tall, red headed boy who sat next to her. Once the assignment was completed, George asked for her help in studying for the upcoming finals. The young Peterson lad had no problem asking for things from others. He just assumed that everyone else was there for his benefit.

He recognized that, without Cheryl's help, his grades would've been less than acceptable, both to his parents as well as for his ego. He was, after all, a Peterson. He had a certain standard to maintain, considering his theoretically lofty position in the community. George also knew that Cheryl would've gotten into an enormous amount of trouble at home had her insane father found out she was spending time with someone of the opposite sex, even if it was in an innocent endeavor, such as helping him with his studies.

As a reward for her help, George decided that he would ask Cheryl out to the Junior Prom. He knew that her father might not allow it, although he reasoned that, because it was him, George Peterson, who had invited her, her father might make an exception. The fact that no other girls were likely to accept his offer and he would have to go to the Prom alone never crossed his mind.

His lack of humility was a trait that most of his peers despised. On the few occasions he allowed himself to recognize that others might not like him, he would generally attribute it to jealousy. He may not have admitted it to himself, but by the time he'd reached the age of seventeen, the only friend he'd made was Cheryl Bradford, and he had only begun to speak to her a month before.

A week prior to the big event, George approached Cheryl in one of the busy corridors in their school.

"Cheryl, I want to thank you again for helping me pass this year."

Cheryl looked up at George and smiled.

"You're welcome. It was no problem."

"Still, all the same, I feel as if I owe you one."

He paused for a moment, his eyes wandering away from the young girl standing three feet in front of him. Suddenly he felt nervous, even scared. He was uncomfortable and almost aborted the entire endeavor. He quickly recognized that this was his moment to step up and not be such a coward. Taking a big breath and swallowing hard, he gazed directly into Cheryl's dark brown eyes.

"How would you feel about going to the prom with me?" he blurted out.

Cheryl felt instant butterflies in her stomach. No one had ever asked her out before. She liked George, but hadn't thought he was interested in anything but her help with his grades. In all of the time they had spent together, he'd been all business. He hadn't even flirted with her. Now, all of a sudden, he unexpectedly sprung this on her, and she found herself speechless.

The moment of silence became awkward, and George jumped in, "Well, I…"

"Of course, I'll go with you," Cheryl cut him off before his offer could be rescinded.

She'd waited a long time for this, and she wasn't going to let it slip through her fingers now. As soon as the words crossed her lips, she felt a sinking feeling inside.

"Well, I mean I want to go with you," she said. "I just don't know if my father will let me."

George was relieved when she agreed to be his date, and even if her father wouldn't allow it, she'd at least said yes. Still, he reasoned, unless her father agreed to let her go with him, that wouldn't change the fact that he'd be going alone.

"Do you think it would help if I asked him directly?" he offered.

She thought about it for a minute and concluded that his idea was pure genius. She didn't think her father would ever let her go out with a boy, any boy; at least he wouldn't if she were the one to ask him. Cheryl presumed that her father wouldn't let her do or have anything if she were the one who was doing the asking. Now, if George Peterson, of the highly regarded Peterson family, went to Brother Luke and asked, it might be different. Her father was dirt poor and pretended not to care, although she knew this was just an act. The way her father glorified her brother's athletic accomplishments told her just how much he wanted recognition for his family. She reckoned George's plan just might work.

"It might, but you'd have to do it right," she concluded. "He's very strict and very traditional. He'll probably make us go with a chaperone. I can't ask you to go to all that trouble. Besides, I don't really have a proper dress to wear."

"I think it's worth a shot. I'll come over this evening after school and we'll see. That is, if you still want to go."

"Of course, I want to go."

As their eyes met, Cheryl smiled and blushed. George smiled in return, feeling a little flushed as well.

"Then, I'll see you tonight. And I'm sure that no matter what you wear, you'll be beautiful."

The school bell rang, bringing them both back down to earth. The couple parted and George strode down the hallway toward his class with a spring in his step. Cheryl was still frozen to the spot, unable to catch her breath. She would replay that moment in her life many times in the years to follow. Those were the most wonderful words that anyone had ever spoken to her. This was the first time in her life that she felt pretty, and she liked it.

The rest of the school day was a blur. She couldn't think; she couldn't focus. The only thing on her mind was what was going to happen that evening. Excited and scared, she both dreaded and anticipated the upcoming meeting. Eventually, the dismissal bell rang, and she made her way to the bus.

When she got home, Cheryl quickly tended to her chores and helped set the table for dinner. Excusing herself, she made her way to the bathroom to wash up and brush her hair. During dinner, she could hardly eat. Her stomach was tied in knots. Her mind wandered as she considered all of the possible scenarios that might enfold shortly. Would her father lose his temper and start quoting the scriptures in an effort to rain hellfire down upon the wayward youth? Would her brother threaten the much smaller George with bodily harm at the very mention of an unseemly courtship with his sister? Would George abruptly change his mind and become hopelessly smitten with Cindy when he saw how beautiful Cheryl's younger sister was?

By the time she found herself clearing the table at the meal's conclusion, an even worse scenario occurred to Cheryl. What if George didn't show up at all? What if he changed his mind, or worse yet, what if the whole thing had been some cruel joke? She fought back the tears that began to well up behind her stoic expression.

The disheartened girl's ears pricked up when the sudden barking of their aged mutt, Barkley, broke the silence. The sound of a car engine coming to a stop, followed by a car door slamming, made her heart jump and got the attention of the entire family.

"I wonder who that could be?" asked the patriarch of the family.

Big Luke and Little Luke looked at each other with concern and bewilderment over an unexpected visitor. After a pause, there was a soft knock on the door, and Luke answered, acting casual.

The door swung open and George Peterson stood in the doorway, displaying as much confidence as he could muster.

"Hello. Mr. Bradford?" George said in his deepest manly voice.

"Yes?" answered Big Luke, nodding slightly.

"I'm George Peterson. Is it okay if I talk to you for a minute?"

By this time, Luke Jr. and Cindy were gathered around the small entrance way, peering curiously at their unexpected visitor. Even Cheryl's mother glanced around the corner from the kitchen to take a look before noticing her eldest daughter's feigned lack of interest in the occurrence. Mrs. Bradford smiled to herself knowingly, then dried her hands and made her way to her husband's side, ready to run whatever interference might be required.

"Come on in, young man," Mr. Bradford replied, standing aside and waving George into the modest living room. "What can I do for you?"

George made his way awkwardly into the small room and steadied himself.

"I came to ask your permission to take your daughter to the Junior Prom, sir," George replied, trying to sound as mature and respectful as he could.

"My daughter?" asked Big Luke.

He was caught off guard. Cindy was too young to have a suitor show up at the door. To even his own shame, Luke had momentarily forgotten he had another daughter. As his wife made her way to his side and introductions were made, he was able to regain his composure and consider the situation in front of him. He glanced toward the kitchen and saw Cheryl standing there. Luke had ignored and dismissed her for so long out of habit that he'd missed the fact that she was growing up. The girl standing alone in the kitchen, meekly staring down at her feet, would soon be a woman. This was a fact he could no longer overlook. He turned his attention back to the young man standing awkwardly in his living room.

"Cheryl, sir, your daughter – Cheryl? I'm in her class at school, and I would very much like to escort her to the Junior Prom – with your permission, of course, sir."

The cat was out of the bag now, but to the surprise of almost everyone, there wasn't a hint of a refusal coming from Brother Luke. Of course, they would be accompanied by a suitable chaperone, and, naturally, they would have to return at a reasonable time, but his permission was granted.

There were vague, but serious threats that there'd be grave consequences if anything were to go awry. George had no intention of incurring the wrath of these hillbillies. Although he may have put on his bravest face and mustered sufficient confidence to ask Cheryl out, in no way did he possess enough courage to not bring her back in one piece and on time.

The Prom came and went; they'd had a good time at the dance and shared their first real kiss that night. The summer break began, which provided nothing in the way of organized entertainment. Without Robert E. Lee High, the two had little chance to see each other over that long summer. George worked, if you could call it that, at his uncle's insurance company in downtown Petersonville. His duties consisted of running errands and assisting with whatever might be needed around the office. It didn't require much effort, although it did take up most of his time. He thought about Cheryl often, but was unable to see or talk to her until the school year resumed in September.

Cheryl had felt elated at the dance. George was the perfect gentleman, attentive and kind. The night went by too fast, and she'd assumed that it would be the first of many more dates. As June progressed to July, the Prom and her first date drifted further into the past. She understood that George had to work for his uncle for the summer, way over in Petersonville, but she was disappointed that he made no effort to see her on the weekends.

As the summer drew to an end, she was worried that when they saw each other again at school, he wouldn't be interested in her anymore. Maybe he met another girl over the summer, someone who was pretty and came from a more respectable family. She couldn't blame him if he had; they'd only been on one date. All the same, she'd be crushed. He was the only boy who'd ever shown any interest in her. He'd even gone the extra mile to approach her father, an effort that had greatly impressed her. If he snubbed her now, she was afraid that no one else would ever ask her out again. She'd be trapped in her unhappy home forever – unwanted and unloved. She couldn't wait for the school year to begin.

The first day back, they found themselves sitting side by side in their homeroom class. It was a powerful moment for both of them when they saw each other again. It was hard to believe that they'd only known each other for a few months and had only shared one date. Neither one of them had any true friends or close confidants, but they had each other. No words needed to be spoken. George and Cheryl were now best friends, boyfriend and girlfriend, and high-school sweethearts.

That last year at Robert E. Lee High went by fast. They attended homecoming together, exchanged meaningful, though meager, Christmas gifts, and he even presented her with a promise ring on Valentine's Day. By the time of their Senior Prom, even Big Luke allowed them to attend without a chaperone, although he was less than comfortable doing so.

George still thought of himself as superior to others, and occasionally desired one of the prettier cheerleaders he eyed discreetly, but he wasn't stupid enough to risk losing his only friend in the world. Besides being his friend, Cheryl was the reason he was graduating at all. It wasn't that he lacked the ability to get decent grades; it was more that he was lazy. He expected life to be easy and he believed that, even without great effort or hard work, he was entitled to a reasonable standard of living. He was, after all, a Peterson, living in Peterson County, and that should count for something.

Thanks in large part to Cheryl's help, he managed to graduate high school. Although his grades were anything but stellar, they were good enough to enable him to be accepted to the University of Alabama. The convenient fact that his family had bequeathed a considerable amount in the way of financial contributions to that fine institute of higher learning over the years hadn't hurt his chances of gaining admission, either. The important thing was that George was going off to college in the spring where he would earn a degree and carry on the family tradition of becoming a successful and respectable businessman.

Cheryl wasn't as lucky as George. Without question, she was far more intelligent and diligent in her studies, but she was a woman and she was poor. College wasn't cheap, and the very idea of sending any of his kids to college had never occurred to the head of the Bradford family – with the exception of Cheryl's brother, of course.

Luke Bradford always held out hope that Luke, Jr. would earn an athletic scholarship to a suitable college, and he had been proven correct. His eldest boy's talent on the gridiron had earned him admission to the University of Georgia, where he was currently pursuing a degree in horticulture.

Although, no one disputed that while Luke Bradford, Jr. was as dumb as a sack of hammers, he could play ball. The idea that a university diploma was an academic achievement was lost on the elder Bradford. Brother Luke was never partial to snobby intellectuals or elitist college boys. In fact, he was intimidated, and thus, distrustful of them. On the other hand, he enjoyed sports, and saw college as a provider of entertainment and a diversion for his unsophisticated amusement.

He felt it was unfortunate that his boy was now a *Bulldog* instead a member of the *Crimson Tide*, but he kept his disappointment to himself so as not to discourage the boy. Brother Luke understood that sometimes sacrifices had to be made for the sake of his children's future.

The summer came and went, and George left for college in the early fall. Cheryl found employment at the local grocery store as a cashier, and felt abandoned all over again. Although George wrote an occasional letter to her, they were few and far between. He'd never been particularly poetic or romantic, and his correspondence was unfulfilling for a lonely girl. Luckily for George, she'd garnered little interest from other suitors. Despite his lack of amorous creativity or diligent effort, she waited patiently for his return.

When the Thanksgiving holiday break came, George came home to visit. The young couple spent all of their time together. Cheryl was happy to feel wanted again, although she could sense that he was under a great deal of stress. Near the end of his short visit, he confided to her that his grades were poor and that he didn't think he would pass his courses that semester. She gave him all of the support she could, ensuring him that everything would turn out alright. He broke down in her arms and, for the first time in his life, allowed himself to be vulnerable in the presence of another person.

That night, before his return to the university, they gave themselves to one another. It was scary and awkward and wonderful. They pledged their love and swore that they would be faithful to each other forever. Afterwards, she went back home and he returned to the university to complete the fall semester. They would see each other in less than a month, over the Christmas holidays.

Christmas came with little joy that year. George had, as predicted, not passed the majority of his classes. His family was not amused. Tuition was not cheap, but, more importantly, the Peterson family had a reputation to maintain. George was not pulling his own weight and his bright future was becoming dim. Just when it looked to him that his problems couldn't get any worse, Cheryl informed him that she had missed her period. It took him a few minutes to understand what she was trying to tell him, but when it hit him, it was like a ton of bricks.

How could she do this to him now? He bitterly contemplated this unfortunate and untimely turn of events. He could see she was terrified, and he snapped out of it. No matter how much he resented her for this, and probably would for years to come, he was wise enough not to show it. He took a deep breath and told her it was going to be alright, trying to give her the same level of comfort that she'd given him a little over a month before. He recognized his responsibility in this situation, and he knew that he was going to have to deal with it whether he wanted to or not.

Once the pregnancy was confirmed by the doctor, things had to happen quickly and in the proper manner. George understood immediately the short-term ramifications of having a child, even if a deeper understanding eluded him. He had little in the way of savings and his collegiate career was in considerable doubt, so he would have to enlist the help of his disapproving family and pray they would help.

George asked Cheryl for her hand in marriage, and she readily accepted. He hadn't approached her father yet and dreaded the meeting, but he knew he had no choice. He decided to settle things on his end first, a task that proved to be even more unpleasant. The Petersons were not happy with his choice of the Bradford girl and had no problem conveying that information. George used this to his advantage by insinuating that his failing grades were, in part, due to Cheryl's pregnancy. He was the martyr, sacrificing his promising future in order to honorably accept responsibility for his actions and provide for his imminent family.

This line of gibberish was well received by the distinguished Peterson clan, and George's success with his parents gave him a new sense of confidence. He was offered a position at the insurance company and was able to purchase a small, but suitable, engagement ring for Cheryl. He would present it to her with appropriate fanfare as soon as he officially asked her father for her hand in marriage.

The afternoon that he went to the Bradford house to discuss his future with Cheryl, Big Luke immediately became suspicious. George quickly got to the point and asked for Luke's daughter's hand in marriage, a move that probably saved his life. At that point, Luke believed that his daughter had acted in an immoral fashion and that her sinful actions pre-empted the engagement. When it was announced that the wedding would be just around the corner, he knew this to be the truth.

Cheryl's father reasoned that, in the end, she'd done well for herself, and that this scenario was best for everyone. Conveniently, his rigid moral attitude, in his mind, justified the shabby treatment and poor opinion of his eldest daughter that he'd always held. He figured that the little harlot wouldn't be his problem much longer. The biggest setback that he had now was how to pay for a decent wedding so as not to completely embarrass his family in front of the prestigious Peterson clan. Since the event was to be held on Valentine's Day, Big Luke only had a matter of weeks to put it all together. He would sit down with his wife later that night and put a dollar amount on what he would spend. His wife would just have to deal with the rest.

In the meantime, he gave the young man before him permission to wed his daughter, and he wished them both luck. He even managed a friendly handshake, smile, and pat on the back for his future son-in-law. As for Cheryl, she received the usual icy glare and cold shoulder.

The nuptials were held at the Living Word Pentecostal Church on Jasper Road, and the reception was held next door at the Church's community center. Being a deacon and long-standing faithful member of the congregation allowed Big Luke to use the facilities at little cost. This, in turn, enabled the Bradfords to scrape together enough funds to host a small, but adequate, wedding. Big Luke was able to save face and stand tall amongst the upper crust of Peterson County society, and even he had to admit his eldest daughter looked beautiful in her home-made dress. The Peterson family commented on Junior's athletic prowess, and this recognition went a long way in charming Cheryl's father.

After the wedding, the happy couple moved into a small apartment over George's office. He told people that, as his wife's pregnancy progressed, he felt more comfortable being close by, in case of an emergency. In typical George fashion, even though he convinced others that was the reason, he knew in his heart that it was a lie. If an emergency were to occur, he wouldn't have the first idea of what to do.

Time flew by and George became increasingly anxious at the thought of being responsible for a wife and a newborn child. No matter how hard he worked, there was never enough money, and he felt as though he'd made a major blunder by not taking his college education seriously when he had the chance. It started to occur to him that maybe his role as a martyr was more accurate than he at first believed. Real or imagined, the seeds of this idea had taken root in the depths of George's psyche, and it was only a matter of time before they grew to fruition.

On a hot August day, George and Cheryl Peterson welcomed the first addition to their family at Crestview Medical Center. She was a healthy baby girl, with bright green eyes and soft auburn hair. Agatha Marie Peterson was the apple of her father's eye, and he showered her with all of his attention. On her part, Cheryl loved her little angel and swore she would do everything to make her feel wanted and loved, feelings she'd always been denied as a child.

The new father was forced to mature quickly, and he took a greater interest in his work and his future in his uncle's business. For his expanded efforts at work, his new status as a father, and, as always, his being a Peterson, he was rewarded with an increase in salary. The apartment he shared with his wife and infant daughter was now too small, and it was time that they bought a house of their own. For the first time in his life, George worked hard so that he could save enough money to find a more suitable home for his family.

Most of the Petersons had lived on inherited land or rented cheaply from others in the family, but that was not going to work for George, and those choices were quickly deemed unsuitable for his needs. Unfortunately, he couldn't afford anything he believed to be suitable for his perceived status, so compromises were going to have to be made. Fortunately, he had a decent income and was able to procure suitable credit because of his family's name and business, so he figured, if he played his cards right, he could somehow manage to start off right and grow from there.

After some inquiry, he was referred to a realtor by the name of Barney Spencer. Barney proved to be quite useful to George, and, before long, he was purchasing a lot in a new subdivision and having a brand new house built for his growing family. The property was a bit out of his way, but there were only a few other houses on the street and almost all of them were newly built.

He wanted something a bit more upscale than the others, so he bought a double-sized lot down at the end of the road so that he'd have a little space away from the other houses. The only thing that he found troubling was that there was a curious looking shack tucked away in the bushes just past his property. The odd little house looked abandoned and was facing in the wrong direction, which only added to its strangeness. George wrongly assumed that this aberration would only be a temporary problem with an easy fix.

*

March 7, 1963

"Useless."

It was the one word that Robert Stallworth thought could best describe the report he was reading. The reports from Sheriff Gaskin's office were pertinent to the investigation, but almost always proved to be worthless. To the detective, this was just another example of the sheriff's incompetency in doing his job and a great source of frustration in having to work with him. He hated the fact that he required Gaskin's assistance at all. The fact that this assistance came with such a lack of quality only further grated on the detective's nerves.

The very existence of these reports was a major bone of contention between the two men. The sheriff didn't think his office should have to provide them to the state authorities in the first place, and he did everything he could to avoid the issue. It was only the persistence of Detective Stallworth and the intervention of Captain Warner that forced his hand in the matter, and the sheriff never forgave the detective for it.

Gaskin was never fond of filling out forms even though this comprised a large part of his job. Being sheriff afforded him the opportunity to delegate the majority of his paperwork to others, with only his signature required. Unfortunately, the reports the detective demanded required his direct participation. This forced Gaskin to not only do some actual work, but have that work examined and critiqued by someone else. There was no up-side for him that he could discern in the scenario, so he resented the entire undertaking. The lack of quality in the reports reflected this attitude.

The thing that really got under Sheriff Gaskin's skin about the situation was that it looked to him like he was doing all of the detective's work. He had to canvass the locals and do the interviews in order to find viable leads, just so the detective could follow up on any that he felt were worthwhile. Unfortunately, when dealing with the local yahoos, most of the information the sheriff was able to obtain was rubbish, and this made his task almost impossible. The result was a report that made the sheriff look incompetent and gave the detective plenty to complain about. The fact that these reports were on paper, with his signature on the bottom and filed away for posterity wasn't missed by the sheriff, either.

Robert understood Gaskin's position better than the sheriff realized, but that didn't mean he cut him any slack. The detective had no choice but to rely upon the local authorities, who knew their constituents personally, in order to get inside information. Uneducated, rural hillbillies were never going to tell a jacket-and-tie-wearing government agent anything. More than once, he had been threatened at gunpoint to get off someone's property because he was 'trespassing'. All of these hicks thought they somehow were qualified attorneys and informed him with great authority how they had some 'right' or another to demand his immediate departure. It was futile to argue with such stupidity since he was there to get their help and cooperation. Clearly, that was not going to happen.

When it was all said and done, what he had left were the reports stacked neatly on his desk.

"Useless."

Chapter Five

The money Purvis received from the sale of his property was enough to satisfy the tax man. Unfortunately for Sue, it was also enough to keep Purvis from having to seek out gainful employment. The Johnsons had just enough to get by on, and getting by was all that Purvis required. Sue, on the other hand, always wanted more.

When she had first begun to flirt with Purvis, all she desired was a stable relationship; her highest aspiration was to find a place for herself and her son to live in peace. She had that now, but it was no longer enough. Sue wanted excitement. Sue wanted romance. Sue wanted a bigger house, a nicer car, and finer clothes. Sue wanted things.

It wasn't long before she realized that she just needed something. She needed a change. After much discussion and a few heated exchanges with Purvis, she began to work part-time, picking up the odd shifts back at Lil' Ray's. Sweet Sue was always welcome at the little watering hole, and her old customers were happy to see her again. The innocent flirtations that came with the job made her feel like her old self, and the little bit of money she was able to make helped out. She never thought she would've missed working at the run down little bar, but she was happy to be back.

Within a few weeks of her return to Lil' Ray's, Harry Lejuine showed up for happy hour. They greeted each other cordially and she casually served him his beer, but they both knew it was all for show. Harry left about ten minutes before the end of her shift, and they met in the empty parking lot of the body shop a half mile down the road. She climbed into the cab of his truck and they tore at each other's clothes as soon as the door slammed shut. It was hot and exciting and over much too quickly. They both knew it wouldn't be the last time they sought each other's company.

When their romantic encounter was finished, she straightened her appearance and made her way back home to her husband. He barely even glanced up to acknowledge her arrival as she entered the little house and went into the bathroom to take a shower. She muttered something about how tired she was from work, but there was only some vague muffled response from her disinterested husband.

She thought to herself that she should feel guilt and shame for what she'd done, but instead, she felt attractive and sexy. She felt like a woman again. Her husband was the guilty one, she reasoned. He's the one that had deprived her of what a woman needs. He's the one who forced her to find it elsewhere. She remembered the shame she'd felt when she was single and Harry was the only married one. Now she understood why Harry didn't seem to share her feelings of guilt at that time. Maybe his wife was like Purvis. Maybe his wife was the one responsible for his actions as well.

By the time she said goodnight to Jimmy and lay down beside Purvis, he was already snoring. Sue stared up at the dark ceiling of their tiny bedroom and thought about Harry. With longing anticipation, she wondered when she'd be able to be with her lover again. Purvis grunted in his sleep, bringing her back to reality. She hated the stupid, lazy, ugly old man beside her. She wished he'd go away and never come back. She knew this would never happen. Leaving would require effort, and her husband avoided anything that might require effort. She was glad she'd cheated on the lazy son of a bitch and hoped she could do it again and again. She rolled over with her back to her husband, smiling secretly to herself as she drifted off to sleep.

Purvis's eyes popped open when he heard Sue's breathing settle into a sleepy rhythm. He knew her sleep patterns well enough now to be absolutely sure that she wouldn't wake up. He let his vision acclimate to the darkness as his ears listened to the ambient sounds of the night. During the war, he had learned to use all of his senses to stay alive in the trenches – a skill he'd lost the ability to control a long time ago.

He never slept more than an hour or two at a time, and even then, he never rested. He figured that this was one of the reasons he felt so tired and lazy all of the time, but he cared little about that. He got things done when he wanted to get things done. Anything he didn't feel like doing, he figured, could wait.

He lay still for twenty minutes. He thought about his wife, and he knew in his gut that things weren't right. She'd been acting strange lately and stranger still tonight. He knew she wouldn't hesitate to talk to him if she wanted something or had something to complain about. The fact that she did neither told him a great deal. She was hiding something. He knew there were only a few things that she'd have to hide from him, and it didn't take a genius to guess which one was the most likely.

This possible turn of events hadn't come as a complete shock to Purvis. He'd lived long enough to know that such behavior was common. It's the oldest story in the book. The problem he had now was what to do about it. As it stood, his wife had no idea he suspected anything. He thought that maybe he could use her ignorance to gather some more information, but he'd have to be cautious. If she sensed that he was on to her, things could get ugly, fast.

Although Sue was only supposed to be working part-time at Lil' Ray's, her hours away from home began to increase. Purvis stopped arguing about it with her; in fact, they hardly discussed it. That was fine with her. She didn't care what he had to say about it anyway, so it was pointless to bring it up. Besides, he was becoming more preoccupied with all of the new neighbors who'd been moving in lately to show any interest in what she was up to.

Harry and Sue were starting to see each other with some regularity. The excitement of an illicit affair was heightened now that both of them were married. It was harder to find a place in which to fool around, which meant they often risked getting caught in the act. In reality, the danger posed by their voyeuristic encounters made their heated rendezvous more thrilling.

After their encounters, Sue dreaded returning to her husband and her mundane life. She yearned for the opportunity to run away with Harry for good, but knew he was never going to leave his family. She avoided mentioning the idea to him for fear of scaring him off. If she could only figure out how she could get away from Purvis and still be able to provide for herself and her son, she would be much happier. She remembered how much she'd struggled to make ends meet before Purvis came along, and she had no desire to return to such a life. For all of his faults, Purvis had provided for her and her son better than she'd hoped. He'd done her a great favor, and she despised him for it.

Purvis successfully played ignorant to his wife's affair. It was easy to find out the awful truth with only the slightest bit of detective work. He'd staked out Lil' Ray's one night near the end of her shift, and watched as his wife and Harry Lejuine left together in Harry's Ford pickup truck. He vaguely remembered Harry as being some kind of plumber, or electrician, or something or other that had come to Lil' Ray's from time to time. He knew that Lejuine was married with kids but liked to step out when he had the opportunity. Purvis didn't care a bit what Harry did in regard to Harry's wife, but he wasn't too pleased with what Harry was doing with his Sue.

There was little doubt as to what the two were doing. Purvis managed to follow them to a dark country road not too far away from his house where he watched them park and turn off the lights. He damn near walked right up on them going at it, without either one of them noticing his presence only ten yards away. They didn't care if they got caught, thought Purvis.

"God damned slut," he muttered under his breath.

After awhile, he made his way back to his truck and drove in silence back to the house he shared with a wife who didn't give a shit about him and the child that he was playing daddy to. He bottled up the rage he felt growing inside and sat out on the front porch, listening to the country music playing on the radio. He was working on his fishing tackle when Sue got dropped off by Bubba after her shift. She had to wait for a ride home and Bubba had been running late, she casually explained to her husband as she sauntered past him into the house. Purvis glanced up for a second and nodded before returning to his work, seemingly unconcerned and unaware.

Sweet Sue was having the time of her life, and, for all she knew, her husband didn't have a clue. As for Purvis, he knew everything he needed to know except what he was going to do about it. While it took him awhile, he eventually admitted to himself that he was going to have to put her out. He knew it would be a hard thing to do, and even harder on the boy, but it had to be done. He didn't relish the idea of living alone again, but anything was better than this.

By this time, Purvis had gotten to know a few of the new neighbors. Houses had sprung up almost overnight up and down the road that used to be his driveway. Nice houses with nice families that were happy to see him when he came knocking on their door, introducing himself with a peach cobbler or hot apple pie and welcoming them to the neighborhood. Once Sue and Jimmy were gone, he wouldn't necessarily be alone or lonely in his little shack anymore. He had the residents of Johnson Road to provide him with company and amusement.

One late Tuesday night, things came to a head. The night wore on and Sue still hadn't returned home from work. It was one thing to come home an hour or two late, but this was too much. As Tuesday night turned into Wednesday morning with his wife nowhere in sight, Purvis had had enough. Something had to be done. He slipped out of the house and set out in search of his wife only to find himself back home within hours.

As the sun rose and it was time to send the boy off to school, Purvis was beside himself. Hell, Jimmy wasn't even his, and now he had to take care of the slut's child while she was with another man. Once the boy was off, he found himself pacing. Maybe someone saw her, he thought. Maybe there was someone that knew something.

He drove down to Lil' Ray's in the early afternoon to see what he could find out. Jimmy would be coming home soon and would almost certainly be asking questions – questions Purvis could not answer. Lil' Ray's wasn't open yet, but Danny Boy was around the back, emptying a mop bucket.

"Hey, Danny Boy. How's it going?" Purvis asked.

Danny Boy jumped, startled to see Purvis almost beside him. He was always a little jumpy, and he'd blanked out while tending to his mindless chores.

"Hell, Purvis, you got to stop sneaking up on fellas like that," he grumbled out of one side of his mouth while clenching his unfiltered Lucky Strike in the other.

Danny Boy stopped what he was doing and looked at the old man, his head cocked sideways and his eyes squinting as a result of the ever-present cigarette smoke drifting up into his face.

"Sorry. I figured you seen me comin'. Any chance you seen Sue 'round here?"

"Course I seen her. She works here."

Danny paused for a moment. He knew what Purvis was asking, but he didn't like to meddle in the affairs of others. Danny Boy was pretty dumb, but he didn't mind playing dumber when required.

"Ain't seen her today, though. She worked last night. Pretty sure she left at the usual time, but couldn't swear to it."

He saw that Purvis was agitated and felt sorry for the poor fool. Everyone knew Sue was stepping out on the old man, even after everything the stupid redneck had done for her. Still, it was none of Danny's business. Purvis should've known what he was getting into before marrying the little whore.

"I'm sure she'll turn up. Got that boy to look after," he added.

In no way was he even remotely sure of that, but he reckoned it was the thing to say.

"Yeah, I s'pose so."

After an awkward moment, Purvis nodded to Danny Boy and walked back toward his truck. Danny Boy picked up his mop bucket and quickly returned to the relative safety of Lil' Ray's before the old man wanted to ask him anything else. Purvis climbed back into his truck and began to exit the parking lot when he saw Sheriff Gaskin's cruiser parked discreetly across the road just off the highway in the shade of a big oak tree. He pulled up alongside the sheriff's car and rolled down his window.

"Sheriff," Purvis nodded.

"Purvis," Clifford nodded in return.

"The wife didn't come home last night," Purvis said as matter of fact as he could. "Getting worried 'bout her. Got that little boy to look after."

"Hmmm," Clifford grunted, letting the situation sink in.

The sheriff already had a good idea what was likely going on, but figured Purvis could use a little nudge in the right direction.

"Not like her to just not come home," Purvis added after a pause.

He could see that everyone already knew about his wife's extracurricular activities. He wasn't sure how to address the issue and have anyone take him seriously under the circumstances.

"Well, I'll ask around a little for you and let you know what I find out. In the meantime, let me know if she shows up so I don't waste my time."

"I'd sure appreciate that, Sheriff."

"You take care now, Purvis."

"Yes, sir."

Purvis drove off and Clifford rolled up the window to his cruiser. Poor son of a bitch, thought the sheriff. The old man deserved a hell of a lot better than this.

Later that evening, just as Clifford was headed home for the day, a call came into the station. It appeared that Sue wasn't the only one that hadn't made it home last night. A Mrs. Lejuine was calling to report her husband had stayed out all the previous night and had not shown up to work today. She told the deputy that she'd called everyone they knew, and no one had any idea where her husband could be. Deputy Bryce took down the information and kindly informed Mrs. Lejuine that at least twenty-four hours would have to go by before the sheriff's office could file an official missing person's report. The deputy tried to console the poor woman, telling her that he'd do everything he could to get to the bottom of her husband's disappearance, whether it was official or not.

Once he passed this latest bit of news around the station house, the sheriff told everyone about the conversation he'd had with Purvis Johnson earlier that day regarding his missing wife. This would be one of those unfortunate situations when the sheriff and his deputies would have to investigate the obvious and become the bearers of bad news to the desperate families.

Clifford relegated the task of asking questions at Lil' Ray's that evening to Deputies Bryce and Willis, with clear instructions to act appropriately official and not take any crap from the drunken yokels who were sure to find the whole scenario amusing. Clifford was going home to eat dinner and would follow up on the information in the morning.

The entire situation disgusted him. What kind of man would run out on his wife and kids without a word? Clifford thought that whatever trouble Harry had coming from his soon to be ex-wife was nothing compared to what the sheriff would like to do to him if he caught up with him first. Leaving the dirty work for him and his men was pretty low, even for a low down son of a bitch like Harry Lejuine, thought Gaskin. What the sheriff thought of Sue he didn't care to acknowledge even to himself.

By the next morning, Clifford found out pretty much what he figured he'd find out from his deputies. The rumor that they'd been engaged in an extramarital affair was common knowledge at the barroom and, although there was no way to completely confirm it, the evidence at this point spoke for itself. Harry and Sue had been seen together at Lil' Ray's and had, most likely, met up soon after each had left that night. Neither one of them had returned home nor been seen in the area since.

The missing person's report for Harry Lejuine was now official. Sheriff Gaskin put a call in to the neighboring counties to keep a look out for the couple and told the two deputies to check around at some of the local motels to inquire if anyone remembered seeing either of the missing people. He instructed Deputy Stevens to check into whatever vehicular information he could find and put out an APB on the plates. He would personally pay a visit to Mrs. Lejuine before swinging by the Johnson place to follow up with Purvis.

The visit to the Lejuine residence did not go well.

"Mrs. Lejuine, I understand that your husband didn't come home from work last night. Do you have any idea where he might've gone?" Clifford asked.

He knew where this was headed, and he tried as well as he could to go easy on the poor woman.

"Any relatives he might've stopped by to see?" he continued, "Maybe a hunting cabin he liked to go to on occasion?"

"No, nothing like that. I already told this to one of your deputies. I tell you, something's wrong. Harry would've been home by now."

"Yes, yes, I understand. We checked around. It looks like the last place he was seen was somewhere called Lil' Ray's. Ever hear of it?"

"That place over on Riverside? Why would Harry've been there?"

"Lots of guys go there after work to have a beer or two and unwind."

"Not my Harry. He doesn't drink. Works too hard and doesn't cotton to drunkards and bums."

"We have several witnesses that place him there."

"Several drunks, I bet; can't take a drunkard's word for nothin'. Is that all you and your men been doing, Sheriff – tossing back cocktails while on the taxpayer's dime? No wonder you can't find my Harry. You and your lackeys been looking in the one place my Harry wouldn't be caught dead in."

"Mrs. Lejuine, I assure you my department has taken your husband's disappearance seriously, and we've been investigating it thoroughly. In fact, during this investigation, we've uncovered some uncomfortable information regarding your husband that I'm afraid you may be unaware of."

"Is that so?"

"Unfortunately, it is. Do you know anyone by the name of Sue or Susan?"

"No, I do not, and I don't care for the implication, Sheriff."

"We have concrete knowledge that your husband was last seen with Susan Johnson. She's a barmaid at Lil' Ray's, which also happens to be the last place your husband was known to be."

"That's ridiculous. Why would Harry be at a bar with some harlot barmaid?"

"I'm only stating the facts, ma'am."

"The facts? You wouldn't know the facts if they hit you over the head. I'm telling you my husband doesn't drink and certainly doesn't sleep around with loose women. Are you calling me a liar, Sheriff?"

Clifford remained silent. He knew the poor woman was distraught and taking it out on him. He'd learned long ago that this often came with the unpleasant task of bearing bad news to people who didn't care to hear it. All the more reason he intended on making Harry sorry he ever left it up to his department to relay the coward's absence to his unsuspecting wife. He felt confident that when he caught up with the two-timing loser that there would be a charge of resisting arrest and the subsequent forceful restraint that was generally required when dealing with offenders who refused to go quietly.

"Of course not, Mrs. Lejuine. I'm just doing my job. Sometimes, that means telling people things they don't want to hear."

"I'm sure it does, Sheriff. I bet most people don't want to hear your excuses for not doing your job."

Clifford bit his lip and remained silent. This was getting to be a bit much. Man, is Lejuine gonna pay for this shit.

"If you're so certain about this alleged affair, why don't you ask the whore where my husband is? I guess that never occurred to you or your men, did it?"

"Her husband reported her missing the same time you did."

"Her husband? She's married? Yet you still think she's sleeping with my Harry?"

"We have reason to believe that they ran off together."

"What? So now it's not just an affair. You're saying that they ran off with one another? My Harry wouldn't do that. We have three kids. Say what you want about me, but Harry would never run out on his kids."

The distraught woman stopped herself, choking back tears. How could that sorry bastard do that to me, she thought. I knew he was up to no good. I'm going to kill that no good son of a bitch!

"Nevertheless," Clifford continued, "It's all we have to go on for the moment. I've contacted some of the neighboring counties to keep a look out for your husband's truck, and my men are canvassing the area for any sign of the two."

"That's all you have to go on? How do you know he wasn't kidnapped? You don't know that he ran off with this slut. You're just guessing – taking the easy road. Have you checked with the State Police or the FBI to see if any other businessmen have been abducted in the area? I bet not. No, instead you come here and accuse my husband of being a philanderer, telling me he ran out on his family to be with some floozy we all know he wouldn't even give the time of day to. It's a disgrace; you're a disgrace. You and your whole department."

"Mrs. Lejuine, I…"

"What about the other woman's husband? How do you know he didn't have something to do with it?"

Clifford almost laughed at the thought. Old man Johnson barely had the energy to get off of his front porch, much less carry out some elaborate plot for revenge.

"Mrs. Lejuine, I assure you…"

"You don't! You assure me of nothing. I'm telling you something bad has happened. My Harry wouldn't do this to me."

"Mrs. Lejuine, I…"

"He couldn't have."

He did, Clifford thought. He didn't have the heart to say it aloud. He was relieved to get out of the line of fire from Mrs. Lejuine's tirade. Once he'd gotten a small taste of Harry's wife's temper, the sheriff had to admit that maybe the man's behavior was understandable. Following up with Purvis would seem almost a pleasure compared to his visit with Mrs. Lejuine.

Pulling off of Riverside Highway onto Johnson Road, his police cruiser slowly drove down the pleasant little street. As he glanced back and forth at the neighborhood, he thought to himself that the brightly painted houses and their neatly trimmed lawns could be used as an advertisement for the suburbs. The homes were identical in size, with only two exceptions – the big house located near the end of the road and the tiny shack hidden among the trees just beyond.

The houses couldn't be more different from each other, and neither could the inhabitants – the Petersons and the Johnsons. Odd neighbors, thought Clifford. Chuckling to himself, Gaskin wondered just how much it bothered George that the street he lived on was named Johnson Road and not Peterson Place. The thought reminded him of the time that George had unsuccessfully petitioned to name the road after himself.

Purvis Johnson was sitting on his front porch when the sheriff pulled up. The old man's rusty pickup truck was parked on the front lawn, the small garage in the back serving more for storage than for parking a vehicle. The two men greeted each other stiffly, followed by a short, awkward pause. Purvis was the first to speak.

"Heard anything 'bout my wife, Sheriff?"

"Nothing yet. Was sorta hoping she was going to turn up by herself."

"Nope. Not a word. Don't know what to tell the young'un."

Clifford frowned and nodded in recognition of the old man's predicament.

"Damn shame when a little one's involved. I'll never understand how a mother could leave her own baby," the sheriff replied.

He paused for a few seconds before breaking the bad news.

"Ever hear of a fella by the name of Harry Lejuine?"

"Name sounds familiar, but not sure I can place the face. Why you askin'?"

"I'm not sure how to tell you this, Purvis, so I'm just going to come out and say it. Rumor has it that Sue and this Lejuine character been seeing each other on the side. We have reports that they were last seen together the other night before they both turned up missing."

A few minutes passed while Purvis mulled this over. He steadied his composure and quietly asked, "They both turned up missing? I take it that fella' didn't go home, either."

"Yep, that's what I'm sayin'. Turns out he's married, too, with three kids to boot. We think he and Sue ran off together."

The two men went silent, both staring off into the distance, while the gravity of the situation sank in. Purvis muttered one word under his breath, so muffled Clifford could barely make it out.

"Bitch."

Clifford nodded in agreement.

"Well, I appreciate you looking into the matter for me, Sheriff. Feel free to pass on by anytime you want."

"I surely will. You take care of yourself and that little one. He's got a heavy load to bear now, and you're all he's got."

"Yep, I'm afraid so. I gotta go in now and get myself prepared for when he gets home. Gonna' be a tough one."

Clifford walked back to his patrol car and drove down the street. The neighborhood didn't look quite as pleasant as when he'd arrived earlier. He repeated the word that he'd just heard, somewhat louder, but with the same emphasis. It seemed to be the most fitting word he could think of at the moment.

"Bitch!"

*

March 6, 1963

"Hot today," Clifford commented.

"Hot every day, Sheriff," Purvis answered.

He had a pretty good idea why the sheriff was here again today, and he was getting annoyed by the whole thing. The fact that Gaskin was going to beat around the bush just made Purvis think that the sheriff thought of him as a fool who had to be dealt with as such. This did nothing to improve his mood on this hot afternoon.

Normally, he would've played along like he usually did, acting dumb so that the sheriff would have to explain even the most inane detail to him while trying not to show impatience and blow the whole 'interrogation' or whatever police term was appropriate. Purvis wasn't in the mood today.

"How's your boy?"

"Why don't you just get to the point, Sheriff? I got things to do today," Purvis quickly interrupted.

The outburst took Gaskin by surprise. The old man was usually slow in speech and thought, and definitely not one to be so short with him. This, added to the fact that the sheriff didn't care much for anyone who questioned his authority, made him change his attitude.

"Well, your boy is the reason I'm here," the sheriff answered coldly in return.

"What about my boy?"

Clifford didn't care much for the tone Purvis was using and he could see things were going to get ugly, fast. He took a deep breath and figured he'd start over and try to de-escalate the situation. Just then, the two men's attention turned to the car coming to a stop in front of the tiny house.

"Oh shit," muttered Clifford under his breath. This was the last thing he needed right now.

Detective Stallworth's car stopped inches from the sheriff's bumper at the end of Johnson Road. He got out, slammed the door shut, and nodded to the two men on the front porch as he walked up to the shack, side-stepping an old tire hidden among the overgrown weeds in the lawn just in time. Falling into the dirt would have made the two country bumpkins' day, thought Robert. Well, they would just have to do without the added entertainment this afternoon.

"What can we do for you today, Detective?" asked the sheriff before the old man could say anything and get this meeting off on the wrong foot. "Purvis, you remember Detective Stallworth, don't you?"

"Detective," Purvis said, nodding to Robert, the neighborly effect muted by his icy glare.

"Mr. Johnson," replied Robert sharply.

Robert figured since he looked official, he was better off acting that way. Any attempt on his part to be personable was going to appear insincere and would not be appreciated. He had learned the hard way that he was never going to be looked at with anything other than suspicion by the locals, and he always got better results by acting professionally.

Purvis eyed the detective coldly, then turned and addressed the sheriff with a warmness that had been lacking just minutes before.

"Seems like you pulled out the big guns today, Sheriff. What exactly do you think my boy is up to? Public Enemy Number One?"

"I'm not here about your boy, Mr. Johnson," Robert quickly answered before Clifford could open his mouth.

"Then why are you here?"

"Actually, I'm not here to see you at all. I just swung by looking for the sheriff."

"Well, here I am, Detective," Clifford answered back as friendly as he could. "Of course, you could've contacted me through the department and saved yourself a trip all the way out here."

"I can think of no better place to meet you than out here on Johnson Road," countered Robert, just as friendly as the sheriff.

Robert paused for a moment, watching the other men's reactions. He found that sometimes it was people's reactions more than their words that told you the most about what they were thinking. He could see by their undivided attention that his words had just the effect he'd intended.

"A lot of things happen out here for such a quiet community, don't you think?" continued Robert.

Clifford stayed silent for a minute to see if Purvis was going to respond, just in case this was some ploy of the detective's. Even Purvis couldn't be that dumb, thought the sheriff; he had determined a long time ago that the old man didn't know anything useful about anything.

"I'm not sure what you're getting at, Detective," Clifford eventually responded. "A lot of things happen all over the county. What things are you referring to?"

Robert ignored the question. He was on the offense now, and he was going to stay that way.

"You know, it just occurred to me that this was the place where we first met. It seems like only yesterday."

What the hell was the detective talking about? Clifford felt out of the loop and didn't appreciate it.

"Anyway, I always thought it was a bit odd that the side of your house faced the street and not the front like all the other houses on the block," said Robert, directing his comments to Purvis.

"That's 'cause Johnson Road used to be my driveway, and my house is facing the highway, which used to be the only street," answered Purvis, an explanation he'd given dozens of times before.

"Well, that would explain it," replied Robert.

"Is that what you wanted to see me about, Detective?" asked the sheriff.

Clifford couldn't resist the chance to mock Stallworth.

"No, of course not, Sheriff Gaskin. I understand you came out here about some neighborly dispute between Mr. Peterson and Mr. Johnson's son. I'm sure that's nothing a fine law enforcement officer like yourself can't handle without the involvement of the state troopers, particularly a pesky detective like me."

He turned back to Purvis and said, "I take it your boy isn't home right now, Mr. Johnson?"

So, he was here about the boy, thought Purvis. Clever fucker.

"Nope, took off awhile ago. Why'd you ask?"

"No special reason. I just noticed your truck parked over there. Didn't know your boy had his own car."

The sheriff's eyes swept the surrounding area. He hadn't even thought about the truck being there until the detective mentioned it. Asshole detective thinks he's so smart.

"Yep. Finally got that old jalopy running. He's been working on it forever. I figured it was a lost cause myself," answered Purvis with an air of pride regarding his son's mechanical skills.

"That old rust bucket you had in the garage all these years?" asked Clifford with amazement.

"That's the one," Purvis answered as the three men glanced over at the garage.

The garage was a mess; the common theme being dirt, disarray, and rust. There were rusted car parts scattered haphazardly all over the ground, and oily tools lay cluttered on a dirty shelf. A child's bicycle was hung on the rusted tin wall, barely noticeable behind an ancient, shadeless floor lamp and a bent up old fan. Broken down lawn equipment was strewn about, covered with thick layers of dirt. Cobwebs were everywhere, testifying to the antiquity of everything in the shed. The only empty spot in the dilapidated building was an area in the very center, with the unmistakable depressions of tire tracks where the previous automotive tenant had once quietly resided.

As the men gazed at the garage for a moment, Sheriff Gaskin said, "That car was in there so long, I thought it was holding the roof up."

"Yeah, that garage was always little Jimmy's space," the old man explained. "I must've told him a million times to clean it up, but the house is so small, I s'pose there was no place else to put all that stuff."

The detective's eyes scanned the decaying inventory in the dirty shed. He couldn't imagine why anyone would keep that junk lying around for so long without throwing it in the trash.

"Now that he's got that car running, maybe he can use it to haul that crap to the dump," said the sheriff.

Purvis and Clifford laughed, and the sound seemed to wake Robert from a trance.

"You okay, Detective?" Purvis asked, but there was no actual concern behind his inquiry.

"Yes, sir. I guess I know who to come to when I need some auto repairs, and where to bring my rusty old lawnmower when it breaks down," Robert replied, playing along.

Small talk was never Robert's strong point and the exchange sounded clunky and awkward even to him. Purvis and Clifford nodded appropriately, but it was clear to all who the outsider was.

"Is that Peterson girl with Jimmy?" Sheriff Gaskin asked directly to Purvis.

"Don't rightly know, but could be. Why? Is Mr. Peterson bending your ear again?"

"You know it. It's his favorite pastime. Man needs to get a hobby."

"Didn't know it was against the law for my boy to date."

"It isn't," interjected Robert. "And since no crime has been committed, I guess my presence is no longer required. It was good to see you again, Mr. Johnson."

Robert shook Purvis's hand, then nodded goodbye to Clifford, "Sheriff."

Detective Stallworth walked briskly back to his unmarked police car and waved briefly as he turned around in front of the old shack and drove down Johnson Road toward the highway. His lunch was beginning to back up on him and he was all out of antacids. Robert contemplated turning on his siren on his way to the drugstore, but talked himself out of it.

"Damn!" the detective exclaimed out loud to the empty seats in his patrol car. In all of the small talk, he'd forgotten to harass the sheriff about the overdue reports.

Chapter Six

"I can't believe I get home late and dinner is still not ready," Jake shouted to his wife in anger. "What the hell have you been doing all day?" He leered at her with that all too familiar menacing look.

"I'm a little behind. The kids kept me running today," Mary answered while diverting her eyes, trying in vain to defuse Jake's anger.

She hated using the boys as scapegoats for her husband's wrath, although lately they made enough mischief on their own that it seemed justified. Jake mused over the last comment for a moment while he popped open a beer, slung back a big gulp of the cheap brew and stared out of the window down the street. He was already working on his second six-pack, and the effects of the fermented hops on what was left of his brain cells only made his demeanor more unpleasant.

"What the hell have the little bastards been getting into now?" he asked, the muscles in his jaw twitching.

Mary hesitated before answering, not sure if the question was rhetorical. She hastily prepared supper with her head down and eyes averted, hoping that Jake would take his sorry ass outside and give her a small reprieve. She exhaled when she heard the screen door slam shut behind her and caught sight of her husband through the window, staggering across the yard in search of the boys.

The Bickmans were the first family to live on Johnson Road, not counting the old man and his boy who lived in the rickety shack at the end of the lane. They had moved into their new house almost ten years ago and had watched the neighborhood grow around them. A few of the houses had been constructed around the same time as theirs, and some of the families, such as the Jenkins, had been living there almost as long as they had, but the Bickmans still considered the street theirs – as if they had discovered a new territory and planted their own flag.

The remaining houses down the block had been built in spurts; one or two were still in the on-again, off-again construction phase. The surrounding region had undergone significant growth over the last decade, and the housing construction industry responded with gusto. The result of the construction boom was that there was a seemingly endless choice of newly built neighborhoods throughout the area. Unfortunately, this had caused the overall value of each house to decrease.

Jake strutted drunkenly down the street in search of his boys. They were fast becoming delinquents, terrorizing the little neighborhood by bullying the other children and pulling childish pranks. He blamed their bad behavior, like he blamed almost everything in his life that displeased him, on his wife. If only she would step up and contribute properly to the family's well-being, they would all be better off, he reasoned. He tried as hard as he could to set her on the right path, and he'd continue to do so as long as was necessary. 'Till death do us part' – Jake took his marriage vows seriously and was proud of the commitment he had so generously made to someone he considered beneath him.

He spotted Gladys Jenkins watching over her little girl, Elizabeth, as she rode her tiny bicycle back and forth in front of their house. Gladys waved at him as he strode down the quiet street, and he reciprocated.

"Have you seen Jack or Frank around?" Jake called out to the woman sitting on her front steps.

"They were roaming around earlier. I think they headed down by the creek, past the Johnson place," replied Gladys.

She knew boys would be boys and gave them a certain amount of leeway for their misbehavior, but Gladys didn't care much for the Bickman boys. They weren't just mischievous – they were mean. Although she loved to spend time with Elizabeth, there were times that she would have liked to get some housework done while her little girl played outside in the yard, but she didn't like to leave her daughter unattended for very long, primarily due to the proximity of the two boys. Maybe she was being over-protective like her husband often told her, but better safe than sorry, she thought.

Jake muttered to himself under his breath. Gladys and Elizabeth watched him stagger down the street, and Gladys shook her head in disapproval.

"What's wrong with Mr. Bickman?" Elizabeth asked her mother.

Gladys thought about the question for a moment, but remained silent. She didn't know where to begin.

"I'm glad he's not looking for me," the little girl said to herself, shrugging her shoulders as she resumed riding her bike.

"So am I," answered Gladys.

Jake staggered down the street, his blood-shot eyes scanning the houses on either side, hoping to catch the boys committing whatever misdemeanors they were into at the time. He paid particular attention to the newly completed house on the right, which was still unsold and unoccupied. Jake wished they would hurry up and get the house off the market so that Barney would stop coming around.

He distrusted the real estate agent ever since he closed on his house and caught him flirting with Mary. The arrogant bastard even had the nerve to give her one of his pens after the signing as a 'memento'. Just a coincidence the pen had his name and phone number printed on it, Jake thought suspiciously. He wasn't that stupid, and he later broke that pen in half in front of his chastised wife to make his point hit home.

The boys were nowhere to be found, and Jake felt his anger rise with every additional step. They were not at the new house, nor at the property in mid-construction. They weren't even in the two empty lots still waiting to be purchased. There were only a few options left, and none of them bode well. Either they were harassing one of the Peterson kids, which always meant trouble, or they were bullying the Johnson boy, which Jake didn't appreciate much.

Jake actually liked old man Purvis, and he didn't like too many people. The old man was always respectful to him and kind to his family, and he was probably the only male in the county who Jake knew wouldn't dare make a pass at his wife.

Jake knew that his boys routinely made the shy little Johnson boy's life hell, and, even though he punished them severely every time they got caught, he knew they weren't going to stop. Although he could never pinpoint exactly why, he always thought that the Johnson boy seemed a little odd, and he had to admit that it made the child a prime target for the boys. The boy needed to grow a pair, thought Jake, and maybe everyone's life would be easier. Jake Bickman always liked to cast a considerable amount of blame on the victim of any transgression, with the exception being the frequent times he thought himself being persecuted.

When he didn't spot the boys at the oversized and pretentious Peterson house or at the small, disheveled Johnson shack, Jake figured they were down the ravine in the woods, getting into Lord-knows-what.

He was in no mood – or condition – to scramble through the brush in pursuit of the duo and called out for the pair as loudly and menacingly as he could. After more yelling, laden with profanities and threats, the two appeared before him. He raised his hand to take a swat at them as they drew near, but the boys ducked past their drunken father and ran home.

The boys knew they were in line for a whipping later that evening, but experience had taught them that later would be better. The old man was already worn out from work, and, with his excessive alcohol consumption, by the time he remembered about their punishment, he would have very little left in the tank. Besides, Jake always saved a little energy for berating his wife for some shortcoming, which favored the two youths more often than not. Unfortunately, there were exceptions, and those punishments were still frequent and brutal.

Once inside their home and out of sight of the neighbors, Jake let them all have it.

"I hope for your sake dinner is ready now!" he barked at his wife as she hastily served dinner for the family. "Where'd those two little bastards get off to?"

"They're cleaning up for dinner," Mary answered while setting the table, avoiding his glare.

Jake stared at his wife for a moment, contemplating his next nasty comment, when the boys scampered by out of reach and quickly sat down. Mary finished serving dinner, making sure that Jake's plate was first, and sat beside the boys. The three quietly remained there with their heads bowed and their eyes fixed on the spaghetti on their plates.

Jake stood over his family and waited, letting them feel the weight of his presence. He towered over them, fancying himself the lord and master of his kingdom. It was his house; they were his family; all belonged to him. He was their master, and he wanted them to know it. He felt he had to be hard just to keep everyone in line. He was responsible for the entire family, and it was his duty to do what was best for everyone, and he had no qualms about performing his duty.

After a brief moment, he sat down, hiding a smile at the collective sigh of relief that issued from his family in response to his seemingly calm disposition. It didn't take long for the terror to resume.

"What were you boys up to in the woods?" he asked.

The boys sat quietly for a moment, each waiting for the other to answer first. Jack was the eldest of the two as well as the undisputed leader, so he knew it was his unfortunate position to speak up.

"Nothin'. Just messin' around, I guess."

"Nothin', huh?" Jake replied, twirling his pasta around his fork before lifting it to his mouth and taking a bite.

"What about you, Frank? Were you doing nothin', too?"

"Yes sir," Frank answered. There was no right answer to his father's question, but he knew that there were many wrong ones.

Jake took another swallow of his beer to wash down his pasta. Realizing that he was leaving his wife out of the conversation, he turned his attention to her for the moment.

"Not much of a dinner tonight, huh, dear? I guess with everything else you had going on today, feeding our family just wasn't all that important."

Mary knew not to say a word. Jake wasn't finished berating her, and she was sure the interrogation was only getting started.

"So if you weren't watching over the kids, and you weren't diligently preparing our meal, what were you up to today? The house is a pig sty, so don't even try to tell me you were busy cleaning."

Mary remained silent. She hated this. It just seemed to get worse and she longed to have a normal life without the abuse. She knew she was trapped, and she knew that Jake knew it, too. He could be so cruel sometimes, especially when he was drunk.

Jack hated his father, hated everything about him, and he'd had enough of this. He felt it was up to him to step into the line of fire and save his mother from the monster she'd made the mistake of marrying.

"Why don't you just leave her alone?" he blurted out, surprising even himself with the force of his words.

Jake's head spun toward his eldest son, his eyes becoming daggers aimed at the boy.

"What'd you say?"

By now, Jack's blood was boiling. He'd inherited his temper from his father and, just like Daddy, he didn't know when to shut up.

"I said 'why don't you leave her alone'? Too drunk to hear me the first time?" Jack answered defiantly. He stared into his father's eyes with daggers of his own.

Jake started to rise from his chair; Jack rose to meet him. Suddenly, the doorbell rang, stopping them both in their tracks.

A brief moment of silence engulfed the house as all four inhabitants held their breath. The doorbell rang again, this time accompanied by a knock at the front door. The sounds from the outside world temporarily brought the entire family back from the brink of disaster, and they quickly re-assumed the 'happy family' roles they presented to outsiders. The Bickmans had become excellent thespians by necessity and sheer repetition when these moments arose.

Mary answered the door with a smile, Jake standing next to her with a blank look on his face. To the visitors standing at their doorway, Jake and Mary appeared to be the model of a loving couple.

"Good evening. I hope we're not disturbing you," said Gladys Jenkins with a warm smile.

Thomas smiled as he stuck his hand out to Jake.

"Good to see you again, neighbor," Thomas said as friendly as he could.

"Thomas." Jake answered as he shook his neighbor's hand.

Jake glanced at Gladys and her daughter, "Gladys. Elizabeth. It's good to see ya'll again."

"Hello, Jake. Good to see you, too," Gladys replied. "Did you find the boys?"

Jake let out a little laugh before answering. "Yep, playing in the woods. I should've known they'd be down there messing around."

"How are you doing, Mary?" Gladys turned her attention to Mrs. Bickman.

"Everything's just fine. How are you doing, dear?" she asked Elizabeth, who'd been silently standing between her parents, clutching her mother's hand.

"I'm doing good, ma'am," the child answered politely.

"Awe, she is such a little angel," Mary said and smiled at the proud parents.

"Yeah, she's alright," Thomas answered jokingly.

Gladys poked him with her elbow and shot him a playfully dirty look while Thomas, Jake, and Mary laughed. Little Elizabeth rolled her eyes, gazing up at her father with the same expression on her face as her mother's.

A brief moment passed by before Mary spoke again.

"Now, where are my manners? Please come in," she stepped to the side and opened the door wider to allow the Jenkins clan inside.

"Oh please, we don't want to disturb your dinner. We just popped by to see if you've seen our dog, Bo. He must've gotten out again and we can't find him anywhere," Thomas explained.

"I'm sorry to hear that, but I haven't seen him anywhere," Mary replied.

"Me neither," Jake added. "Hold on a sec, I'll ask the boys if they've run across him."

Jake turned toward the inside of the house and hollered, "Jack. Frank. Come here for a minute."

The boys came out of the dining room with innocent expressions on their faces.

"The Jenkins's dog got out and they were wondering if y'all might've seen him?"

The boys looked at each other for a second as if searching their memories.

"Sorry, ma'am," Jack answered for both of them, addressing Mrs. Jenkins directly. "We haven't seen him. Did you ask the neighbors down the block? They might've come across the little mutt."

The Bickmans looked sympathetically at the Jenkins, who were clearly disappointed, if not surprised, by the answer to their inquiry.

"Well, thanks anyway. Please let me know if you see him," Thomas spoke up as they turned back and started to walk down the walkway.

"We surely will," replied Jake. "I'm sure he'll turn up sooner or later."

"I hope so. He's my best friend," the little girl answered despondently.

"We're sorry again for disturbing your dinner," Gladys said as the family departed.

"No problem," Mary said as she closed the door.

No one spoke a word as the Bickman family sat back down to what was left of their dinner. The interruption had diffused the tension that had previously had the two eldest males about to come to blows, but everyone knew that the night's disturbing activities were far from over. As the family was finishing their last bites of pasta and tomato sauce, Jake addressed his sons directly.

"Now, tell me the truth. Either of you seen that dog today?"

Jake stared at Jack first, who by now had lost his previous boldness and bravado.

"No sir," Jack answered as sincerely as he could muster. The unexpected visitors had delivered him from a certain ass-beating, and he wasn't going to press his luck now. His only hope now was that Frank wouldn't give anything away when Dear Dad stared him down.

As predicted, Jake turned toward his youngest son. "What about you?"

Frank sat in silence, too terrified to answer his father.

"Well? Cat got your tongue about the dog?" Jake was proud of his clever line and savored it for a brief moment while his eyes bore holes into Frank. He knew that the boy was the weaker of the two and would crack under interrogation if he pushed it far enough.

"No sir. Haven't seen him," Frank finally answered, looking up into his father's eyes.

Jake had a feeling that the boys were lying to him, but he didn't give a shit about that stupid dog, so he decided to let it go. One less mutt on the block to bark in the mornings and wake him up when he was hung-over, Jake thought. That damn family was just too fucking perfect. Let them lament their poor, long-lost dog.

Jack and Frank were relieved when the meal was over and they were sent to their rooms to get ready for bed. If their father had known what they'd done to that little brat's dog, there was no telling what he would've done to them. It was ironic that it was the Jenkins's search for their little mutt that had saved them both from a serious beating. This only made the scenario even funnier to the cruel boys.

They turned out their lights and tried to fall asleep as fast as possible – before the unspeakable noises from the master suite could disrupt their slumber.

*

February 27, 1963

"Can I top you off, Sheriff?"

The waitress cocked her head while holding the pitcher of hot coffee in her left hand, her right hand fidgeting with her apron pocket. Janet had always been the nervous type, long before she took up waiting on tables to make ends meet soon after high school. The job was only going to be temporary; though she inadvertently made it a career by never pursuing any other opportunities. In all fairness, opportunities rarely came knocking for someone like Janet, stuck in a place like Peterson County. The fact that she never actively searched for new opportunities sealed her fate.

"Sure, why not?" replied Clifford.

He was already working on his third cup, but was in no hurry to leave the relative peace he found at the Olde Towne Diner. It was a slow time at the establishment and there was little to distract him from his work – unlike the endless interruptions he had to deal with at his office. Clifford needed to finish the latest report due to the state office and had procrastinated long enough.

Janet filled his cup with the steaming brew and left the officer to his work. The sheriff added a spoonful of sugar and a drop of cream and stirred his coffee for a few seconds, not paying attention to what he was doing. He managed to spill a few drops on one of

111

his forms, which snapped him out of his daydreaming and aggravated him further. Damn, he hated filling these out, even as half-assed as they were.

Clifford read through the couple of paragraphs he'd previously written, hoping to jump-start his memory. He had interviewed a few of the locals himself and hadn't gotten much that he deemed worthwhile out of it, so naturally he found that he couldn't remember enough details to make it look good on paper.

He'd never gotten into the habit of taking notes while talking to people, as his style was more casual conversation. He considered this one of his strengths; he figured that people would be more forthcoming if they felt they were just having a friendly chat than if they were being interrogated by the authorities.

This belief had some merit, although the fact that Clifford almost never followed up with notes later and that he had a poor memory to boot ended up sabotaging most of his efforts. Since the sheriff was never particularly adept at admitting his own shortcomings, this fatal flaw in his method continued to haunt him throughout his career.

Luckily, a few of the deputies had questioned some of the witnesses and provided the sheriff with reports that were actually filled out appropriately. They were devoid of any useful data as far as Clifford could ascertain, although the deputies had used professional terminology and written down dates, times, and names, which meant the sheriff could copy the information into his report, sign his name at the bottom, and make the paper appear, at least outwardly, to be good solid police work. Well, until the detective got a hold of it

"Damn it, what the hell was that comment that Mrs. Jenkins made about that dog?" he wondered aloud.

It was bad enough that he couldn't remember the date when she said it or why she had said it, but to not even be able to remember the context of the statement at all was ridiculous. If any of his deputies had performed their duties so poorly, he would've chewed their asses out for a month.

As it stood now, all the sheriff could do was to pretend it never happened and keep it to himself. Clifford couldn't shake the notion that it might've been important and a real clue in the case when they had almost nothing to go on.

"Fuck it," was all he could mutter to himself as he took another swig of coffee.

Clifford rearranged the papers that lay on the table in front of him and once again re-read the report he'd started. This time around, he took out his pen and filled out the rest of his report with worthless rubbish that sounded official. If the detective demanded reports, he would get reports. Never mind the quality of the information, reckoned Clifford. If Stallworth needed something more, let him go get it himself.

The sheriff would have Mabel type it up and correct any grammatical mistakes he may have made, put it in a fancy file-folder with an official stamp on it, and send it on over to the state office in the morning. Sheriff Clifford Gaskin had better things to do with his time

Chapter Seven

"They seem like such a nice family," Thomas commented as they walked back down the block in search of their wayward canine.

"Don't be so naïve, dear," answered Gladys.

Her lips were turned down at the corners and she rolled her eyes at her husband's comments. Although she realized that Thomas was gone most of the day and had only met the neighbors sporadically in the years that they'd lived there, Gladys also knew that, like most men, her husband could be oblivious to the obvious.

She didn't think for a moment that she really knew what most of her neighbors were like behind closed doors – nor did she care. She did, however, know too much about the Bickmans to describe them as 'a nice family'.

"What's naïve mean?" asked Elizabeth, looking up at her mother.

"Nothing, dear. It's a grown-up word," answered Gladys.

"It means that your mother doesn't think I know what I'm talking about," Thomas explained.

Gladys and Thomas laughed. They enjoyed conversationally sparring with each other, and even Elizabeth's constant questions didn't annoy them. They felt that it was a mark of intelligence that their little girl was so inquisitive, and they tried to explain things to her as well as they could. Of course, she was all of eight years old, so some things could never be explained to the child's satisfaction. In those cases, the interrogation could go on relentlessly until all parties were left frustrated and exhausted.

As the trio strolled down the quiet street, they resumed their efforts to find Bo. They scanned the horizon for any sign of their lost dog, occasionally calling out his name. They paid particular attention to the last two empty lots on the block as well as to the empty house still up for sale next to theirs. Gladys shook her head in disapproval at the very sight of that house for reasons she kept to herself. The beagle was nowhere to be found.

Thomas was curious about his wife's comment about the Bickmans, but knew that it was not the time to delve into it further. Elizabeth would want to know every detail, and Gladys would never gossip in front of the impressionable child.

Adding even further to his curiosity was his wife's apparent displeasure with the empty house next door to their own. She never discussed her feelings or thoughts in regard to the matter, although Thomas knew his wife well enough to sense her misgivings about why the house had been on the market for so long.

"Look, Daddy. It's Mr. Purvis," Elizabeth said with delight while pointing down the street. "Maybe he knows where Bo is."

Thomas and Gladys were hoping that this would be the case. They were running out of options the further down the street they walked. If their dog roamed out onto the highway, he was sure to be run over by a speeding vehicle, and the last thing Thomas wanted to see on his way to work in the morning was their beloved beagle's battered carcass rotting on the hot asphalt.

Unfortunately, if Bo had wandered down into the ravine behind the Johnson place, his fate could've been much worse. The slope was steep in spots, and there were all kinds of unsavory wild things roaming around in the thick brush. The tiny stream at the bottom was murky and probably filled with toxic waste from the aged septic systems that lined its banks, along with the few industrial entities upstream.

Environmental regulations were extremely lax in Peterson County. In areas where there was little opportunity and rampant poverty, any source of employment meant little oversight by the authorities whose favor was usually easy to purchase at a bargain rate.

"Hello, Mr. Purvis," Elizabeth said with delight as they drew near to the old man.

"Hi there, my sweet little angel," Purvis greeted the child with a warm smile. "Hello, Gladys. Thomas."

Purvis shook Thomas's hand and nodded toward Gladys before stooping down and patting Elizabeth on her head.

"Y'all going for a nice stroll this evening?" Purvis asked.

"Looking for our dog, Mr. Purvis," Thomas answered. "Have you seen him?"

Purvis shook his head. A look of concern crossed his wrinkled face.

"Sorry. I ain't seen him nowhere. How long's he been missing?"

"He was in the back yard this morning, but when I went looking for him this afternoon he was gone," Gladys replied.

The four of them remained silent for a moment. Things weren't looking good now. If Purvis hadn't seen Bo, it was unlikely that the dog had strayed down to his end of the road. The old man usually took up permanent residence on his front porch early every morning, and it was unlikely that the dog would have gone unnoticed if he'd wandered by.

"Maybe one of the Petersons might've seen him," Purvis suggested.

They all knew this was an unlikely scenario. Although Cheryl and the two children seemed friendly enough, George Peterson was a snobbish jerk. If he'd found the dog, he would've complained to anyone that would've listened to him whine. Most likely he would've called the pound and demanded that animal control report to his place immediately to apprehend the vicious beast. At the very least, he would've called the poor sheriff and had a deputy reprimand the Jenkins family for their failure to

117

secure the animal. In no way did Thomas or Gladys consider knocking on the Peterson door during their evening meal to inquire about their poor, lost dog.

After another moment of silence, the three adults could sense Elizabeth's anxiety at the thought of never finding her pet. She had Bo from the time he was a little puppy and would be devastated if anything happened to him – an outcome that was becoming more likely by the minute. Purvis broke the silence first.

"I'll let Jimmy know Bo got out. Maybe he can search 'round tomorrow in the daylight and see if he can find him."

"We'd appreciate that," Gladys answered.

"Ain't no problem. I'll ask 'round myself 'n see if anyone's seen anything. I'm going to bring some of my famous chicken soup to Cheryl for Georgie's lunch tomorrow. Poor child is sick again. I'll ask 'em to keep an eye out for Bo – discreetly, of course."

"Poor child is always sick. I feel bad for Cheryl, too; always trying so hard to take care of him without much help from that awfu…from her husband."

Gladys stopped herself from expressing her true feelings in front of Elizabeth, although it hardly mattered. Everyone felt the same way about George Peterson.

As if it weren't bad enough for Cheryl to be married to a man like George, she had the thankless task of caring for her daughter and ailing son. Everyone that knew the situation sympathized with the poor woman. 'A martyr and a saint, married to Satan hisself' is the way old man Purvis had exclaimed once – an estimation that summed it up best.

"Is Mrs. Peterson sick, too?" asked Elizabeth.

"I don't think so. Why'd you ask that?" replied Thomas.

"Cause sometimes sick people get sick from other sick people. Like the time I got the chicken pox from Francine at school," Elizabeth answered.

"I don't think what little Georgie has is contagious, dear," said Thomas.

"What's contagious?"

"It's when you can catch something from someone else."

"Oh. Well, maybe Georgie got it from someone at school."

"I don't think he's gone to school much lately, with him being ill all of the time," Gladys chimed in.

Elizabeth thought about this for a moment before asking, "Maybe he's catching it from his mama?"

"I really don't think he has that kind of illness, sweetie. Sometimes people just get sick all on their own," answered Gladys.

"I can see ya'll have your hands full with that one," Purvis finally said.

The three adults laughed while little Elizabeth was still mulling over little Georgie's predicament.

"I'll pass on by tomorrow and let ya'll know if I find out anything," Purvis said.

The Jenkins thanked him again and walked back toward their house before it got too dark to see. The three of them were worried about their lost pet and sad that they hadn't found him yet. Hopefully he would turn up the next day. If not, Gladys and Thomas knew their little girl's heart would be crushed.

After they put the distraught child to bed, the young couple lay together discussing the evening's events.

"What was that comment about the Bickmans all about?" Thomas asked.

Gladys took a moment to think of how to answer before replying. "I just have a feeling all is not well over there."

Thomas remained silent, waiting for his wife to elaborate further.

"I think Jake beats on Mary."

There, she spoke her misgivings aloud for the first time.

"Really? What makes you think that?" Thomas asked in surprise.

"There are days at a time when she doesn't come outside at all, and, when she does, she has those big sunglasses on or tons of makeup. With your schedule, I know you aren't around a lot during the week, but surely you must've been thinking the same thing. Just look at the way she acts. She's either jumpy or withdrawn, or she overdoes putting on a good face in front of others when Jake is around. And then, there's those boys…"

"Yeah, those boys…"

Thomas let his wife's words sink in. They'd both been having the same ideas about the Bickman situation, although this was the first time either one of them had talked about it openly.

"Thomas, I really think those boys might've had something to do with Bo missing."

"Do you really think so? Why do you say that?"

"Earlier today I saw the younger one talking to Elizabeth out in the front yard, so I went out there to keep an eye on them. He left almost immediately and walked down the street toward the Johnson place. When I looked for Bo later, he was gone."

"I'm not sure I'm following you. You said he walked down the street alone? Bo wasn't with him, was he?"

"No, but neither was Jack. Those two are always together. Besides, Frank wouldn't do anything unless Jack was there to tell him what to do. Maybe Jack was snatching Bo while Frank was being the look-out?"

"Dear, just because the two boys weren't together at that exact moment is hardly incriminating. How do you know Jack wasn't at home?"

"Because, when Jake came home later, he was looking for both of them. He wanted to know if we'd seen them. Then he went down toward the ravine to look for them. I mean, you should have seen him, honey. He was drunk and slurring his words and staggering around. It was a disgrace. Anyway, after a while, he came back up to his house with both of the boys. Don't you see – they were together when they came back, but not when they went down there."

"Maybe Jack was already down there and Frank was just looking for him. You didn't see either one of them with Bo."

Thomas could sense his wife's frustration with him for not agreeing with her. He knew that she didn't care for the boys and would naturally try to blame them for anything bad that happened on the block. He didn't care that much for the two hooligans himself, but remembering what a handful he'd been for his parents when he was a boy their age, he afforded them more slack than his wife did.

"Look, honey, I'm not saying you're wrong. Maybe they did have something to do with it. All I'm saying is that we don't have any proof. No one saw them with Bo that we know of. Maybe tomorrow Purvis can find out something for us. Little Jimmy can search down by the creek and see if there's any sign of him."

Gladys sighed. She knew he was right; just like she knew that she was right. She had a gut feeling about those boys and Bo, and she trusted her feelings. Still, there was no real proof, and it was possible they had nothing to do with the dog getting out.

Thank God Jimmy could take a look around down there tomorrow. Her mind would never be at ease until someone searched down the ravine. Poor little dog, she thought, all alone down in those scary woods in the dark.

"It's been a long day, honey. Let's just try to get some sleep and hopefully he'll turn up before long," Thomas said at last.

"You're right, dear. I hope so for Elizabeth's sake – and for Bo's."

The next day came and then the next. Purvis had no news to report, either good or bad. Jimmy had found no sign of the dog in the woods, and none of the neighbors reported seeing the little beagle.

Fortunately, Thomas had not spotted any canine road-kill on the highway. He had some flyers printed and they posted them on some telephone poles in the area, but no one ever contacted them.

Thomas went to the dog pound to inquire about the lost dog, but there were no reports of any dogs even close to Bo's description being found. It's as though their pet had just vanished off the face of the earth.

As hard as they both tried, Gladys and Thomas could never truly understand how a living creature like their dog could just disappear. Someone had to know something. Someone had to be responsible somehow.

After a few months, Thomas reluctantly took down the few remaining posters of their dog scattered around the neighborhood. It broke his heart every time he saw the picture of his missing friend – the puppy staring back at him with those sad eyes. He fought back the tears as he ripped the last one off of the rough creosote soaked wooden pole and tossed it into the trash.

Gladys never wavered in her belief that the Bickman boys had something to do with Bo's disappearance. She tried as hard as she could to keep an eye out anytime she thought those two might be creeping around outside. Outwardly, of course, she remained as friendly as ever, but she was determined to catch the two in the act of committing some criminal mischief.

*

August 9, 1961: 3:37

"The sheriff's not in, Detective," Mabel informed Robert as he walked into the station house.

It wasn't that she disliked the detective. In fact, she had no personal opinion of the man at all. She knew he had a good reputation for solving difficult cases, and she could see that he was considerably more competent than the officers that she'd grown accustomed to at the sheriff's office. Still, ever since he'd been coming around, her work load had increased dramatically. Lord knows he got under the sheriff's skin, which meant she heard about it relentlessly.

Detective Stallworth stood in front of Mabel's desk, gazing around the room, pretending not to hear her pronouncement regarding Gaskin's absence. She looked up from her desk and started to repeat herself, but Robert interrupted her.

"Yeah, the sheriff's not in. Any idea when he'll be back, Mrs. Crawford?"

"No sir. Sheriff Gaskin pretty much comes and goes as he pleases. He is the boss, you know," Mabel answered.

"I see. Well, in that case, may I speak with Deputy Sean Willis, please?"

Mabel hesitated for a moment. How the hell did the detective know Sean, she thought. She scanned her memory for a moment before realizing that his name must've been mentioned in one of the reports that the sheriff was always having her type up to send to the state office.

"He's in back, I believe. Wait here. I'll go see if I can find him," she told Robert before getting up from her chair and disappearing into one of the back rooms.

Mabel would normally have just buzzed the deputy on the phone at his desk and told him to come to the front, but she wanted to give the unsuspecting officer a little heads-up. She wondered what on earth the detective could want with Sean, and she knew that Sheriff Gaskin would not be pleased when he found out that Stallworth was questioning one of his deputies without his presence, knowledge, or consent. Still, there was no reason to deny him access. He was, after all, an officer of the law, and if the sheriff didn't want these kinds of things to happen, he should spend more time minding the store.

Robert knew that Mabel could've called the deputy on the phone, and he figured that she went to fetch the deputy in person because his visit wasn't expected or particularly desired. He was happy that his presence was intimidating to the deputies. He remembered when he was just a deputy starting out and occasionally came in contact with the detectives from the state office. He was so eager to be noticed that these events motivated him to elevate the quality of his work. He hoped that his involvement with these deputies might have the same effect. In his opinion, Sheriff Gaskin set a poor example for his deputies, and his laziness encouraged incompetence on every level.

After a few minutes, Mabel walked back to her desk, with the deputy not far behind. After the two introduced themselves, Deputy Willis invited the detective to have a seat at his desk in the back office. The others in the room pretended to be busy with official business and did their best to conceal their interest in the surprise visitor. Robert smiled to himself at their not so subtle pretense.""Detective Stallworth, what can I do for you today?" the deputy asked.

"Call me Robert. May I call you Sean?"

"Sure Detect…, I mean Robert."

"Well, Sean, I came down here with the intent of talking to the sheriff, but unfortunately, he's nowhere around."

"Yeah, he's over on Johnson…," Sean began to answer before catching himself. He was so unnerved by the detective's visit and eager to please that he blurted out the answer to a question that hadn't been asked. Damn, he thought, Gaskin wasn't going to like this at all. Sean felt that he'd already dug himself a sizable hole by even talking to the detective without the sheriff's presence. Giving out the big man's whereabouts was likely to get him an ass-chewing of monumental proportions.

"Over on Johnson Road," Robert finished for him. "That's okay, Sean. I'd rather talk to you, anyhow. Do you mind if I ask you a few questions?"

Sean shifted nervously in his chair. It was bad enough to be talking to the detective like this, but sitting in the middle of the sheriff's office, surrounded by the other officers, and chatting away with Stallworth was not going to go over well at all. He was sure that this would be like a slap in the face to the sheriff, and he felt like an unintentional accomplice. The detective might not care whether or not Gaskin liked it, but the sheriff was his boss.

"Sure, you can ask me whatever you want. I'm not sure there's anything I know that might be helpful to you, though," the deputy answered.

"As you know, Sean, I've been getting reports from Sheriff Gaskin. As I've read those reports, I couldn't help but notice your name come up a time or two. When I read between the lines, I get the impression that you're more involved in the investigation than you're getting credit for."

Robert let this sink in for a few minutes. He knew this was a dangerous game to play, one which could blow up in his face. Still, he was getting nowhere playing nice, and he needed to shake things up a little. Having this talk with the deputy in the middle of the station house without the sheriff's presence would definitely rattle a few cages. Only time would tell if his strategy would help or hurt the investigation.

"Unfortunately, those reports are proving to be almost worthless. The biggest fault is mine. As you know, a lot of the leads we get come from questioning people in the community and possible informants. Since I'm perceived by the locals as an outsider, most of the people I come in contact with are somewhat reluctant to even speak with me. This puts me at a distinct disadvantage, which makes me rely upon you and your fellow officers, which brings me to why I'm here."

As Robert paused for a moment, he noticed that the 'pretend work' noise in the room had diminished considerably. It seemed that he'd gotten more than just Sean's undivided attention.

"Every good cop knows that a lot of the information we get comes from non-verbal communication. It's not just what people say, it's also what they don't say. It's the way something is said, the expression on their faces, their body language, and stuff like that. A good interrogator uses all of these, not only in the course of interrogation to get facts, but also to get feelings and ideas that can prove to be just as useful. None of these things are in the reports."

The detective paused for another moment to let the deputy catch up before continuing.

"Now, I want you to understand, I'm not blaming the sheriff. He does the best he can to gather all of the information he feels is pertinent to the investigation and convey that information to me. It is unrealistic to expect him to do any better than he's already doing." Robert lied.

"I need to know your thoughts, your ideas, your feelings, and any theories you or your fellow officers may have about this case. I know you report these things up the chain of command, but I'm not so sure that Sheriff Gaskin is reporting them to me."

Sean shifted in his chair, his eyes glancing down at the papers on his desk. The rest of those nearby in the room suddenly became busy again, performing their assorted duties, and Robert could sense he was losing them all. He changed his tactics accordingly.

"Look, Sean. This isn't about taking credit for success or taking the blame when something goes wrong. This isn't about just 'doing your job'. I know the sheriff isn't going to like me being here, and he's more than likely going to take it out on you. I understand you may feel like you're sticking your neck out here, and I can appreciate the fact that you might think you're even risking your job, but this is your job."

Robert saw he had the room again and laid it on even thicker.

"Your job, my job, everyone's job here is about solving this crime. It's about catching the monster that did this and preventing him from doing it again. This is about protecting our community and punishing the guilty. It's about justice."

The detective's locker room speech had the effect he wanted. The room was silent; the deputy in front of him was focused on every word. Now, for the finish, he thought.

"We're all in this together, Sean."

Deputy Willis felt a lump in his throat. For the first time in a long time he remembered why he'd wanted to become a cop. Why didn't the sheriff ever talk to his deputies like this instead of making them feel like bumbling, incompetent fools? Instead, he threw his weight around and derided them, achieving the self-fulfilling prophecy of ineptitude in his workforce. Sean felt empowered; he felt as if he could crack this case wide open at any moment.

He looked at the detective who was staring at him, waiting patiently for a response. Sean felt his heart drop as reality came crashing down on him. He tried desperately to think of something – anything – to say.

"I'm sorry, Detective, uh, I mean Robert. I just can't think of anything that might be helpful right now," he mumbled.

"That's alright, Sean. I just want to make sure that if you think of anything, no matter how unimportant or insignificant it might seem, you let me know."

"I surely will, Robert."

"I guess I better go see the sheriff," Robert said, getting up from his chair.

The room was abuzz again with a steady influx of phone calls, errands being run, and the staccato sound of typewriters churning out the endless stream of paperwork required in law enforcement. Deputy Willis walked out with the detective.

"Let me guess. Gaskin is down there right now responding to some complaint by George Peterson?" asked Robert.

"Naturally, Mr. Peterson always has some complaint or another that requires immediate attention," Sean replied.

Both men laughed. Stallworth knew that George Peterson had quite a reputation as a needy citizen that could not be placated no matter how much attention he received.

"That man is never happy about anything. Right now, his major issue is with his daughter dating the Johnson boy," explained the deputy.

"Agatha, right?"

Sean nodded. The detective could remember every name he'd ever heard, or so the deputy thought with amazement.

"Dating Purvis's boy, Jimmy, I think," Robert stated.

Sean nodded again before adding, "Yeah, he smothers that little girl ever since all that happened with his little boy."

The men went quiet for a moment. Robert was the first to break the silence.

"It sure was tragic. Poor man."

Robert never thought he'd use the word poor in reference to George Peterson. The hard lesson to be learned was just how often the phrase 'money isn't everything' could turn out to be true.

"The sheriff talks to Purvis a lot, or so it seems by the reports," stated Robert.

"Yeah, but I'm sure it's not all official police work," Sean conceded. "They've known each other for quite a while. Still, I think old man Purvis is the only one on the block that ever knows anything."

"Probably because he just sits on that front porch all day," Robert mused.

"Yeah, that he does. Unfortunately, he's not exactly the sharpest tool in the shed."

"I know what you mean. I guess that explains why we're not getting anywhere with the reports," laughed Robert.

"Could be," Sean agreed.

"Thanks again, Sean. I look forward to working with you in the future. Maybe we can make a difference by working on this together."

"I appreciate that Detect…, I mean Robert. I'll do my best."

Detective Stallworth drove his cruiser down Riverside Highway, heading toward Johnson Road and the sheriff. He knew that there'd be repercussions from his visit with the deputy, but figured he'd deal with them when he had to. He had no intention of mentioning it now; it would just further incense Gaskin. Oh well, he'll just have to get over it, Stallworth thought.

He was hoping he'd get there in enough time to see Purvis with the sheriff. Maybe he could get something useful out of the meeting if he played the two right. He had no qualms about manipulating his fellow law enforcement officer under the circumstances. They weren't getting anywhere with Sheriff Gaskin's approach, so something had to be done – and he was the one to do it.

Chapter Eight

The construction of the Peterson domicile proved difficult for all involved. George wanted everything just so. He had unrealistic standards and demanded anything and everything be done immediately. He didn't intend to spend any more money than was originally quoted by any of the contractors. The fact that the original quotes didn't contain most of the items that George would later insist upon didn't seem to matter to him, although they mattered a great deal to the contractors. All of this resulted in costly delays, threats of lawsuits, and more than one bout of flared tempers.

As the on again, off again project lumbered on, a pattern emerged. Construction would start at a swift pace until George would inspect the progress and find it unsatisfactory. He then insulted anyone within earshot and demand that something be done. The hard working and generally broad-shouldered laborers on the receiving end of his tantrums didn't take kindly to his attitude and things often got out of hand. On occasion, the sheriff's office was called in to break up the ensuing melee.

After the threats of bodily harm were resolved, there would follow a pause in production. This brought on threats of lawsuits and the need for remediation to resolve differences. It was in everyone's interest to complete the project, so reluctant compromises and half-hearted apologies were always followed by an unenthusiastic return to work.

The house was finished eight months after the original estimated completion date and over-budget by thirty-five hundred dollars. Most of the additional money was tied up in litigation for years and had to be written off by the various contractors, who vowed to never do any work for George Peterson again. George didn't care.

The small family moved into the big house on Johnson Road within weeks of the birth of their second child. George Harold Peterson, Jr. was born ten days premature at Riverside Memorial Hospital. Cheryl had a difficult time with the pregnancy – a situation that was not helped by her husband's immature handling of the construction of their house.

By the time she went into labor, Cheryl was already exhausted. Her contractions began unexpectedly and George could not be reached, which required an ambulance ride to the hospital with her daughter in tow. Cheryl remained in labor for fourteen long and painful hours before she heard the cries of her son for the first time. Not long after that, she gave in to her fatigue and slept for two days.

As Cheryl recovered from the effects of a difficult delivery, she was only able to see her little bundle of joy for brief periods. George, Jr. was small and sickly and required extra care by the health care professionals. All of the nurses fell in love with the tiny little red-headed boy and doted over him despite their dislike of his father.

For his part, George, Sr. only saw his wife and son on rare and brief visits. These were usually accompanied by harassment of the doctors, nurses, and hospital supervisors concerning the myriad of grievances that he always had. Everyone was delighted when Mrs. Peterson and son were discharged to their new home on Johnson Road.

When Cheryl returned home, things didn't get much better for her. George refused help around the house, and she had her hands full with George, Jr. and little Agatha. Her husband had stopped paying attention to her since Agatha was born, and the only affection she received was from her children.

Her daughter was ten years old now, and Cheryl loved her dearly. But over the years since her birth, the little girl took precedence over George's wife's needs. Agatha was always 'Daddy's little girl', and, in some ways, her mother resented the affection her husband showed her. The situation with her daughter reminded Cheryl of the jealousy she'd experienced with her sister while growing up. She knew it was wrong and she felt guilty that she harbored those feelings, but felt helpless to control them.

Georgie was a fussy baby, whose cries woke the couple up every two hours almost every night. His father wasn't much help, preferring to roll over and press his pillow over his ears in an effort to block out the helpless wailing from the newborn. George would nudge his exhausted wife with his elbow or kick her under the covers until she got up to comfort the poor baby. Later, he chastised the bleary-eyed Cheryl about her lack of urgency to go to the child in need, thus allowing the unwelcome noise to waken him. After all, he explained, he was the breadwinner and worked hard to support them all, so, therefore, he required a good night's sleep.

He figured his wife had all day to catch up on her rest. She was merely a housewife with almost nothing to do. The fact that 'nothing to do' entailed taking care of two children, cleaning the house, doing the laundry, cooking the meals, going shopping, and doing all the rest of the endless and thankless tasks that could never be completed was beyond George's comprehension.

Fortunately, there were others in Cheryl's life that occasionally recognized her plight, and she did get some attention when her pregnancy was taking its toll. While her husband was preoccupied with work and all of the problems that he caused with the new house, Cheryl's mother and sister comforted her and tried to help out with Agatha whenever they could. Unfortunately, those moments were infrequent because both women had their own families to tend to. Nevertheless, Cheryl appreciated the recognition and emotional support that their few visits provided.

Once the baby arrived and they were settled into their new house, Cheryl became isolated from the few people she had that might've given her support and recognition. She was exhausted, struggling to keep up, while her husband criticized and complained. She became increasingly depressed, regretting the choices she'd made in life and her roles as a wife and mother.

A few of the neighbors came to the house when they first moved in to welcome them to the neighborhood. The cheerful guy from down the street with the quiet wife and two polite boys brought them an apple pie. The nice couple with the cute little baby girl came by with a casserole. The friendly old man and his son that lived in the strange little shack next to them brought over some delicious chicken soup. George was gregarious and gracious to all of them when they first came knocking, although in short order he ran most of them off.

George didn't like the two boys. He considered them hooligans and a menace to the neighborhood. He referred to their father as a drunkard, and he never bothered to recognize their mother's existence. He didn't care for the cute couple with the beautiful baby girl. He thought that they were pretentious for people of lesser means than the Petersons. Most of all, he despised the old man and his son who lived in the tiny house next to theirs.

George had a problem with the Johnsons even before he'd met them. He hated that eyesore of a shack that they lived in; hated that it was next to his beautiful new house. Thank God, he thought, the trees, bushes, and shrubbery hid the odd dwelling from plain view, but he still knew it was there. He made an offer to buy the property just to rid the block of the monstrosity, but the stubborn old fool who lived there wouldn't even consider it. When he met the old man in person and pressed the issue, the dumb redneck responded by laughing in his face. This incensed George. How dare that ignorant hick dismiss him so casually! In the end, he found there was nothing he could do about the situation.

He came up with the idea that the street name should be changed. Why should they all live on a street named after the poorest and least prestigious family on the block? He pushed the idea to the city council, which wasn't interested; so he took it up with the county office.

In order to achieve a name change, he was informed he would need the approval of most, if not all, of his neighbors. This proved impossible since George was the one guy on the block everyone hated. His idea to rename the street Peterson Place only served to unite the entire block into keeping the current name. Johnson Road it would stay, and he never forgave his neighbors for that humiliation.

Unlike all of the other neighbors, old man Johnson still came around despite George's objections. Purvis took to helping out the overwhelmed, depressed mother when her son was ill, which was more often than not. He recognized the woman's unappreciated efforts and complimented her. He also spread the word of her sweet, selfless nature to the other members of the community. Suddenly, Cheryl had people coming up to her when she was out shopping or running errands. They were friendly and sympathetic and praised her for her motherly sacrifices in caring for her ailing child.

For the first time in her life, Cheryl was noticed. The poor woman had suffered in obscurity for a long time, and she'd longed for acknowledgement and support. She was finally being recognized for her unselfish nature, and she was grateful that she was getting some attention at last. She was thankful to the old man for seeing her as no one had before and for introducing the real Cheryl to the world. Purvis became more of a father to her than the pious Brother Luke Bradford ever had been.

George Peterson was not pleased with his wife's friendship with his nemesis, and he let her know it. The problem was that Purvis was always nice to him no matter how mean and ugly he was in return. To make matters worse, his kids loved the old man, and his wife appreciated the help and support Purvis provided – support that he was too lazy or indifferent to provide himself.

He knew it was a losing battle to try to keep the old man out of their lives completely, so, over time, he relented. He continued to talk bad about the Johnsons whenever he could, but ceased his efforts to eliminate their presence entirely.

As Georgie grew from a baby into a toddler, his frequent bouts of illness lessened. He became mobile quickly, progressing from crawling to walking to running in what seemed like a matter of weeks. Cheryl was relieved by his development and didn't mind the extra effort it took to chase him around. He'd been sick for so long; she thought he'd never be anything but a bedridden, ailing child. Now, he was becoming a healthy growing boy, full of energy. She noticed her own energy increasing with her son's.

Georgie's return to health wasn't all good news for Cheryl. Much of the help and recognition she'd received from others began to fade away. Purvis's help was no longer needed, and her husband seized on that fact in order to eradicate the old man from the family's affairs.

The couple began arguing nightly over George's renewed demands that Purvis not come around, but Cheryl would stand up for the old man over her husband's wishes. This was a slap in the face to George. He was furious over his wife's defiance, but felt helpless to do anything about it. For a control freak like George Peterson, this feeling of being helpless was untenable.

The urgency of the problem with their neighbor declined when the boy unexpectedly fell ill once again. It started one night as a slight fever and general malaise that the couple dismissed as the effects of a common cold. By the next morning, however, Georgie's symptoms grew worse. His temperature remained elevated and he developed a cough. Cheryl thought they should just keep the child comfortable until he shook the cold off, but she was overruled by her husband's insistence on bringing the child to the doctor's office.

"I think little George will be just fine, Mrs. Peterson," Dr. Garrett reassured the worried mother. "It looks as though he has a touch of that nasty stomach virus that's going around. Give him the medications I wrote down for you and let him get plenty of rest, and I'm sure he'll be alright."

"He hasn't been eating well over the last couple of days. How long do you think it will be before he can get down any solid food?" Cheryl asked.

"Depends on how he feels. Start off slow with some broth or soup and see how he does. It shouldn't be too long before his appetite returns."

"I see that these are just over-the-counter drugs. Doesn't he need any prescriptions?" asked George, Sr., waving the medication list at the doctor.

"No. There's nothing I can give him that will cure a virus. It'll just have to run its course. The best thing we can do is to treat his symptoms and keep him comfortable. If he doesn't improve in a few days, come back and see me," Dr. Garrett explained.

The pediatrician didn't care much for George Peterson, who'd developed quite a reputation amongst the local health care workers. He was known to be a difficult man to deal with – one who liked to question everything even though he had no medical training or knowledge. Still, Dr. Garrett had been seeing George, Jr. since the boy first went home from the hospital after he was born, and he was worried about the youngster.

The little guy was sickly and presented a challenge to the doctor at times, but his mother seemed to be a good caregiver and doted on the child. The physician had developed a good rapport with both mother and child, and he was optimistic about the boy's health. He chose to overlook the patriarch's off-handed remarks and endless whining in the best interest of his patient.

With George, Sr. away at work and her daughter at school, Cheryl once again found herself tending to a sick child. The next day the child's condition didn't seem to improve, although Purvis did drop by with a batch of his famous chicken soup. She was grateful for the soup her kind neighbor brought over, as it provided both her and her son some much needed nutrition when they seemed to need it the most.

The boy managed to get some of the delicious broth down, but his nausea prevented him from eating enough to get his strength back. Worse yet, Cheryl seemed to catch whatever her son had, and it was all she could do to tend to the sick child while fighting her own illness.

"Don't you worry now. Ol' Purvis is here to take care of you two," the old man reassured her when he looked in on the ailing pair the next day.

"I can't thank you enough for all you've done for us, Mr. Johnson," Cheryl told him.

She'd been weak and nauseated since the night before and was experiencing severe cramps in her lower abdomen. Purvis came by just in time to help out with the boy because Cheryl didn't have the strength to tend to the poor child.

"Now, call me Purvis. Mr. Johnson was my father," he said with a smile. "It's no trouble at all. Y'all get some rest and I'll bring some more soup 'round for y'all in a bit. Just remember to go slow and I'm sure by tomorrow both of y'all will be feeling much better."

She gratefully did as he instructed. She was worried she might have to drag them both back to Dr. Garrett's office, but just as Purvis predicted, the two began to feel much better by the next day.

Slowly, the mother and child regained their strength, and even her husband secretly admitted that he was indebted to the old man. He would never voice the sentiment aloud, of course, but his endless indictments of the Johnson family's substandard living conditions diminished for a time.

Although both Cheryl and her son recovered from their intestinal bug, the youngest Peterson never seemed to stay healthy for very long. The poor child suffered recurrent bouts of illnesses of varying symptoms and severities for years. It seemed that just as he would shake off whatever latest affliction he had, he'd come down with something else within a few months.

George, Sr. accused Dr. Garrett of incompetence and insisted on second, third, and fourth opinions to no avail. He went on tirades and blamed everyone for his son's suffering, including his wife, the Bradford family gene pool, the air and water on Johnson Road, and even poor old Purvis Johnson. None of his actions helped his son's condition improve, but only made his wife's heavy burden harder to bear.

Despite her husband's neglect and abuse, Cheryl managed to care for her son, nursing him back to health each time. Sometimes, her sister and mother would stop by and help out a little; other times, Purvis would drop by and lend a helping hand. Mostly, she carried out her duties alone, sacrificing her own dreams and ambitions for the well-being of her children.

*

August 9, 1961: 1:13 pm

Ring!
Ring!!
The damn phone just won't stop, thought Clifford. He was trying in vain to gather his thoughts, but the constant interruptions were making it all but impossible.
Ring!!!

"Sheriff Gaskin here," Clifford snapped into the receiver.

He listened intently for a brief moment before losing interest in the call. It turned out to be yet another insignificant complaint. The sheriff was an elected official, and it was important to be as personally involved with the electorate as possible, or they might remember it come Election Day.

"Yes, Mrs. Smith, I'm glad you called. Hold on just a minute while I get a pen to take a few notes," the sheriff said politely, considering his level of frustration.

Clifford put her on hold a minute while he found a pad and pen to jot down a few details. He was going to delegate the task to someone else in the department, but wanted Mrs. Smith to think that her abatement issue with her neighbor was the most important thing on his agenda.

Harriet Smith was a grumpy, old widow, who was also very wealthy. Her husband had passed away years ago and left her a considerable nest egg. Eli Smith had been a successful businessman and a shrewd investor before his stroke and early demise. Some said his death was his way of getting away from his nagging wife. The couple had only produced one daughter, who had died as a young child from complications related to diphtheria. In the years that followed, the frugal and unpleasant couple never spent a dime that wasn't absolutely required.

Mrs. Smith now lived in an enormous Victorian mansion near the Old Town Square and didn't mind spending her deceased husband's money if it got her what she wanted. Clifford would do whatever he could legally do to stay on Harriet's good side. He knew she could be generous when fundraising time came around for his re-election.

"Mrs. Smith? Sorry to keep you on hold. Let me have a few of the details, please."

Clifford jotted down the main points of the woman's complaint on a legal pad he kept just for that purpose. Once she was finished, he thanked her and assured her that someone from his department would get right on it. He hung up, set the note pad aside, and attempted to get back to his previous task.

"Now, where was I?" the sheriff asked himself, leafing through the piles of papers and reports on his desk.

The truth was that he wasn't looking for just one specific thing. Clifford had given up hoping for the one clue that would break the case. He knew from experience that cases were solved using an accumulation of many facts, evidence, and clues. His philosophy was that the boxer who hit his opponent with a multitude of punches throughout a fight was more likely to win the match than a boxer who depended on a single knockout punch.

He knew that, the majority of the time, a criminal was caught because he couldn't keep his mouth shut. He believed that talking to people and listening to their gossip was the best way to gather leads, and he engaged in mundane chit-chat with the local yahoos in order to be in a position to obtain valuable information when it mattered. The problem was that, once people thought the authorities were listening, they'd stop talking. It irked him. Now, when he needed it the most, no one was talking.

He gathered a page here and a page there from the pile scattered on his desk. Most were parts of reports that contained summaries from interviews with the local gentry. As he flipped through the papers, he tried to envision the actual interviews as they took place.

He could see it all playing out in his mind – where they were, who they were talking to, how they answered, and what they were eager to say. Clifford tried to consider what they may not have been so eager to say, or what they weren't going to say at all. He tried to remember the essence of the conversations. Once he'd rummaged through a half-dozen or so of the reports, he spread them out in front of him and tried to look at them from a distance. Somehow, he thought, they were all related in one way or another.

Ring!

"Jesus Christ!" blurted the sheriff to no one in particular.

Ring!!

Clifford picked up the phone, "Sheriff Gaskin."

The voice on the other end belonged to Wilford Hopkins. Wilford owned a small auto parts store out on the highway and was always complaining about people leaving their abandoned, broken-down automobiles in his parking lot. Hopkins would generally call Randy, the tow-truck driver, who'd eventually oblige him and go remove the offending vehicle, although, on occasion, he couldn't be reached quickly enough to appease Hopkins. This was one of those times.

"I understand, Wilford, but there's not much I can do about it at the moment."

Wilford didn't care much for the sheriff's response and continued to babble on about how much the situation was putting him out.

Clifford gave him a few minutes to vent before replying, "Okay, now listen to me, Wilford. Give it about a half hour and then try Randy again. If he doesn't answer, call me back, but speak to Mabel. She should be back by then, but, if not, ask for one of the deputies. I'll pass the word around to make sure someone can help you if need be. I won't be here."

Wilford was only minimally appeased by the sheriff's answer, and he hung up abruptly. This did not amuse Clifford, and he had a good mind to call the ungrateful old coot back and give him a piece of his mind, but he thought better of it for the sake of positive community relations. If Mabel didn't get back here soon to screen these calls, he was going to lose it.

The sheriff once again stared at the papers on his desk. He needed to get a handle on the situation and put all of the information together in a report. The state office and that pesky detective had asked the sheriff to provide these reports in order to assist in the investigation. Once the investigation had stalled, the reports were all anyone had to go on. So far, he was unable to write a single report that was worth anything, and it was making him look bad. In his mind, he was becoming the scapegoat for the failed investigation – a situation he was, unfortunately, unable to change unless he could come up with something useful.

Ring! Ring!

"Fuck it."

The sheriff gathered up the forms he'd been staring at for the past forty-five minutes and stuffed them into a binder. Ignoring the continued ringing of his phone, he made his way to the front of the station just as Mabel was returning from lunch.

"Mabel, Mrs. Smith called about one of her neighbors illegally using the abatement behind her house. The info she gave me is on a big, yellow pad on my desk. You know the one I'm talking about. Please send one of the boys over there ASAP to see what they can do. Make sure whoever goes over there mentions that I'm personally seeing to this matter and for her to call me if she has any more problems."

"Is it time for your election fundraisers already?" Mabel asked sarcastically.

"Isn't it always?" he replied with a sly grin. "I'm heading out to try and get some work done. I can't think in here with all the interruptions. If anyone calls, you don't know where I am."

"Before you go, there was a call for you earlier," Mabel replied before he could slip out the door. "Some detective from the State Troopers' office wanted to come over to talk with you. He said he'd be here this afternoon sometime."

"Great," Clifford replied. "Well, it's a shame that he missed me."

With that, he was out the door and in his car before anyone could interrupt him again. Time to get some work done, he thought, as he pulled out of the parking lot and headed to the diner where he might be able to work in peace. He only then remembered Wilford's request, but he wasn't about to turn back now. Damned if he was going to go out of his way for the old man after he'd hung up in his face.

"Fuck it!"

Chapter Nine

Jimmy was a quiet boy; by all accounts, a loner, who kept to himself most of the time. He never got into trouble and his grades were acceptable, if not remarkable. In fact, there was almost nothing about him that people remembered.

Shy and awkward, the boy had an unfortunate quality about him that made others uneasy and left almost everyone he met to describe him with one word – weird. One of Jimmy's eyes was slightly blue, the other slightly green. The subtle difference wasn't obvious enough that most people noticed it, but they came away thinking something about the boy was odd. He had no friends, yet made no enemies. He had acquaintances at best, and the Bickman boys at worst.

Jimmy was born a Magee; although, after his father abandoned him at a young age, he never came in contact with his many extended relatives that inhabited the county. Once his mother married Purvis, he went by the last name of Johnson. Only on official documents was the last name of Magee used, and, in time, everyone just assumed he was Purvis's flesh and blood. Jimmy never met any of Purvis's kin, and none ever came around. After his mother left, the old man was all he had.

Purvis took care of the boy's material needs, providing a roof over his head and three square meals a day. The elder Johnson never abused nor neglected the youngster, and he taught the child many things about hunting, fishing, and self-reliance. What Purvis could not do was to provide the things that only a mother could.

Always a quiet and somewhat withdrawn man, Purvis spoke little to the child and rarely showed him affection. Having been abandoned by both of his natural parents, Jimmy needed someone to talk to and confide in. He needed someone to ease his loneliness and soothe his despair. Purvis, who had for so long suppressed and ignored his own demons, was simply not up to the task.

There were some things that the old man passed on to the boy by example and proximity. Jimmy was able to function on his own without supervision although, most of the time, he felt uncomfortable around other people. Like Purvis, he was able to be friendly and polite when conversing with the neighbors so that most people had no reason to think ill of him.

The young man was, however, at an awkward stage and looked odd. George Peterson wasn't the only one on the block who thought the child was strange, although he was the only one who voiced his misgivings aloud.

The biggest problems Jimmy had in his early teens were named Jack and Frank. The Bickman boys were bullies, and Jimmy was a prime target for the terrible twosome. The trouble started not long after the Bickmans moved into the neighborhood.

Purvis, of course, went calling on the Bickman household with Jimmy in tow, welcoming the new family into the neighborhood. The fact that there were two boys around Jimmy's age at first looked like a godsend. The shy Johnson boy needed a friend or two to help bring him out of his shell, and what better opportunity than the boys who just moved in up the road. The introductions went well and everyone assumed that the boys would become fast friends, everyone except Jack and Frank, who had other ideas.

The Bickman boys had their own special relationship and didn't feel the need to include others. Instead, other children were seen as victims for their sadistic amusement. The fact that Jimmy lived so close and was such an odd and quiet kid made it easy for the pair to dish out their favorite forms of abuse. They pretended to be his friends the first few times they met, but the ruse wouldn't last.

Jack and Frank decided to start slowly and see how far they could push Jimmy until he broke. One day, the three boys were walking down the road when Frank turned to Jimmy.

"See that new house they're building over there?"

Frank pointed to one of the houses under construction. The frame and some of the siding was up and the roof just beginning to take shape. All of the workers were absent at the moment, either off at lunch or called to another job site that day.

"Yeah," Jimmy mumbled suspiciously as the three boys stared at the abandoned dwelling.

"I dare you to set fire to that wood pile in the back," Jack said.

Frank and Jack's eyes met for a brief moment, a glint of malevolent joy in their eyes, before goading Jimmy further.

"Come on. You ain't scared, are you?" Frank joined in.

"No," Jimmy answered, but made no move toward the property.

"Well then, what you waitin' for?" asked Jack.

Jimmy remained silent, his eyes wandering around as his heart raced.

"I think he's chicken," Frank said to Jack.

"Yeah, I think you're right," Jack replied in disgust.

"So are you going to do it or not?" Jack turned to Jimmy.

Jimmy stood by silently, not knowing what to do. He couldn't see himself doing what they asked, but was unsure how to handle this unexpected turn of events.

He finally raised his eyes to Jack and muttered, "Why don't you do it?"

The Bickmans laughed. This wasn't going to work on them. Jack nodded to Frank and handed him the Zippo he'd stolen from his old man. Without a word, Frank snuck over behind the house and lit the odd assortment of wood chips and sawdust, then turned to jog back to where the other two boys were standing.

Jimmy felt a sharp blow to the back of his head. Before he knew it, he was on his hands and knees on the hard concrete of Johnson Road. He stared up at Jack in shock and disbelief as the world began to spin around. Jack was smiling his evil smile as he glared down at the helpless boy.

"That's what you get for being such a pussy! I don't know why we even thought about hangin' out with you." Jack laughed. "If you tell anyone about this, we'll tell everyone you did it. It's two against one, and don't you ever forget it, Crazy-eyes."

They laughed in unison and ran back down the street toward their house, leaving Jimmy all alone in the middle of the road. He felt like he was going to throw up. After a few moments, his dizziness abated and he was able to get himself up, although his head was still pounding from Jack's punch.

By this time, the small flame was beginning to grow and a cloud of smoke was billowing into the sky. Jimmy panicked and ran to his house. He wasn't sure if Purvis would be sitting on the front porch like he often did, so Jimmy took a slight detour around some bushes and made his way into the garage.

The small garage had become Jimmy's private space. He tinkered with the old machines that sat rusting on the shelves and often made new contraptions out of the discarded parts of the broken-down equipment and appliances. The boy's imagination allowed him to envision all kinds of amazing inventions that he could create alone in his workshop. The garage was his sanctuary and the one place that he felt safe.

When supper time came, he quietly snuck into the back door of the small house and sat at the table where Purvis waited. The two ate dinner in silence until the elder Johnson calmly addressed the shy boy.

"Sheriff came 'round this afternoon."

He let the boy stir on that while he ate a few more bites of his meal. Jimmy avoided all eye contact and that told the old man a good deal.

"Someone set a wood pile on fire behind one of the new houses they buildin' up the block, but I'm guessin' you already know that. Turns out someone saw you runnin' away not long after."

Jimmy's heart sank. He tried hard to keep his composure and not cry in front of his father. After a moment, he took a deep breath and tried to explain.

"I didn't...," he began before his father cut him off abruptly.

"No, you didn't. It was them Bickman boys." Purvis took a bite of his meatloaf and chewed it slowly, giving the boy time to compose himself. "You wanna know how I know?"

Jimmy was shocked. He looked up at his father astounded.

"They was the ones who ratted you out. I hinted that to that idiot sheriff until it took. Once the fat guy saw the obvious, he figured he thought of it first and was so pleased with himself – almost like he discovered an abandoned box of fresh donuts."

Purvis chuckled at his little joke while Jimmy sat stoically at the table. The boy wasn't sure how to react in front of his father. On one hand, he'd always been taught to respect his elders and authority and to stay out of trouble. On the other, he knew the old man didn't like the way the police tried to intimidate and belittle him, and he took joy in fucking with the sheriff whenever he had the opportunity. If the sheriff wanted to think Purvis was dumb, the old man had no trouble with providing the sheriff with an education in stupidity.

"Them boys gonna come at you again, ya know," Purvis continued. "They'z two of them and one of you. So seems like you're gonna have a rough go of it."

Jimmy knew the old man was right. Even if Purvis tried to intervene – something that was unlikely, knowing the old man – he couldn't be there to protect him all of the time.

"Yes sir, I know."

The old man finished his meal before continuing. "Any idea how you gonna handle things?"

"Don't rightly know just yet. Can't avoid them forever, and always gonna be outnumbered. I don't s'pose you got any advice?"

Purvis contemplated the question for a few minutes before getting up from the table. He walked to the front porch to rock in his favorite chair and have a smoke. Jimmy tended to the dishes before joining the old man on the porch, hoping his father might be able to share something useful with him. After awhile, the old man began to speak – deliberately and unhurriedly.

"When I went away to the war, I weren't all that much older than you. I learnt a great deal about being afraid over there. I also learnt about how to act and how not to act. I only learnt the real lessons about the consequences of those actions much later, when it was too late. It'll be the same for you."

This was no help at all, thought Jimmy. He had no idea what the old man was babbling on about, but he knew all too well the problems his father had with nightmares. The house was small; Jimmy had been woken up many times in the night by screams of terror that he'd learned to ignore them. Still, what he needed now was some practical advice he could act on, suggestions of things to do or not to do. Purvis's reminiscences about the war weren't going to help him with the bullies down the street.

As if the old man had read the boy's thoughts, his conversation took a different turn.

"Thing you got to remember is that fear works both ways, boy."

Purvis rocked in his chair and lit another Camel. After taking a big puff, slowly exhaling a cloud of white smoke and watching it drift through a spider web above their heads, he began again.

"War ain't like shooting ducks. Ducks don't shoot back. Them Germans were some badass motherfuckers, I tell you."

He paused to take a long drag off of his cigarette, savoring the rich flavor before blowing the smoke toward the arachnid poised overhead. As if speaking to the spider, Purvis recounted the glory days of his lost youth with pride, "Of course, I was a badass motherfucker myself."

There was a twinkle in the old man's eyes as he relived memories he'd suppressed for so long. Jimmy felt a chill; this was a side of his father he'd never seen before. Maybe the old man might have some good advice for him after all.

"Them boys are tryin' to learn how far they can push you before you push back. Wanna' know how far you're willin' to push back when you do. They ain't too worried about it, 'cause they outnumber you. You gotta figure out them answers yourself before they do, and make the most of the surprise."

Purvis sat quietly for awhile, and Jimmy could see that he was going to need a little prodding to go on. The old man gave him a lot to think about. His head was buzzing with thoughts, although they were too scattered and unfocused to do him much good. He was going to need something more specific, and he eventually pressed his old man further.

"I'll have to think on all of this, I s'pose. Don't really know what my options are," the boy said, hoping his father would take the hint.

Purvis knew he was going to have to be less vague for the boy, although was unsure how much he wanted to share. He felt it was his duty to prepare the boy for moments like this as best he could, and he understood the child's predicament. Still, he wanted the boy to figure out as much as he could on his own. He knew this was a big step in Jimmy's growing from a boy to a man. Purvis was also aware that if he was too specific in his instructions, he would be responsible for the consequences of the boy's actions; if he was too vague, his son's problems could get exponentially worse.

"Them boys set you up today. You fell into their trap. Bet they would walk right into a trap like that themselves – as long as you weren't too obvious about it."

"But there's always going to be two of them and one of me."

"In the war, you learnt quickly that it's better to be outnumbered than out armed. Now don't get the wrong idea. Don't do anything stupid. I don't want that fat sheriff knocking on my door lookin' for you. You got to be more subtle than that."

"Well, if I can't shoot 'em, and I can't stab 'em, not sure what that leaves me."

Purvis was starting to get tired of this. Damn boy was going to have to think of some things on his own eventually. It was bad enough it was taking him so long to grow a pair of balls; he better grow a brain even quicker. He stared at the boy before glancing back at the old garage where he hung out most of the time.

"I bet you got all kinds of tools back there in that shed; tools for all kinds of jobs."

Jimmy followed his father's gaze toward the garage. The old man was right. There must be something he could come up with to even the odds a little.

"Whatever you do, wait just a little while to do it. Got to catch them boys off-guard. Catch 'em where and when it's right for you, then act, quickly and decisively. Things may or may not work out, but at least from then on, them boys will know fuckin' with you comes with a price. Just don't kill anyone or leave any permanent damage; don't maim 'em or mark 'em up too bad. You just want 'em to hurt a little. Point is to have them learn what fear feels like. Do it right, I'll back you up. You might wanna remember their drunken stumblebum of a father ain't goin' to back 'em up as long as you're smart about it."

Purvis sat back and smiled, pleased with himself. He noticed a subtle grin creep over his son's face as he mulled over the advice he'd given him. The boy's evil smile on such an innocent face made the hair on the back of the old man's neck stand up. The little fucker might get through this alright after all.

After the discussion with his father, Jimmy heeded the advice and set about plotting his revenge. The first order of business was to find a way to even the odds. He looked around the old garage and tried to come up with the perfect weapon. He knew any kind of gun or knife was out, which, unfortunately for him, eliminated most of his initial ideas. He was going to have to get creative before he could get even.

He thought of making some kind of blow-gun with poison darts like he saw in the movies once, but quickly realized that it was unrealistic. Any devices, such as spears, harpoons, or bayonets, caused virtually the same results as a knife and weren't going to work, either. The only thing he kept coming back to was using a pipe or club of some sort. This didn't really appeal to Jimmy, and he envisioned a much more devious weapon of grander proportions. In the end, he had to admit he was stumped, so he went to work on his club concept.

He figured that he couldn't go around carrying a baseball bat, or the two boys would notice right off. So, he came up with an idea of how to disguise his weapon until he was ready to use it. He took some pipes of different thicknesses and made a collapsible tube, much like the radio antennas on some of the cars he saw around town.

He made it small enough to hide down the side of his pants, but accessible enough to pull it out quickly. He practiced his moves over and over so that when the time came, he would be ready to act quickly and decisively –just as the old man had instructed.

Jimmy wasn't very pleased with his choice of weapons, but couldn't think of any viable alternatives, so he watched and waited for the opportunity to strike. Unfortunately, none seemed to arise that looked promising.

In the meantime, he had to lay low, and he resented it. Prior to the incident with the Bickman boys, he was more than happy to waste the hours away by himself in the small garage. Now, it felt like he was trapped in the small building, and he didn't want to be there.

The bullies made him feel like a coward and he hated it; he hated them for it, and hated himself for it, too. He longed for the day he could finally get even with the duo.

As time went on, Purvis began to think maybe the boy didn't have it in him. He didn't want to push the issue. He wanted Jimmy to act on his own. In the meantime, the boys had the run of the neighborhood.

Houses sprouted up all down the block until almost every lot was filled. The Bickman boys started running out of empty territory, and Purvis knew that they would start fooling around down by his property soon, and he didn't care much for that idea.

Purvis Johnson didn't like to have his back exposed. In the war, his platoon had been outflanked once, and a surprise attack from the rear had cost them dearly. The hand to hand combat that dark, miserable night went on for hours. He could still hear the screams coming from the adjoining fox holes in his nightmares. He could still smell the rancid aroma of burnt flesh and stale blood. He could still see the haunted expressions of the three men next to him in his own, their intestines and blood covering his boots while their lifeless eyes bore into his guilty soul.

Since then, he never sat with his back to the door, and even his house was at the end of the block, facing the highway. He could sit on his front porch and survey everything at his leisure. The only thing behind him was the ravine that dropped off, treacherously at times, to the polluted creek at the bottom. Shit Creek, it was called, and was to be avoided at all costs. He gave strict instructions to his own boy to stay out of the woods behind the house, and he was damned if he was going to have the Bickman boys rummaging around back there, doing who knows what.

When the double lot at the end of the block next to his was finally sold, Purvis was more than a little curious to see who and what was going to move in there. He could see right away that the house was going to be much bigger than the rest of the houses, almost twice the size. This made it almost three times the size of his, but he didn't care about that at all. What he didn't care for was the attitude of the man who was building it.

One day, while he was rocking in his chair on the front porch, the weird little creep came calling. George Peterson was his name, and Purvis took him for an asshole at once. The man actually had the gall to suggest he sell his property to him. Turns out, he thought Purvis's home was an eyesore and didn't want it next to his. The arrogance of the man astounded Purvis, who replied by just laughing at the absurdity of the request. This response only seemed to incense the pretentious jerk, a reaction that pleased the old man to no end.

In the years that would follow, Purvis would ingratiate himself with Mr. Peterson's wife and kids in order to get under the rich jerk's skin. This task would be made all the easier because the man's poor, unfortunate spouse was overwhelmed with a sick infant. He would ignore all of George's insults and warnings to stay away, and try to help out the ill-fated woman as much as he could. He knew his efforts were working when the idiot unsuccessfully tried to have the name of the street changed. In the meantime, he amused himself by watching the antagonistic idiot and the ridiculous obstacles that he managed to put in the way of the construction of his over-sized house.

The construction project took a life of its own; the crew starting and stopping over and over again. He sat on his porch day after day, watching the entire endeavor unfold before him like some kind of Greek comedy – or tragedy – depending on your viewpoint.

The old man made a point of letting Jimmy know just how particular Mr. Peterson was in regards to his property, and just how easy it would be to set him off. He could see the wheels spinning in the boy's head, and he sat back to get ready for the show.

By this time, Jimmy had moved on from his iron wand idea. The collapsible pipe was demoted to plan

B status. He'd created a much better instrument of revenge. He'd gotten the idea once when he visited the feed store with his father. A certain item was displayed on the wall, and he studied its simple design while the old man shopped, pretending not to notice his son's fascination with the dangerous instrument.

When he got home from the store, Jimmy got to work immediately. He already had the components that he needed laying around, so all that was required was a little ingenuity, experimentation, and hard work.

When he was finished with the product, he was delighted with the results. Now, all he needed to do was to set the trap. Thanks to his father's advice and keen observations, he was ready to roll.

One afternoon, Purvis called to his son from the porch. Jimmy came out to see what his old man wanted, and his father nodded toward the two bullies up the street.

"Ain't that them Bickman bullies down there?" he asked Jimmy.

"Sure is." Jimmy stood still, staring at the two boys. "Well, I got things to do out back," Jimmy replied before slipping around the side of the house and out of view.

Almost an hour passed before Jack and Frank made their way up the street. They were almost in front of the Peterson house when Jimmy strolled up to them.

"Well, well, if it isn't the little fire-starter," Jack remarked to his brother.

"I tawt I taw a puddy tat," laughed Frank in return.

Jimmy ignored their taunts, feigning surprise at the duo's presence.

"I got a can of spray paint. I dare you to write your names on the Peterson's wall," he boldly declared while holding a can of red paint out for the brother's inspection.

Jack and Frank were taken off guard. The Peterson house was not yet completed, although most of the walls were up and some of the drywall was hung. The site was off limits, even to the Bickman boys. Mr. Peterson's wrath was well known to everyone on the block and, in particular, to Jake Bickman. The boys had taken a severe beating already over the arson incident even after they'd blamed it on Jimmy. The idea of stepping foot on the Peterson property was going to spell trouble.

Jimmy saw their hesitation and taunted sarcastically, "What's the matter? You guys chicken?"

Jack and Frank weren't about to stand for that. They'd rather take a beating from their old man than have the weirdo Johnson boy call them out.

"If I remember correctly, you're the only pussy here, Crazy-eyes," Jack said.

"Shit, I ain't scared. I'll go in there right now," Jimmy replied.

He turned toward the house and started walking to the opening where soon there would be a front door.

"Y'all comin'?" Jimmy asked.

The brothers looked at each other, then followed suit. As they entered the unfinished house, they grew wary and excited at the same time. The two boys preferred to control the situation and felt that wasn't the case here.

The three boys went from room to room, before walking over to the bottom of the staircase.

"Wonder if they left any tools upstairs?" Jimmy whispered.

Jack took the bait.

"Let's go see," he said excitedly.

Jimmy motioned toward Jack and said, "You go first."

Jack hesitated a moment while Frank slipped past them and started up the stairs. Jack's eyes never left Jimmy's face, whose expression never wavered. Jack motioned for Jimmy to follow Frank up the stairs. As they proceeded up the stairs, the Bickmans had Jimmy sandwiched between them. They would be all alone and out of view upstairs in the Peterson house. Stupid kid never learns, thought the two bullies, as they prepared for the beat down they were about to bestow on unsuspecting Jimmy.

Once they cleared the stairwell, Jack and Frank let Jimmy take the lead. Most of the upstairs was still comprised of exposed studs, with only a few walls bearing unfinished sheetrock. They started down the hall, peeking into each doorway. Jimmy led the way into one of the large bedrooms upstairs.

When they got into the room, the Bickman boys were shocked to see that Jimmy had already been there with the can of spray paint. They were stunned by what they saw and walked further in the room, past Jimmy, to investigate closer, leaving Jimmy standing in the doorway behind them. On the far wall in front of them, in freshly painted dripping red letters, they saw:

JACK AND FRANK WERE HERE

They stood with their mouths open, reading their own names painted on the wall in big red letters. Suddenly, something hit Frank on his shoulder. He screamed in agony as he hit the floor, biting his tongue. Blood started running out of his mouth and down his chin.

"What the hell?" Jack exclaimed at the unexpected sight on the wall before hearing his brother's shriek.

He spun around in time to see Frank collapse on the floor and Jimmy coming at him with something in his hand. He quickly lunged at the advancing boy, but Jimmy poked him in the gut with the pole he was holding, sending a shock through his body. He flew back against the wall, his knees buckling as he landed on the ground, and he felt like he was going to puke. When he looked up, he saw Jimmy standing over him, holding some kind of homemade collapsible cattle prod.

Frank, recovering from the initial shock, tried to get up. Jimmy turned toward him quickly and kicked him square in the face, breaking his nose and sending more blood gushing down the front of his shirt. Frank fell back again, his hand held to his nose, and started to cry. He looked over at his brother propped against the opposite wall, and he didn't like what he saw.

Jimmy turned once more toward Jack. Jack's eyes were wide with fright, his gaze transfixed on the torture devise in the Johnson boy's grasp. Jimmy smiled when he saw Jack's eyes glued to the cattle prod. The distinctive aroma of ozone permeated the stale air, coupled with the unmistakable smell of fear.

His revenge was everything he'd hoped it would be, and he savored the moment. He slowly walked toward the terrified Jack, waving his horrific invention in front of him.

Frank saw his chance and ran, leaving his pride and his older brother behind. All he felt was fear, and he reacted without thinking. He tumbled down the stairs, holding his hand to his broken nose, before slipping on the sawdust on the bottom step and landing against a pile of wood scraps in the corner. The side of his face scraped against the jagged edge of one of the random pieces of lumbar, tearing a gash from the middle of his chin to just below his right ear. Warm, sticky blood oozed out of the open wound, covering his shirt.

He panicked at the sight of his blood-soaked garment and weakly stood up before staggering out of the open doorway. Tears ran down his face, mixing with blood and spit, as he stumbled across the lawn toward the street.

Once outside, the bright sunlight and fresh air relieved the unbearable tension he'd endured for a brief moment before high-pitched howls rang out from the upstairs bedroom window and stopped him in his tracks.

"Jack!" he whimpered to himself in horror.

On all fours, Jack tried in vain to crawl away from Jimmy and his electrical device. He felt a painful jolt on his buttocks and fell face down on the plywood floor. This time, Jimmy kept his torture stick pressed down on Jack's body for a few seconds. The terrified bully screamed in pain, pissed on himself, and began to cry. Suddenly, there was silence.

After a few moments, Jack carefully turned to see that Jimmy was gone and he was all alone. He picked himself up and cautiously made his way down the stairs and toward the exit.

Frank had pulled himself together at the sound of his brother's agony and headed back inside, only to be met by Jimmy, who was casually walking out alone. Frank backed away from the terrifying sight and gave Jimmy plenty of room to pass.

"What did you do to my brother?" Frank angrily shouted at Jimmy's back.

Jimmy paused and turned toward the slobbering Frank. He made a quick motion with his arm toward the boy, and Frank jumped back in terror. Jimmy laughed, making the motion again, and, this time, tossing the empty can of paint to the terrified boy.

Frank caught the unexpected item in his hands, exposing the nasty mess that was his face. The spectacle almost made Jimmy queasy, and, for a fleeting moment, he thought that maybe he'd gone too far.

Jimmy looked at Frank, put his finger to his lips, and smiled.

"Now, don't tell anyone," he laughed.

"You won't get away with this," Frank answered defiantly.

"I already did. Who's gonna believe you? Besides, my dad already knows where I am."

Jimmy nodded toward the little shack behind him, hidden amongst the bushes. Frank looked over and saw Purvis rocking in his chair on his front porch, smoking a cigarette. The old man took a big drag off of his Camel and slowly exhaled, a cloud of white smoke billowing up as he watched the two boys, seemingly enjoying the show.

"What's your drunken Dad goin' to do when he finds out what you two been up to?" Jimmy asked the younger Bickman boy, nodding toward the paint can in Frank's hand.

The sudden realization of the situation dawned on Frank and he felt sick to his stomach all over again. He glanced down at the incriminating item in his hand. He and Jack were screwed. Frank watched with hatred as Jimmy sauntered down the street back toward his own house as if he didn't have a care in the world.

"You're going to pay for this," Frank said under his breath before turning back toward the house to retrieve his brother.

When Jack met Frank at the doorway, the pair looked at each other with fear and shame. Deciding that they'd better get out of there in a hurry before anything else could happen, they turned and ran down Johnson Road, trying to distance themselves from the humiliation that engulfed them.

Once they left the construction site, Frank realized he was still holding the empty can of spray paint, and quickly stopped at a neighbor's garbage can by the curb to dispose of the evidence. As the brothers were walking back home, they spotted the Peterson's Cadillac slowly cruising down the street toward the big, unfinished house.

"Shit, its Mr. Peterson," exclaimed Jack.

"Do you think he saw us throw the can away?" whispered a worried Frank.

"Probably. Maybe. Doesn't really matter anyway, does it?"

"I guess not."

At that moment, neither one of the boys remembered what Jimmy had painted on the upstairs wall.

The Bickman boys hurriedly walked on and avoided looking at Mr. Peterson, who was staring intently at the two hooligans as he drove past. There'd be a lot of explaining to do later.

Unfortunately, neither of them could supply a believable alibi. The whipping their father was going to put on them was going to be severe, even by Jake Bickman's standards. Even that was nothing compared to what the Johnson boy had done to them.

The two boys swore their revenge on Jimmy, although neither of them would ever dare to make a move against him. Purvis was right. The bullies now knew that there was a heavy price to pay for fucking with a Johnson.

*

August 9, 1961: 12:25 pm

"So basically, you're telling me you don't know shit!" said Robert.

He'd been at Lil' Ray's for almost an hour and was tired of getting the runaround. The detective knew that the local drunks were just toying with him for their own amusement, and he didn't appreciate it. He knew this was to be expected when dealing with uneducated, shit-for-brains alcoholics.

"Yeah, basically," Danny Boy blurted out before bursting into laughter with the others seated at the bar.

Even Bubba was grinning as he wiped a beer mug with a rag of questionable cleanliness and stared at the confrontation through blood-shot eyes. Robert let the boys have their moment at his expense. When the hilarity of the moment died down, he reminded the good 'ol boys of why he was there.

"I'm glad that y'all can find so much amusement in the matter. You'll excuse me if I don't share in your fun because I have to face those poor people and explain why I can't find them justice."

With that, the saloon fell silent. There was nothing as effective as a dose of harsh reality to ruin everyone's good time.

"I'm sure they won't be any more amused than I am. I guess it's too bad not everyone is in on the joke," Robert went on. "Now, if any of you fine gentleman can think of anything that might be of use,

I'd surely appreciate it if you'd give me a call. I'll leave my card on the bar – just in case."

Stallworth placed his business card on the counter, looked everyone in the eye, one at a time, then turned and walked toward the exit. He was almost to the door when Bubba spoke up.

"Detective, the sheriff and his boys been down here already – many times. Why don't you just get with him and see what he says."

Robert turned and looked at the man behind the bar. He could see that his words had the effect he'd intended. No one was laughing now. He exhaled slowly before answering the complicated question as best he could.

"I appreciate the suggestion, sir. The sheriff and I have been working together on this from the beginning. We just haven't gotten anywhere up to this point and sometimes people remember things later that they may have left out originally. I'm not trying to be a nuisance to you or harass any of your customers. I'm just trying to do my best for those poor people – same as I'd do for you and yours if it came to that. Sometimes even the smallest of details can be important in a case like this, and I'd appreciate it if anyone could help us out. I'm doubly sure that the family over there would be most appreciative as well."

Everyone nodded, agreeing with the detective's sentiment. Robert nodded in return before putting back on his hat and heading out the door. He'd taken the wind out of their sails with a heavy dose of reality before he'd left. The locals sat there for awhile, silent and ashamed at the immature way they'd behaved, given the circumstances. Bubba turned up the volume of the baseball game playing on the television over the bar, hoping his customers wouldn't sober up enough to go home to whatever families they had that might be waiting for them.

Detective Stallworth got back into his unmarked cruiser and fired up the engine. He adjusted his seat, kicked on the air conditioning, and sat back for a few minutes.

This case was wearing on him. He'd had cases like this before – cases that went nowhere. Sometimes, despite how hard everyone worked, a case could grow cold – no suspects, no leads, no nothing. Robert had been on the force long enough to learn to accept this fact, even if he despised it. This time, he felt that this wouldn't happen. It couldn't happen. He wouldn't allow it.

Robert sighed in frustration as he gazed out of the window of his car and down Riverside Highway. There was something there, hidden underneath it all. If only he could figure out what it was that he kept missing. He racked his brain and scanned his memory, hoping that something would jump out at him. There had to be some outlier there, he thought; something out of place that just didn't fit. In the end, he was always led back to those useless reports.

The files consisted mostly of interviews with people – people who didn't know shit. Robert believed that someone knew something; they just weren't talking. He was pretty sure that, in this case, it was unlikely that more than one person knew anything of value. After all, it wasn't the sort of thing people would hide from the authorities just to be neighborly.

The only way someone would cover for someone else in a crime of this nature was if the witnesses were either implicitly involved in the crime, or closely related to the perpetrator. Even then, it might be a stretch. Of course, there could and would be threats to any potential witnesses, regardless of who they were – threats that would be very effective and definitely be taken seriously.

There had to be clues, just waiting to be uncovered. Subtle clues, to be sure, but clues nonetheless. If only he'd been able to be there when the interviews took place, able to participate without all of the bullshit attitudes his presence always seemed to illicit from the rednecks involved.

Robert sighed again and shifted his car into gear. He turned around in the parking lot and headed back toward town, changing his mind and his direction. It was time to make a personal call on the sheriff and his deputies.

Bubba gave sound advice; the sheriff and his boys had been everywhere, multiple times. They'd put their bumbling fingerprints on everything. If he wanted to shake things up, there was no better place to start.

Chapter Ten

Jack and Frank never discussed the incident that happened with Jimmy. It had been their single biggest moment of humiliation, and both had suppressed it as best they could. They avoided Jimmy for a good while, concentrating their reign of terror on the other inhabitants of Johnson Road whenever they felt they could get away with it. Their sadistic games were curtailed a great deal by the lack of available targets in the area and their father's severe punishments for the slightest infractions, but boys will be boys.

As time wore on, the terrible two learned to confront Jimmy in less extreme fashion. They'd never approach the boy alone, or let him lead them into any possible traps, but they'd taunt him just enough to satisfy their cruel urges, while being careful not to push the boy too far. Jimmy was an odd and quiet sort, much like his father, so it was easy for the Bickman duo to subtly harass him without the fear of retribution, as long as they didn't get careless.

As for the rest of the block, there were the Peterson children and the little girl across the street. The youngest Peterson child, George, Jr., always seemed to be sick and was rarely seen outside, which left his sister, Agatha. Agatha was tom-boyish and assertive, although cute and girly enough to make the Bickman boys hesitate before giving her any trouble. The fact that her doting father was George Peterson dissuaded them from any possible mischief aimed in her direction. The pair had gotten a taste of Mr. Peterson's wrath by way of the sheriff and their drunken father after the paint can incident, and neither wished to relive it.

Elizabeth Jenkins was the beautiful little blond girl that lived across the street from the two boys. She was much younger than the pair, and as cruel as the Bickman boys were, they hesitated to mess with a child of Elizabeth's age. Besides, the child's mother rarely let the girl out of her sight, so the opportunity for them to interact with the child was considerably limited. Still, the boys were often bored, and they tried to initiate trouble on the block whenever they felt they could get away with it.

When the Bickman boys decided to dognap the little girl's pet, the two had planned it out beautifully. Frank approached Elizabeth, which, in turn, drew her mother's attention, thus allowing Jack to snatch the beagle from their backyard and carry him along the back way, down to the woods. Frank then walked away from the little girl and scurried on down to the designated spot, where the two boys met up a short time later.

The Bickman boys only occasionally went down past the Johnson place into the woods. The ravine was off-limits, and, although they didn't mind testing their father's boundaries, the two never wanted to be caught down there by Jimmy in some trap.

They both fantasized about getting the better of the weirdo in that remote place, but were petrified that the situation might backfire on them. The fact that Jimmy's old man was adamant about having no one trespassing on his property minimized the boys' visits. Old man Purvis was the one man on the block who routinely visited with their father, and he would undoubtedly rat them out.

When the two started terrorizing the little mutt, both thought that the other one would set the limits. Unfortunately, since neither wanted to look like a wimp, the amount of cruelty they inflicted kept escalating.

Things got out of hand quickly, and the meek and gentle little dog began to whimper and then howl loudly. Scared that they'd be discovered, the boys tried to shut the poor little mutt up, only to have him snap at them in desperation. This incensed the two bullies, and they started kicking and beating him unmercifully with sticks. After a few minutes, the dog lay still in the dirt at their feet, motionless except for his labored panting.

They had no choice but to get rid of the evidence, so they tried to dig a hole in which to bury the dying animal. The ground was soft enough for them to get the grave started, but a multitude of roots and hard stones impeded their progress. They couldn't make a sizable enough hole without tools, and they were concerned that they'd been away too long. They panicked when they heard their father call their names.

"Jack! Frank!" Jake Bickman shouted angrily.

The brothers looked at each other with wide eyes and then down at the bloody dog.

"You boys better get up here! Now!"

Frank stood up, his eyes darting about indecisively as he wiped his dirty hands on his pants. Jack sprung into action and grabbed the injured dog by his tail, slinging him around, and launching him through the air and into the polluted creek below. They heard a heavy thud and brief splash, and then they turned and raced up the side of the ravine toward the sound of their irate father's voice.

When the night passed and there came no reprisals for their horrendous deed, the Bickman boys were elated. The perfect little girl across the street with her perfect little family now had a taste of anguish, which pleased the tortured youths to no end. Why should they be the only ones who suffered a painful existence when everyone else lived the good life?

To the boys' relief, the dog's remains weren't discovered, although the Jenkins's searched long and hard to find him. The brothers saw a few posters with a picture of the lost mutt hanging on telephone poles around town, which they found hilarious. They knew the dog was gone forever and the family's stupid search for him was pointless.

The boys felt that the little girl's mother suspected their involvement in the dog's abduction, although neither could see how she could've possibly known. The pair figured that she had no evidence anyway since they'd never been confronted directly about the incident. Unfortunately, Mrs. Jenkins's suspicions led her to spy on their every movement, making any future mischief much harder to accomplish.

Since the boys were forced to be more subtle in their devious ways, the two began to split up when they roamed the neighborhood in search of trouble. One of them would typically let himself be seen in order to provide a distraction while the other tended to business. It worked so well with the dog's abduction that it became their modus operandi. Wisely, they remained cautious enough to keep away from the Johnson boy; there was no reason to tempt fate.

One afternoon, while Jack strutted down the street to talk to Agatha Peterson, who sat out front on her lawn, Frank snuck around the back of the empty house that was for sale next door to the Jenkins's place. Being extra careful not to be spotted by the nosy Jenkins woman, Frank hid in the bushes in the backyard.

After hiding for a few minutes, Frank looked through one of the back bedroom windows. He wanted to see if it had been inadvertently left unlocked so he could possibly gain entrance to the house without being detected. What he didn't realize was that, while he was looking for a way in, the real estate agent had pulled up to the front of the empty house and was making his way in through the front door.

Barney Spencer had been trying to sell this last empty house on Johnson Road for quite some time. Nowadays, he concentrated most of his efforts on the newer and bigger subdivisions closer to town, where the asking prices were higher and his commissions more lucrative. Every once in awhile, he would pass by the house on Johnson Road to make sure it remained in good shape in case he had to show it to possible buyers if the opportunity arose.

The agent looked around, inspecting each room quickly and efficiently. As he walked through the empty house, Barney made mental notes as to what he might do to improve his chances of moving this property. When he got to the back bedroom, he paused.

He thought he heard a noise outside and peered out of the back window to take a look. He saw nothing, and, after a few minutes, he turned his attention back to the room, satisfied that there was no one in the backyard. Sometimes these empty houses made more sounds than the full ones, he thought.

Before he could lift the window, Frank spied the real estate agent unexpectedly stroll into the empty room. He ducked back into the bushes and held his breath, trying to keep as still as possible.

Frank's heart raced, and he was breathing hard. The boy remained quiet, composing himself. He pressed against the side of the house, hoping that Barney wouldn't see him hidden beneath the window ledge. He remained motionless for a while to be certain that the man had moved on before cautiously raising his head to peek through the window to make sure that the coast was clear.

The man was still there, although he was no longer looking out of the window. Frank could see that the agent was distracted by something, and he could safely make his getaway. Suddenly, Frank froze in place.

He stared through the window in disbelief at the unexpected spectacle before him. He felt nauseated and wanted to turn away. He wanted to run as fast as he could and forget everything that he'd seen, but was unable to move, unable to look away from the awful sight before him.

*

June 25, 1959

"Good to see you again, Sheriff," Captain Warner said as he firmly shook Clifford's hand.

"Captain," the big man replied before turning to look at the detective who was approaching from behind him.

The men were meeting in the parking lot of the old grain mill located ten miles Northeast of Hidden Springs. The mill had been closed for decades; the large, unoccupied buildings left to rot in the desolated area. Each had arrived separately from different directions. Each would exit likewise when their business was completed.

Captain Eddie Warner arranged to meet the two officers at a neutral location on purpose. There were always problems when different jurisdictions had to work together, and this case was no exception. Experience taught him that, despite all of the 'we're in this together' speeches he gave, people were set in their ways. Type-A personalities were common in law enforcement; it's what made the authorities the authorities. Nevertheless, the captain wanted results and wasn't interested in hearing excuses, or complaints.

"Glad you could make it, Robert," Eddie greeted the detective. "I believe you've met Sheriff Gaskin."

Detective Stallworth and Sheriff Gaskin shook hands. The men had previously met, albeit briefly.

Each knew that they'd be forced to work with the other, much to the displeasure of both.

"I want to thank you two gentlemen for meeting me out here on short notice," Captain Warner began. "We are all incredibly busy so I figured this was the best place for the three of us to get together. I'm sure you both know why you're here, so let me just get to the point. This investigation is going to require that we all work together intimately and efficiently. I know that there are always problems with interdepartmental dynamics, and, frankly, we can't afford that here."

Eddie looked squarely at the two men and continued, "I guess you know that this all depends on the two of you. Sheriff," the captain addressed Clifford directly. "Detective Stallworth here is the best man I have. He's assigned to this case because I have the utmost faith in his abilities. I expect you to do everything in your power to assist him with his work, whether you agree with him or not. Am I making myself perfectly clear?"

Clifford didn't care for the captain's tone and cleared his throat before exercising his right to dissent.

"Captain Warner, with all due respect, I don't work for you, or the detective," the sheriff began before Eddie abruptly cut him off.

"Don't even start with that bullshit, Gaskin. You work for the people of Peterson County, and they expect results. As the ranking officer of the State Police in this investigation, I'm telling you right now that your office better not sandbag me here or, come election time, you'll be out on your fat ass. I already have the federal authorities breathing down my neck, and believe me, if they get involved, there will be hell to pay for all of us."

Clifford remained silent and let the captain continue.

"Now, as for you, Detective, I want results and I want them now. I expect you to work with the sheriff and his deputies, and don't forget that they're not yours to command. Sheriff Gaskin knows his job and knows his officers. More importantly, he knows his people. Ain't no one going to talk to you, so you'd better appreciate what the sheriff and his men do for you, or it'll be your ass."

Robert was smart enough not to say a word. The detective knew Eddie long enough to know it was always best to keep your mouth shut and do what you were told. Captain Warner had worked his way up the chain of command, solving crimes before the young detective could walk. Robert considered the captain's endorsement of his abilities to be the greatest professional compliment he could ever hope to achieve.

"Have I made myself clear to both of you?" Eddie asked.

The captain didn't expect a reply, so he continued. "Well, then, if either of you have any questions, you better ask them now."

The captain paused for a moment for show. He knew that neither man was going to ask him a damned thing.

"If either of you have any complaints, feel free to write them down. You can drop them in the closest complaint box or garbage can before getting back to work," Captain Warner concluded before shaking the two men's hands and driving off down the dusty road.

"I understand that you and your men have been questioning a number of people," Detective Stallworth addressed the sheriff.

"Yep, you understand correctly," Clifford answered before letting Robert continue.

"Any leads or promising suspects?"

"Not yet. You'd know it if I had something. Tell me, Detective, what would you like from my department?"

Clifford hated the way Captain Warner had talked to him, especially in front of the cocky detective, but he knew Warner was right. At least with the State Office, the Sheriff's Department could be involved in the investigation. They may even get some of the credit if they managed to catch the perpetrator. If they were unsuccessful, Clifford could always scapegoat the detective and state authorities. Once the feds were involved, all of that was out of the window. They'd all be painted as backward, incompetent yokels no matter what the results.

"For now, I need some detailed reports of your investigation," Robert answered.

"Detailed reports?" the sheriff asked with irritation. "What kind of detailed reports are we talking about here?"

"I want transcripts of any interrogations or questioning of witnesses or suspects. Timelines of events, including background checks and pertinent bios of any and all persons involved. I need a category of evidence, any details about the acquisition of such evidence, and the conclusions derived from that evidence. In addition, I'd like summaries attached with any impressions or theories from you or your men regarding this case. Please feel free to relate it to any other crimes or incidents in the area, or implicate any persons who may be involved if you feel they are even remotely relevant."

"Is that all?" Clifford responded sarcastically.

Robert ignored the sheriff's tone before finishing. "When can I expect the first report on my desk?"

Oh, this was going to be fun, thought the sheriff. This shit's going to be a thorn in my side from here on out.

"Well, it might take a little while, Detective. We do have other things to attend to."

"Two or three days should be fine; the end of the week at the latest. After that, I'll need updates at least once a week and as the investigation warrants. I don't need to remind you how important it is to get things moving fast on this one, Sheriff."

"Or you'll be out on your ass. Right, Detective?" Clifford replied with a disgusted grin.

"Or we'll be out on our asses. Right, Sheriff?"

There was nothing left to be said, and, after the two men exchanged contact information, they got into their patrol cars and drove off, each going in a different direction, hoping to arrive at the finish line before the other.

Chapter Eleven

June sixteenth, nineteen fifty-nine was a hot, muggy Tuesday on Johnson Road. The sporadic cloud cover allowed for some temporary breaks in the heat, and the neighborhood was bustling with activity. Elizabeth Jenkins was riding her bicycle up and down the block, under the watchful eye of Gladys, her mother, who was alternately tending to the stew brewing on her stove and keeping an eye on her active daughter. The Bickman boys were fiddling around in the tree house perched in the willow tree behind their house, and Agatha Peterson was sitting on her front lawn talking with Jimmy Johnson.

Old man Purvis must've been looking in on the young Peterson boy, thought Gladys, and Jimmy was using the opportunity to visit with the sick boy's older sister. She knew that the poor Johnson boy was smitten with the Peterson girl, and she was sure that George Peterson wasn't going to like it if his daughter returned the interest in the poverty-stricken youth.

"Look, Momma. I can ride really fast!" exclaimed Elizabeth as she raced past her mother on her bike.

"Good, honey, but slow down a little. I don't want you to get hurt."

"I won't," replied the little girl as she turned around in the driveway and prepared to race down toward the end of the block.

Gladys watched her daughter speed down the street. She waved at Purvis as he left the Peterson house with an empty container of soup in his hands. Little Georgie had been suffering from one of his frequent bouts of abdominal issues, and Purvis's chicken soup was famously delicious – hard to pass up even when nauseated. Old man Johnson was a godsend for Cheryl Peterson, who was having a tough time caring for her little one without much help from her neglectful husband.

Gladys ducked inside to stir the family's dinner before it boiled over. She took a few moments to dice an onion to add to the stew. Just then, she spied the youngest Bickman boy from her kitchen window. Frank was creeping suspiciously around behind the empty house next door, getting into Lord-knows-what. She hurried out of the front door to check on Elizabeth, who was down the street talking with Agatha and Jimmy, much to her mother's relief.

Gladys believed that the only thing worse than the Bickman boys together was the Bickman boys apart. Her suspicions about the two juvenile delinquents and the family's long-lost beagle had not faded, and she was certain that they were up to something whenever she saw only one of them and not the other.

She saw Jack fooling around with some rope by the tree house in his back yard; she knew that the younger brother was looking for trouble behind the empty house next door. Gladys stood on her front lawn for a few moments to let her presence be known when she saw the mailman turn off of Riverside Highway and onto Johnson Road.

She walked out to the curb to greet Walt, the postman, and gather the family's mail. They chatted about the heat and the possibility of rain for a minute before she turned back toward her house and Walt returned to his duties.

Gladys glanced back down at the Peterson place and was happy to see her beautiful little girl giggling as Agatha showed off her cartwheels. She took the opportunity to duck inside again and continue in the preparation of their evening meal.

As she sliced a bell pepper, she peered out of her window again, but Frank Bickman was nowhere to be seen. She had a gut feeling that he was still over by the empty house, creeping around, but was out of sight for the moment. Gladys hastily threw the pepper into the pot and gave it a couple of stirs before hurrying outside again to check on her daughter.

Elizabeth was riding back up toward the house. Gladys waved and waited for her little girl to reach her.

"Did you see what Agatha can do?" Elizabeth asked her mother with excitement.

"I sure did! It was pretty amazing."

"Can I try it, Momma? She said she would teach me if you said it was okay."

"I don't know. You could get hurt."

"Please. I swear I'll be extra careful," the little girl begged.

"Okay, dear, but be very careful, and do what Agatha tells you to do."

With that, Elizabeth raced down the block to the Peterson house and a new adventure. Gladys stood watching her little girl when she heard the phone ringing inside. She turned to go back inside when she saw Mr. Spencer, the real estate agent, pull up to the empty house next door.

He waved to her as he got out of his car, and she waved back briefly before ducking inside to answer the phone. She wanted to tell Barney about Frank Bickman trespassing around the back of the property, but it would have to wait until she tended to her stew and answered the telephone.

"Hello?"

"Hi, Baby. How's your day?" Her husband's voice drifted up from the receiver.

"Good, honey. Elizabeth is outside playing and I'm fixing our supper. How's your day going?"

"Great, but it'll be much better when I get home to my two girls. I'm going to be a few minutes late tonight because I have to go over some documents with the other managers before I head home. Shouldn't be too late though, so keep my dinner warm."

"Of course, I will, honey. I'll see you soon."

She quickly stirred the pot on the stove again before heading out the door. Mr. Spencer was already inside of the empty house so she waited to give him the news about Frank's trespassing.

She glanced at the Bickman house and saw Mary by the curb, retrieving her mail. Gladys waved to the woman and Mary waved back. She couldn't help noticing that the Bickman woman was reading her mail at the curb, almost stalling a little before slowly walking back into her house. Curious woman, thought Gladys.

She looked down the street again to see Elizabeth try, in vain, to do cartwheels. Agatha and Jimmy were attempting to help her, but all three were laughing hysterically as the little girl tumbled into the grass time and again. Gladys laughed at her child's antics before her attention was distracted by the loud noise of the garbage truck lumbering down the block from Riverside Highway.

The sudden realization that her full garbage cans were still sitting at the side of her house made Gladys spring into action. Damn Thomas, she thought. He'd forgotten to put the trash out by the curb again.

She grabbed each can by its handle and started to pull them down the driveway to the curb, making an awful screeching sound in the process. The two overflowing receptacles were too heavy to drag at the same time so she left one behind and quickly pulled the other down to the street before the garbage truck arrived.

The sanitation workers smiled and waved, and then one of the men jogged up and grabbed the other can and easily heaved it over his shoulder. He emptied its foul contents into the truck before placing both cans on the driveway by the street. Gladys yelled out an appreciative "thank you" to the working men, and they waved back before resuming their task for the remainder of the block.

She glanced down the street and saw Jimmy inspecting her daughter's bicycle. Elizabeth and Agatha seemed to be supervising. Probably a loose chain again, thought Gladys. Another thing Thomas was going to have to attend to when he got the time. She knew her husband worked hard to provide for the family, but sometimes she wished he'd spend a little more time at home taking care of all the odd jobs that always needed doing, but rarely got done.

She spotted the elder Bickman boy wandering down the block alone and wondered what his brother was up to. He's probably hiding out so that Barney won't catch him on the property, she thought. It didn't matter; she was determined to inform the real estate agent of the boy's transgression at the first convenient moment.

She didn't want to take her eyes off of her daughter with Jack Bickman on the prowl, but her telephone began to ring again. She noticed that Mary Bickman was coming out of her front door, and it appeared as if she was searching for her boys. Gladys figured it was a good opportunity to duck inside and answer the phone.

As soon as she picked up the phone, she regretted it. It was her mother-in-law, Shirley. It wasn't that she didn't like Shirley – quite the opposite. She thought that Thomas's mother was a very loving and caring woman, who did a great job raising her children. Miss Shirley had been there for them throughout their infertility crisis, the miscarriage, and the care of

Elizabeth. The problem was, Miss Shirley tended to be long-winded.

"Yes, ma'am."

"No problem."

"I have something on the stove."

"Elizabeth is outside and I need to keep an eye on her."

She tried in vain to get off the phone.

Nothing could get the old woman to shut up, and Gladys was starting to get nervous. A few seconds became five minutes, then grew to ten minutes, then more. The anxious mother took a second or two every couple of minutes to stir the pot and glance out of the window, but, short of hanging up on the gabby woman, Gladys felt trapped.

She got her window of opportunity when Miss Shirley stopped talking for a moment to sneeze, and Gladys blurted out that she had to go check on Elizabeth. Putting the phone down before the other woman could respond, she hurried out to the front yard in time to see Frank run from behind the house next door, a troubled expression on his face. For some reason that she couldn't fathom, this unexpected sight set off alarms in her mind, and she quickly looked down the street to check on Elizabeth.

The block was empty. No mailman, no garbage truck, no Agatha, no Jimmy, no Jack, no Purvis, and, most alarmingly, no Elizabeth. A high-pitched ringing began to chime in her head and her stomach clenched tight as she began to panic. She ran inside, hung up the phone on her mother-in-law without another word, took the pot off of the stove, turned the gas off, and darted out of the front door in search of her only child.

As she reached the sidewalk, she saw Barney Spencer's car driving away toward Riverside Highway and Mrs. Bickman entering her house through the side entrance. Gladys no longer cared about whatever it was that Frank was up to next door – neither of these events concerned her at the moment. She was focused only on finding Elizabeth.

She frantically raced down the street, trying to keep her nerves in check as she scanned her surroundings for any sign of the missing child. Johnson Road was like a ghost town. There wasn't a person in sight. The whole block was eerily quiet, and this only made Gladys panic more. How could the street be so busy just moments ago and now be so empty, she thought. Where was Elizabeth? Memories of the family's missing pet surfaced, and she began to cry. This couldn't be happening. Not here, not now, not to her family.

"Elizabeth! Elizabeth!" she called out again and again, her voice beginning to crack.

She ran up to the Peterson door and knocked loudly. Agatha answered and immediately saw Mrs. Jenkins's distraught appearance. She tried to calm the panicking woman, but when she said that she didn't know where the child was, Gladys began to wail.

Cheryl Peterson appeared suddenly in the doorway, summoned by the sound of Gladys's mournful sobs. There was nothing she could do to help, short of producing the child, but she had no idea where the little girl was.

Gladys pulled herself together and hurried to the last house on the block – the Johnson place. For once, Purvis was not on the front porch, but the door was open, and she could hear the sounds of cooking and a radio playing music through the screen door.

She knocked forcefully on the rickety old door, but no one answered. She banged again and began calling out for the old man, just as Purvis came out of a back room wearing a look of surprise and bewilderment on his face.

"Hold on there, I'm comin'!" he barked with annoyance at the unexpected intrusion before he saw the panic-stricken woman on his doorstep.

"Mrs. Jenkins, what's wrong?" Purvis asked as he pushed open the screen door.

"Purvis, have you seen Elizabeth?"

"Sure have."

Gladys felt a wave of relief sweep over her body at the old man's reply. But then, her hopes were dashed when she heard what he said next.

"She's out front playing with Jimmy and Agatha," he said as he pointed to the empty spot in front of George Peterson's house. "Well, they were just there a little while ago."

He could see the panic returning to Mrs. Jenkins's face, so he said quickly, "Let's see if Jimmy knows where she is. Jimmy! Jimmy!" he hollered.

The thought that Jimmy might know something brought a small measure of hope to Gladys. After a few minutes, Purvis called out to his son again. When there was still no answer, Purvis came out onto the porch, carefully closing the screen door behind him so it wouldn't slam against the doorjamb.

He stepped out into the yard in search of his son, but, before he could call out again, Jimmy came bounding around the corner of the house.

"Yeah, Daddy, did you need me?"

"'Bout time, boy. Mrs. Jenkins here has been looking for little 'Lizbeth. You know where she is?"

"No, sir. She was over at Agatha's with me a little while ago, but I don't know where she run off to"

Gladys's heart sank again, and this time her knees buckled and she landed in the grass at the side of the Johnson house. Purvis and Jimmy helped her to her feet and sat her in Purvis's rocking chair on the front porch.

Jimmy ran inside to get her some ice water while Purvis sat with her, reassuring her that her child would turn up soon. She was inconsolable as the old man questioned her about what she knew of the child's whereabouts and who she had asked on the block prior to knocking at his door.

Knowing that it was unlikely that the child had gone back up the street, Gladys was afraid that the child had just vanished without a trace. She began to hyperventilate. Jimmy arrived with the glass of cold water, which did little in helping her to regain her composure.

Purvis suggested, as calmly and diplomatically as he could so as not to set her off again, that they contact the sheriff's office. Despite his best efforts, this suggestion sent Gladys into a screaming panic. Purvis sat with her and tended to her while he sent Jimmy over to the Peterson's house to use the telephone, a luxury item that Purvis never found a justifiable expense, to call the sheriff's office.

Purvis whispered to Jimmy as he turned to leave that it might not be a bad idea to look around the neighborhood once he'd contacted the sheriff's office. Jimmy could talk to a few of the neighbors and scan the area until the authorities arrived. He wouldn't go near the Bickman place, but that still left most of the block to search. Hopefully, the child would emerge soon and ease her mother's suffering. Never all that comfortable around people, Purvis was uneasy having the hysterical woman on his front porch.

The news of the missing child spread quickly up and down the block. After Jimmy explained the situation to Agatha and her mother, Mrs. Peterson put a call into the sheriff's office while Jimmy and Agatha walked down the street, knocking on doors. Before the two made it halfway down the short block, most of the neighbors were coming out to see what was going on. Even Mary Bickman came out front to find out what was happening.

Purvis convinced Gladys to go back to her house in the off chance that the girl had returned while she was out searching for her. When Agatha returned home to look after her little brother, Cheryl Peterson helped Purvis escort Gladys back to her own house. Purvis asked Cheryl and Mary Bickman to search Gladys's house and yard, but to no avail.

They sat with Gladys on the front steps, waiting for the authorities to arrive. By the time Sheriff Gaskin showed up with a couple of deputies in tow, the despondent mother was sobbing uncontrollably.

Once the sheriff got some preliminary information from the three women, he dispersed his deputies to question the neighbors and search the area. As the deputies began to carry out their assigned duties, Clifford stayed with Gladys and tried to gather more of the details leading up to the girl's disappearance.

Normally, these things ended up with the child running away, or visiting one of their friends without the parent's knowledge, although the sheriff could see that neither scenario was likely this time. Unfortunately, this left only unpleasant alternatives.

Either the child had gotten lost, or had been abducted. The short distance along Johnson Road left little chance that the girl couldn't find her way home, which made the sheriff shudder with the reality of the more likely chance that they were dealing with a child abduction.

The mother's story provided a lot of possible suspects. The way the woman told it, the street was full of people the last time she saw the child. Where there were lots of people, there were lots of suspects, and, hopefully, lots of witnesses.

Clifford hoped that, before long, they would have a lead or two to follow. However, he knew better than to convey either his concerns or his optimism to Mrs. Jenkins. He understood too well that even if they found out who took the girl, that didn't mean they could prove it. He also knew that it was possible they might not find the girl alive, or even find her at all.

Sheriff Gaskin and his men gathered up a few of the neighbors and instructed them to search the area. Deputies Bryce and Willis inspected the empty house next door, but nothing was out of place.

Afterwards, they joined the rest of the men and made their way down the ravine in the off chance that the girl had wandered down there and couldn't get back. He knew it was unlikely, but by looking down there now, he would eliminate that option for later, and the sun would be setting soon enough. He certainly didn't want anyone stumbling down there in the dark, making things worse. Clifford also knew that, as long as the child's mother was focusing on her child being lost, the alternative of her child being abducted hopefully might not enter her mind.

By this time, even more deputies had arrived at the Jenkins's house, and the whole scene was starting to take on a carnival atmosphere. The sun descended below the horizon and the streetlights kicked on, while the sight of waving flashlights and searching neighbors calling out for the missing child set the entire block alive with action.

As more police cars arrived, their red and blue spinning lights produced an awful vision down the block. When the sheriff's men began to unroll the yellow tape to cordon off the scene, Gladys became hysterical and she had to be escorted into her house and out of view of the milling crowd.

When Thomas made the right hand turn off Riverside Highway and onto Johnson Road, he spotted the chaos in front of his house. His stomach flip-flopped and his heart beat wildly as he pulled up behind one of the patrol cars clogging the street.

He sprang out of the vehicle, leaving his door open and the car running. Deputy Bryce tried to catch and stop him on the way into the house, but was too slow. When Thomas spotted his crying wife sitting on the couch, without his daughter by her side, he knew his life would never be the same again.

"Where's Elizabeth?"

Gladys could only look at her husband through tear-filled eyes as she fell into his arms and continued to sob loudly.

"Where's my baby girl?" shouted the anguished father.

Deputy Bryce tried to tell Thomas that he'd tried to contact the man at his office and that everyone was doing everything they could to find his daughter, but Thomas wasn't listening.

All he could do was to hold his wife in his arms, feeling her shaking body against his chest. He closed his eyes tight, hoping against hope that this nightmare would end, and that his beautiful little girl would be returned to the safety of her loving family.

*

June, 1959

Just after nightfall the rain came down. The torrential downpour lasted unabated for almost four days, making the search for the missing girl much more difficult.

Sheriff Gaskin wasn't as concerned about the rain as those around him. He'd worked relentlessly around the clock since the incident and had formed a number of theories. Most of these theories pointed to the chance of little Elizabeth being found anywhere near her home as having only a very small and remote possibility.

As the initial investigation began to grow within the first couple of days, all of the inhabitants of Johnson Road were interviewed and their stories investigated. Despite several 'iron clad' alibis, Clifford considered everyone a suspect, although some more likely than others.

He contemplated the likelihood that someone outside of the area was the culprit and didn't want to expend all of his department's manpower pursuing dead ends. The sheriff gave Deputy Stevens the task of researching similar crimes in the neighboring counties and instructed him to produce a list of possible offenders that they could investigate. To Clifford's consternation, the deputy's inquiries brought the state police to his doorstep in full force.

The disappearance of an eight year old girl was an appalling and uncommon occurrence, so the fact that the authorities upstairs would take notice and want to get involved was to be expected. The state police came to his office and the Jenkins's house by the second day, although they hadn't stepped on his toes just yet.

The additional manpower and resources were appreciated and invaluable to the investigation, but experience had taught him that his luck was going to run out fast with these guys. The sheriff understood that their involvement was a necessary evil, but even so, he knew that too many chefs would spoil the stew.

The FBI was already calling, and they weren't going to be dissuaded by Mabel's runaround. Clifford swallowed hard and hedged his bets. He'd work with the state troopers in earnest, no matter what the cost, if it kept the Feds away.

In the end, he was the one who had to face Thomas and Gladys Jenkins and deliver the bad news. Make no mistake, thought Clifford, no matter how things turned out, the news was going to be bad. They were four days into the search already, and not a trace of the girl. Yes, conceded the sheriff, the news was going to be bad– very bad.

He sat at his desk and pored over the papers in front of him. He'd wasted no time in making lists of possible suspects and comprising strategies for him and his men to follow in looking for the girl. He personally interviewed Walter Brown, the postman, and had Deputy Willis follow up with the man's supervisor as well as canvassing the remaining mail recipients on the postman's route that day to see if they'd received their deliveries. They had.

He made a few preliminary inquiries with the sanitation company, and had reviewed the files of the three garbage men. The driver was one David Garcia, a third generation American whose grandparents emigrated over sixty-years ago from Spain. In the enlightened enclave of Peterson County, Alabama, this made him a Mexican and, therefore, a person of interest.

The remaining two workers, James Jones and Tyrone Letts, were both Negroes. This alone made them prime targets for the boys in the white hoods, and Clifford was going to have none of that. He doubted that any of the sanitation workers had been involved in any way in the abduction of little Elizabeth, and it was of the upmost importance that he nip any guilt by racial affiliation in the bud. Things were bad enough already.

All of the policemen in Peterson County were white. He was aware that a black officer would probably be more effective in pursuing things on the other side of the tracks. For this task, he utilized the state police, who wanted to get more involved. When he discovered that there was a highway patrolman, Clarence Jackson, who was not only black, but highly regarded by his fellow troopers, he paired the man with Deputy Willis and sent them over to Moorestown, the black section of the county, to see what they could dig up.

So far, everything had checked out on all fronts. But to be thorough, he contemplated tracking down the rest of the stops of the garbage truck and having a few men sift through the refuse. Clifford considered farming out this unpleasant task to the state boys, but knew he was also going to have to send at least one of his own, if only for the appearance of fair play. The sheriff hadn't yet decided which unfortunate man he was going to assign, although he figured it was more than likely going to be the first one who managed to piss him off.

The sheriff was keeping his prime suspect for himself. He had met Barney Spencer on many occasions prior to this incident and would never have given the man another thought – until now. By all accounts, the real estate agent was a go-getter, without so much as a parking ticket in his past. All the same, the man's presence in the vicinity and his timely exit coinciding with the disappearance of the girl meant that he would've had the best chance to abduct the child and make his getaway unnoticed. The fact that the girl knew Mr. Spencer meant that it was entirely possible that he was able to coerce her into his vehicle unseen with little resistance.

Clifford had learned through discreet inquiries that the agent's movements were difficult to nail down. He seemed to come and go as he pleased, with little in the way of supervision, making any possible alibi shaky at best. None of this made the man guilty of such a horrendous crime.

The sheriff hated to assign suspicion to Barney based only on his unfortunate luck of being in the wrong place at the wrong time, but something was nagging at him about Mr. Spencer. What, exactly, was he doing down on Johnson Road that afternoon anyway?

Chapter Twelve

When George Peterson turned his luxury sedan off of Riverside Highway and onto Johnson Road that fateful Tuesday evening, he almost went into cardiac arrest. The multitude of police cars parked up and down the block would've been alarming to anyone, but for a nervous sort like George, it was more than a tad bit disconcerting. He drove slowly past the Jenkins house, spied the crime scene tape cordoning off the area, and let out a small sigh of relief. At least it wasn't his house or his family, he thought, feeling strangely guilty for his selfish lack of compassion.

By the time he'd pulled his car up his driveway and into the garage, George had regained some of his composure. Agatha and little Georgie met him at the doorway; Cheryl was still down the street tending to Mrs. Jenkins. Agatha informed her father of the terrible incident that had transpired earlier that day and to the whereabouts of their absent mother. George was visibly shaken by the awful news of the missing girl, and he told Agatha to wait at the house with her younger brother while he went down to the Jenkins's house to retrieve his absent wife.

Most of the neighbors didn't care much for George Peterson and his snobbish ways, but with a child missing, petty differences were largely ignored. He spoke in whispered tones with a couple of his neighbors and the deputies mulling about in the Jenkins's front yard about the day's events in an attempt to get as many of the grim details as he could before spotting his wife emerge from the Jenkins's house.

Cheryl came walking out of the front door with Deputy Bryce at her side, both wearing solemn expressions. She looked up, saw her husband, and quickly ran to him. The couple embraced with more feeling and intimacy than they'd known in a long time. Their moment together ended with the arrival of Thomas Jenkins, who'd just pulled his car up behind the police vehicles blocking his driveway. Thomas jumped out of his car and ran into the house, with the deputy close at his heels.

The Peterson couple stood for awhile in silence until they heard the anguished cries of the grieving father, then they turned and walked slowly back to their home and their waiting children. George listened intently as Cheryl told him about all of the terrible things that had happened that day. When she got to the part about the missing girl's last known location being in front of their house, he noticeably tensed up. This was the last thing he needed, he thought.

Later, inside their home, the Petersons sat at the dinner table together to share their supper. After the awful events of the day, none of them had much of an appetite, although they seemed to take some solace in each other's company. There wasn't much talk among them, but what little there was consisted of trivial things. No one wanted to discuss the missing girl.

When the meal was finished, Agatha went to her room while her parents tucked in Georgie. The young Peterson boy had been suffering bouts of nausea and vomiting intermittently for several months, although today he'd managed to get a little relief.

Cheryl told George about Purvis's visit earlier that day and how much Junior enjoyed the chicken soup that he'd brought. George seemed pleased that his little boy was able to finally keep some food down, and he agreed with his wife that they were lucky that the old man next door took such an interest in the child's recovery. He'd had his differences with Purvis Johnson to be sure, but he was able to overlook any disagreements when it came to the health of his sickly child.

"So, how's my little tiger doing today?" He asked his son as they tucked him into bed.

"Good, Daddy."

"Can you growl like a tiger?"

The boy and his father growled for a few minutes as their mother happily looked on. They broke into laughter, and even Cheryl began to laugh, succumbing to the contagious sounds of her youngest child's giggles.

Once the boy was put to bed, the couple returned downstairs to the kitchen to straighten up before bedtime. Much to Cheryl's surprise, George was acting kind and attentive to her, even helping her with the dishes. The long-neglected housewife relished her husband's affection, enjoying the rare moment that she knew wouldn't last.

The horrible tragedy that struck the Jenkins that day made George take more notice of his own family. He knew he was oftentimes aloof and detached at home, spending his time thinking about work at the expense of those he believed he was working so hard for. What a fool I've been, he thought. He vowed that, from then on, he would take more stock in his life and the blessings that he was lucky to have.

His thoughts turned toward Georgie's recurrent bouts of illness. He realized how long the child had been suffering and how much care that his wife had been providing the boy. He felt ashamed that he hadn't really been there for either one of them. He turned to Cheryl and took his wife's hands in his. Looking into her eyes, he praised her for being a wonderful mother to his ailing son. With tears of happiness in her eyes, Cheryl kissed her husband and held him close.

Cheryl had felt invisible to her husband and to the world for a long time. It felt good to get some recognition, even if it came because of the unfortunate health of her son. Until Purvis came along, she'd borne the brunt of her suffering in silence and anonymity. Thanks to Purvis's help and intervention, she began to get noticed for her unfailing dedication to her sick child; noticed by everyone, that is, except her husband.

George had complimented her on rare occasions in the past, but only when he couldn't avoid it, and

Cheryl always detected a subtle note of insincerity when he did. This time it felt different. She could see that he truly recognized her tireless efforts in the care of the boy. She knew deep inside that this change of heart by her husband wouldn't last and that they'd return to their dysfunctional lives soon enough, but knowing that he'd recognized her devotion just this once made her feel like she was finally vindicated.

The next day, Deputy Sean Willis came knocking at the door before George had even started on his first cup of coffee. George tried to give the officer the brush-off with the excuse that he was running late for work and didn't have much time, but Sean wasn't going along with it. He only had a couple of questions, the deputy explained, and it shouldn't take but a few minutes. In any event, Deputy Willis continued, the investigation was more important, and George was just going to have to be late. George conceded the deputy's point and reluctantly invited the officer in.

Most of the questions were addressed to Agatha since she was the one who'd actually spent time with Elizabeth prior to the child's disappearance. She recited the previous day's events again as Deputy Willis took notes. Sean asked Cheryl a few questions about what she may have known or seen in the hopes that some detail they'd missed might surface. None did.

The deputy attempted to ask the young Peterson boy if perhaps he had looked out of the window, or had any ideas that might be helpful, but the child could think of nothing. Once the interview was finished, Sean rose from the table and walked out, escorted by George.

When the two men were outside, the deputy turned to George and inquired about his exact whereabouts the day before.

"What time was it you said you left your office, Mr. Peterson?"

George was caught off guard by that line of questioning and quickly grew defensive.

"The same time I always leave my office. What exactly are you implying, Deputy? Are you accusing me of having something to do with that little girl's disappearance?" His complexion turned red as his voice grew louder. "How dare you ask me a question like that! Do you know who I am?"

"Now, hold on a second, Mr. Peterson. I'm just doing my job." Sean said evenly, trying to de-escalate the situation. "I'm asking the same questions to everyone that lives near here or is known to have been in the vicinity. I am not accusing you of anything, nor does the sheriff's office consider you to be a suspect in any way. I assure you, it's all part of standard operating procedure and not targeting toward you specifically."

"I left the office at six o'clock as always. Feel free to check up on that any time you want. By the time I got home, y'all were already here, blocking the street with your squad cars and searching the block. Now, if you don't mind, I really need to get to the office. I've answered all of your questions, but I do have a job to get to. If you need anything else, it'll just have to wait."

He turned his back on Sean and marched over to his car without so much as a handshake or a second look. Deputy Willis watched the man's childish display with amusement, shaking his head in disgust. Same ole' George Peterson, he thought.

Once Peterson's car backed out of the driveway and drove off down the street, the deputy closed his note pad, tucked it into his jacket pocket, and returned to his patrol car. The rain began to fall again, so the deputy shut the car door quickly and picked up the radio. As he checked in with Mabel, he watched as an unmarked state police cruiser drove past him and up to the Johnson residence.

Gaskin was not going to like this. The deputy informed Mabel about the unplanned visitor that had just arrived. He knew once she passed that news on to the sheriff, it wouldn't be long before he'd be needed right where he was. He sat back and waited for the sheriff to show up or call. He didn't have to wait long.

*

June 17, 1959: 9:54 a.m.

When word got around to Robert about the missing
girl over in Peterson County, he knew he'd be
summoned by the captain. Warner called him at home
the night of the disappearance with instructions to
'poke around discreetly and see what you can dig up.'
The detective laughed to himself at the absurdity of
the request.

Stallworth was aware that the first time he showed
his face over there, the local authorities would get
defensive and call the captain. Warner would notify
him of the inevitable complaints and reiterate his
impossible instructions about discretion. In the midst
of the ass-chewing, the captain would then offer a
sure way for the detective to redeem himself – solve
the case. It was a game that they both were familiar
with by this point, but because it usually ended up
with positive results, there was little incentive to
change.

Early the following morning, the detective headed
out to the crime scene. He was still in the dark about
almost everything pertaining to the investigation, but
figured he might as well start at ground zero and work
from there. He'd made a few calls before he left the
house and had gotten the address of the missing girl's
family, the location of the last known sighting, and
the name of the last person to see the child.

Detective Stallworth didn't know much about the
boy. His name was Jimmy Johnson, and he lived at

the end of the street where the girl went missing. Jimmy lived with his father, one Purvis Johnson, who'd been residing in the area for a number of years. Purvis was retired, disabled, unemployed, or some combination of the three. It was possible that the father could be of some help as well, thought Robert, since there was a good chance that he was in the vicinity at the time of the disappearance and may have seen something.

By the time he pulled his car off of Riverside Highway and slowly drove toward the back of Johnson Road, the rain had resumed. It had been coming down off and on since the wee hours of the morning and promised to continue for days. The timing couldn't have been worse, as the deluge would definitely make the search for the child more difficult.

There were two patrol cars from the sheriff's office on the block – one by the house where the missing girl lived and the other in front of the big house near the end. The state troopers had one of their own cars positioned at the exit off the highway, although no one was inside.

No doubt whichever officer the car belonged to was inside one of the pretty little houses on the block, trying to stay dry and gather information. When he was through 'discreetly poking around', Robert made a mental note to find out who was involved in the investigation and who would be responsible for funneling all of the available facts his way.

He passed the big house with the patrol car parked out front without acknowledging the deputy sitting behind the wheel, then stopped in front of a curious looking little shack at the end of the road.

The house was easily the oldest, smallest, and most disreputable on the block. To add to its strangeness, the house was facing in the wrong direction, with the front toward the highway instead of the street. Old car parts were scattered about the unkempt yard and a dilapidated tin shack toward the back seemed to serve as a garage, tool shed, or some combination of the two.

He doubted that any vehicles resided in the old building, since there were already two trucks in view on the property. An old Ford pickup was parked halfway up the front yard and an even older rust-bucket of undisclosed origin could be seen in the back yard, which was overgrown with weeds, a testament to the junker's long-standing immobility.

The detective gathered his belongings, put on his hat, and got out of the car into the falling rain. He normally liked to eschew the state trooper's most famous wardrobe accessory. He thought it was a cliché and even a little pretentious, but the precipitation forced him to rethink his stand in favor of staying a little drier.

He turned and walked briskly to the front porch of the house and the old man sitting in a rocking chair, watching his arrival.

"Good morning, sir," the detective greeted the man. "My name is Detective Robert Stallworth of the Alabama State Police. Would it be okay if I had a word with you and your son?"

Purvis sat, rocking in his chair, before exhaling a billow of cigarette smoke into the damp morning air. He nodded toward the empty wooden bench on the front porch next to him.

"Sure thing, Officer," he replied. "Have a seat. We'd be happy to help in any way we can."

The old man called for the boy, and, after a few minutes, Jimmy appeared from inside the small, but dry, shack. The boy let the screen door slam behind him as he walked over to a spot next to his father. Purvis winced at the sound of the slamming door, but he let his displeasure go unvoiced since they had a visitor. Once they were all settled and introductions made, the detective inquired about the previous day's events, taking notes on a small pad he produced from one of the many pockets of his wet overcoat.

Robert directed the majority of his questions toward the boy as Purvis sat quietly by, listening intently. Jimmy told the detective that he and Agatha were outside in front of the big house next door as Elizabeth rode her bike up and down the block.

The detective let the boy go through the day's events with little interruption. He would clarify any discrepancies later in subsequent interviews. He knew that they would be going over this again many times in the upcoming days and weeks, so there was little need for impatience on his part.

As the boy continued, he described how Agatha taught Elizabeth how to do cartwheels on her front lawn. Jimmy paused for a moment, choking back tears, before regaining his composure. He was visibly shaken over the disappearance of the girl as he recounted how much fun they'd been having only moments before she vanished.

The boy told the detective about the malfunctioning chain on the girl's bicycle. He told the detective that he'd gone into the garage to look for some pliers and a wrench to try and tighten the chain; when he returned, Elizabeth was gone.

Detective Stallworth asked the boy who else had been in the vicinity at the time, but, before Jimmy could answer, their attention was diverted toward the two automobiles with the unmistakable sheriff's star emblazoned on their front doors that pulled up in unison to the front of the house.

Deputy Willis got out of his patrol car, which was still parked in front of the big house next door, and joined Deputy Bryce and Sheriff Gaskin. Once together, the three marched through the falling rain toward the little shack.

"Looks like the party's over, Detective," Purvis muttered with amusement.

"Looks that way," Robert replied, rising to greet the approaching officers.

Chapter Thirteen

"Jimmy," Purvis hollered, "I'm goin' next door for a bit. You comin'?"

The boy ran out of the old garage and through the back door. While his father was putting the hot chicken soup into a smaller bowl to bring to the neighbors, Jimmy went to the restroom to wash up and comb his hair. Purvis stalled a few minutes to give the boy time, smiling to himself about the boy's infatuation with the pretty girl who lived next door.

"Come on now. Gotta go," Purvis called out as he walked through the door and onto the front porch, shutting the screen door gently behind him.

By the time the old man made it to the bottom step and into the yard, Jimmy came running up behind him, letting the rickety door bang loudly. Purvis winced and shot the boy a look that required no further explanations.

"Sorry," Jimmy whispered, his shoulders hunched over and his eyes directed to the ground.

The old man shook his head and the two continued toward the big house next door in silence. When they got to the end of their property and turned toward the front of the Peterson house, they spotted Agatha sitting on the front porch. Jimmy's face blushed at the sight of the pretty girl; his heart raced and his stomach filled with butterflies. Purvis was aware of the girl's effect on his son, but he showed no outward sign of it. They smiled at Agatha as they approached the house, Purvis carrying the pot of chicken soup while Jimmy walked a step behind.

"Mornin', Agatha," Purvis greeted her with a smile. "Your Momma home? Got some soup for the young'un. 'Aught to make him feel a might better. Get some strength in him."

"Yes, sir. She's inside tending to Georgie right now," Agatha replied. "I'm sure she'll be happy to see you, too. Georgie's been having trouble keeping anything down. I'm sure that'll change when he gets that soup in front of him. I just hope he leaves a little for me."

"Didn't bring none for you," Purvis teased. "Just enough for the sick one. You feelin' alright?"

Agatha feigned a cough before replying, "Maybe could use a little something."

They laughed. Agatha smiled at Purvis and then at Jimmy, who blushed and averted his eyes for a moment at the sudden attention.

"Well, if you start puking up before long, you let me know, and I'll bring some more over," the old man replied.

"Eewww," Agatha answered with a look of disgust on her otherwise angelic face.

Agatha opened the door and called her mother, "Momma. Mr. Purvis and Jimmy are here with some soup for Georgie!"

"Okay, dear. We're up here," Cheryl's voice drifted down from one of the rooms upstairs.

"You can go on up, Mr. Purvis. They're in Georgie's room," Agatha instructed.

"Jimmy, you stay down here with Agatha for a spell. I don't want to chance you catchin' whatever Georgie has," Purvis told the boy.

Jimmy had no problem complying with the expected request. It was Agatha he came to see. The old man went up the stairs, bringing the much anticipated soup to the ailing boy while Agatha and Jimmy went back outside and sat on the front lawn. They chatted about some of the kids that they knew from school, with Agatha doing most of the talking.

The Peterson girl found herself unexpectedly drawn to the strange boy next door. Agatha was outgoing and popular – all the things that Jimmy wasn't. None of her friends could understand why she even associated with Jimmy Johnson, and she was sure they would be horrified if they knew that she had a major crush on the boy. She didn't understand why she felt the way she did, either. Perhaps it was because she felt totally at ease with him, or maybe it was because she knew that he adored her. Maybe, she thought, it's because I love him.

"Hello, Jimmy. Hello, Agatha!" Elizabeth shouted as she rode up suddenly on her bicycle.

"Well, hello, Princess!" Agatha answered back.

"Wow, you're riding pretty fast on that bike there," Jimmy told the little girl.

"As fast as a rocket-ship!" exclaimed Elizabeth with delight.

Agatha and Jimmy watched as the girl turned around in the Peterson's driveway and raced back down the block toward the highway and her waiting mother. Elizabeth stopped to talk with her mom for a few moments, then turned around and raced back down the block to them again. Purvis appeared, walking out the Peterson's front door, carrying the now empty pot with him.

"You didn't save me any?" Agatha asked in jest.

"No ma'am. You didn't throw up, did you?" Purvis replied.

They laughed. The old man walked back toward his house, leaving Jimmy behind to visit with Agatha. The three turned at the sight of Elizabeth quickly riding up on her bicycle and screeching to a halt on the sidewalk. Purvis glanced down the block, spotted Elizabeth's mother, and waved to her before resuming his trek home.

Agatha showed off her cartwheels, which she had mastered, for her visitors. Elizabeth and Jimmy applauded her success, and Agatha bowed to the adoring crowd. Elizabeth asked if Jimmy could do them too, but he refused to even contemplate the request. The little girl called him a chicken and began to make clucking sounds, but he turned the tables on her and challenged her to try. She was ecstatic at the prospect of learning this new skill, and she begged Agatha to teach her how. Agatha shot Jimmy a sarcastic look of 'thank you very much' before telling the excited little girl that she'd have to get permission from her mother first. Elizabeth wasted no time

221

jumping on her bicycle and racing back to her home as fast as she could.

The mailman drove up to the mailbox at the curb, sliding the assorted letters and advertisements into the waiting box. He waved at the two teens sitting on the front lawn, and turned around at the end of the block in front of Jimmy's house. There was no mail for Purvis today, so Walt, the postman, started up the other side of the street. Elizabeth returned within a few minutes with permission granted by her mother. She set the kickstand down and met Agatha on the short-cut grass of the front yard, ready for her lesson.

Agatha talked Elizabeth through the steps and demonstrated a couple of proper cartwheels to the little girl's delight. When it was Elizabeth's turn to try, things didn't work out exactly as planned. At first, the little girl hesitated, which ended up with her falling to the ground. Determined to succeed, she picked herself up and tried again. Elizabeth managed to finally go for it and to land fully on her hands, but her legs folded and she plopped to the turf with a thump. Jimmy was beside himself with laughter, and Agatha couldn't help from joining in. Even Elizabeth couldn't stop laughing after her third hapless attempt.

Agatha tried a different tactic, having Elizabeth do a handstand while she held the girl's legs straight up. Even though Elizabeth was small, this proved difficult for Agatha, so Jimmy was recruited to help. The three went through a few cartwheels in slow motion, stopping between attempts to giggle and laugh. On the fourth try, Elizabeth was somewhat successful, and Jimmy and Agatha applauded. The encouragement was all that the child needed for motivation, and she did the next one without any help. A loud honk sounded from the garbage truck that was passing, and even the two sanitation workers applauded the girl's new-found gymnastic skills.

The three children took a break from the tiresome antics and sat on the front lawn, talking and laughing. Elizabeth told Jimmy that the chain on her bicycle had been jamming up and coming loose, so the boy went over to examine it. He propped the bike upside down on its handlebars and spun the wheels a few times, tugging at the chain. He was sure that he could fix it, but he'd need a few tools from his garage. He excused himself to go and fetch them.

Jimmy nodded to his father, who was standing on the front porch smoking one of his cigarettes, before ducking around back and disappearing into the garage. The old man glanced over to where the two girls were waiting and waved before crushing the butt of the cigarette on the porch beneath his boots. He looked back down the street just in time to see the eldest Bickman boy amble down the block toward them. Damn troublemaker, thought Purvis. The old man stood on his porch all alone, watching and waiting for a few minutes before disappearing into the house to start preparing dinner.

He was busy in the small, hot kitchen, working on the evening meal, when he heard a loud banging at the front door. The knocking grew louder. He wiped his hands on the closest dishtowel he could find and went up front to see what the racket was about. When he got there, he saw that it was the Jenkins woman, who was in a panic and nearly hysterical. She couldn't find her daughter. Purvis told her that he was sure that the child was around somewhere.

The little girl was just here, thought Purvis. He called out to Jimmy, but the boy explained that when he came back out of the garage with the tools to work on Elizabeth's bicycle, the child was already gone. The old man scanned the neighborhood from the vantage point of his front porch. The street was empty.

The rest of that terrible day was one that both father and son would wish they could forget. Purvis helped tend to Elizabeth's distraught mother while Jimmy went to look around. After Mrs. Jenkins went back to her home and was being comforted by the neighborhood women, Purvis helped the arriving authorities search the area for the missing child.

By the time night fell, they all knew that, wherever the girl was, she wasn't anywhere near Johnson Road. The block wasn't very long, and the area was small. The search was thorough enough, even in that short time, to determine that the child wasn't there.

Once it was dark, the inhabitants of Johnson Road returned to their individual homes, cherishing the closeness of their loved ones – all, but one. The Jenkins's lives would be shattered forever. The rain began to pour down in buckets; even the heavens were mourning the loss of the beautiful child. Four days of rain would never be enough to wash away the sorrow of that Tuesday afternoon.

Early the next morning, a detective from the state police showed up at the Johnson's door. Purvis wasn't surprised. After all, he figured, the girl's last known whereabouts was in front of his neighbor's house.

When the officer wanted to question Jimmy, he grew uncomfortable. He didn't want the boy to become a scapegoat. Once Jimmy had told the detective everything he knew, Purvis felt a little better, although for some reason he couldn't quite place, he still felt uneasy.

Sheriff Gaskin showed up before long, cutting short the questioning by Detective Stallworth. Purvis could see right away that the two men were not fond of each other. Good grief, thought the old man. It's always a pissing contest between authority figures. The sheriff ran the detective off, but he and his men were just getting started with him and his boy.

One of the deputies made a lame excuse that he needed to use the bathroom and disappeared into the house for a lot longer than Purvis figured it required to take a piss. The deputy eventually emerged empty-handed. The sheriff kept the old man outside making inane conversation while the other two deputies accompanied Jimmy to the garage after asking him to show them the tools he'd gone to fetch in order to fix the little girl's bike.

Purvis didn't much care for the haphazard way the sheriff and his men went about their unofficial search of his property. They treated him like he was an idiot. Did they really think that their ploy wasn't transparent? He was even less enthusiastic about the way they doubled up on the questioning of his son without his presence. Purvis chose not to protest this time, hoping that this would put to rest any doubts and clear their names.

The old man discussed the chances that the missing girl was still in the area versus the chances that she'd been abducted and taken away. He was sure that the sheriff would see the obvious logic in the latter scenario. Once Sheriff Gaskin convinced himself that this was all his idea, he would set about tracking the girl in more fertile pastures, or so Purvis imagined.

The detective was another story, thought Purvis. He was sure that the man was going to be incessantly methodical in his methods. The old man respected this, but hoped that he'd soon look elsewhere. He wanted them all to go away. He'd purposely bought his property in the middle of nowhere in order to get away from people, and now he felt like he was in the thick of it.

After the sheriff and his men left, he sat alone with Jimmy and listened to the rain. He talked to the boy about Elizabeth and the previous day's events. He could see that the child's disappearance was upsetting his boy and, after awhile, he let it pass. Purvis found himself staring at the boy from time to time in the days and weeks that followed, wondering if there was something the boy wasn't telling him. Did he know something he wasn't talking about?

The old man knew in his heart that Jimmy was a gentle sort. He remembered how much prodding it took to get the boy to stand up for himself when the Bickman brothers were bullying him. Sure, thought Purvis, the boy eventually stood his ground. Maybe the boy had even gone a little too far in getting his revenge. Maybe Purvis pushed him too hard into a place that he could never come back from.

JOHNSON ROAD

Corporal Purvis Johnson had gone to that place in the war, never to return.

*

June 17, 1959: 5:17 a.m

Clifford was starting on his first cup of coffee that morning when the call came in. He'd been up late the night before and had only slept a couple of hours. The sound of the rain reverberating on the tin roof of his back patio made it all the more difficult for the sheriff to roll out of bed, but there were things to do today. He washed his face and got dressed in a hurry, leaving his house while it was still dark outside. He pulled up to the Olde Towne Diner a little after six and sat in the booth by the window up front.

The sheriff ordered a cup of coffee, black with no sugar, and leafed through the notes he'd made the previous evening. His mind raced as he looked over the pages in front of him, the urgency of the investigation waking him up more than the caffeine laden drink he poured into his empty stomach. He almost jumped at the sound of his radio chirping loudly in the sleepy diner.

"Gaskin here. Over."

"Sheriff, Deputy Willis here. Ten-twenty at the Peterson house on Johnson Road. State Trooper just pulled up to Purvis's place and looks to be questioning the old man and his boy. Thought you'd want to know. Over."

Clifford cringed as the sound of his deputy's voice rang out the unpleasant news through the static of his hand-held radio. Damn, the state boys are already on my case, he thought.

"Ten-four, Deputy. Who else is down? Over."

"Deputy Bryce is down by the Jenkins place. One of the state patrol cars is parked right off Riverside, but no one's in it. Over," the deputy replied.

"Ten-four. Stay put and have Mabel call Deputy Bryce. I'll be there in twenty. Join me when I get there and we'll welcome our new colleague together. Gaskin out."

Clifford gulped the last of his coffee and gathered his papers, stuffing them into his case and putting on his coat and hat. He threw a couple of bucks on the table and headed into the rain toward Johnson Road.

When the sheriff turned onto the little road off Riverside Highway, he spotted Deputy Bryce in his patrol car, waiting for him. Clifford slowed down as he passed the Jenkins house and let the deputy pull up behind him. The two men drove to Purvis's house and parked behind the State Trooper's car.

They got out of their cars and met up with Deputy Willis, who was emerging from his waiting vehicle next door. As the trio marched through the drizzling rain toward the old man's front porch, they spotted the detective. Purvis and Jimmy were sitting next to the man, all three watching in silence as the local authorities approached.

"Mornin', Purvis," said Clifford.

"Mornin', Sheriff," answered the old man, blowing out a billow of cigarette smoke into the damp morning air.

"Jimmy," Gaskin nodded to the boy sitting next to the old man. Lastly, he looked over at the detective and asked, "And who do we have here?"

"Allow me to introduce myself, Sheriff. I'm Detective Robert Stallworth of the Alabama State Police," Robert replied.

The sheriff paused for a moment, giving the detective an icy stare. Robert stood smiling with his hand out-stretched, although his eyes mirrored the same coldness that was present in Gaskin's gaze. If Clifford was trying to intimidate the detective, he was going to have to do a better job.

"Mornin', Detective. I'm Sheriff Clifford Gaskin of the Peterson County Sheriff's Office," he said, eventually taking Robert's hand in a firm grip. "This here is Deputy Willis and Deputy Bryce." He nodded toward the two men at his side.

"Please to meet you, Deputies," Robert answered, shaking each man's hand in turn.

"We havin' some kind of law enforcement convention down here today, Sheriff?" asked Purvis sarcastically. "I don't think my porch is gonna be big enough. If y'all need a bigger venue, might I suggest the Peterson place?"

"Now, Purvis, you know good and well why we're down here this morning," chastised the sheriff. "We got to find that little girl, and this was the last place she was seen."

"No sir. I don't think you're right. I'm no detective or policeman or anything, but I believe 'Lizbeth was last seen next door. Why I suggested the Peterson place," Purvis repeated.

Clifford looked at the old man with contempt, but held his tongue. He could sense that Purvis was getting annoyed at the presence of strangers on his property, and he had every right to ask them to leave.

Clifford wanted to avoid alienating the old man since he was vital to the investigation, so he took a deep breath and reluctantly changed his tone.

"Yes sir, I do believe you're right about that. I'm sorry we came out here so early this mornin'," Clifford said, darting his eyes toward the detective for a moment, "especially since we kept you up so late last night searching down that embankment behind your house."

"We was searching, too, Sheriff," Purvis told the men. He wanted them all to remember that he and Jimmy were more than mere bystanders in the search for the missing child.

"I know that, and we appreciate both of y'all's help down there. It was dirty and unpleasant work, and I'm sure it wasn't what either of you would've rather been doin' on a hot, rainy night," Clifford replied.

"Wasn't doin' it for you; was doin' it for little 'Lizbeth."

The men stood in silence for a minute before Robert spoke. "We're all here for the same reason, and we're all doing everything we can to find her as quickly as we can." He looked at the three men from the sheriff's office before turning back to Purvis. "I appreciate you and Jimmy talking with me this morning. I'm sure that we'll chat again soon."

Robert shook Purvis's and Jimmy's hands and walked down the steps and into the drizzling rain to his car. He paused as he passed the sheriff and his men and addressed them briefly.

"Sorry if we got off on the wrong foot today, Sheriff. I know I should've called you first before coming out here, but I was only following orders. I'm sure you understand. Call me later when you have a minute and we'll try to coordinate any future inquiries."

The detective handed Clifford one of his cards, touched the rim of his dripping hat, walked over to his car, and got in and out of the rain. Sheriff Gaskin stared at the man as he departed, not knowing what to say. As Robert drove off, Clifford glanced at the soggy calling-card in his hand, and then tucked it into his jacket pocket. What arrogance, thought the sheriff. Who the hell does he think he is?

Chapter Fourteen

The days following the disappearance of the little girl were upsetting to everyone on the block. Mary Bickman noticed a change in her boys' behavior, but was unsure what to make of it. The two seemed to be at odds with one another, although neither one would fess up to exactly what the problem was.

Jack was more hostile to others than even his normally volatile personality allowed, while Frank became withdrawn. Mary could sense her youngest child's anguish. No matter how hard she tried, he wouldn't share what was troubling him. In fact, Mary decided that he was mad at her, although she could think of nothing specific that she did that might account for this sudden change in him.

She attributed the subtle differences to the incident of the missing girl across the street. Although the boys weren't the most sensitive creatures on the planet, they were still kids, and other children disappearing could be very upsetting, especially for youngsters unaware of the evils of the world.

She was convinced that whoever abducted the girl was from elsewhere, and it was unlikely that another such incident would occur in their neighborhood, but, all the same, she tried to keep a close eye on the two whenever they left the house.

Things came crashing down at the Bickman homestead about a week after the girl's abduction. Although the sheriff's office had sent a deputy to ask them questions twice in the days following the crime, nothing could prepare them for the onslaught that came the next week. Jake would forever blame that detective for the problems that ensued; Mary was convinced the sheriff was the one at fault.

It was four-thirty on a Wednesday afternoon when the police arrived at the Bickman house. Jake wasn't home from work yet and Mary was busy in the kitchen cooking baked chicken for dinner. The boys were out back in the tree house. Mary was sure of this as they were forbidden to leave the yard without informing her first. Ever since the incident the previous week, Mary insisted that they let her know where they were at all times. This new rule was strictly enforced by Jake Bickman's leather belt and excessive temper, thus ensuring absolute compliance.

Mary heard the doorbell ring and casually strolled to the front door to answer. She was taken aback when she opened the door and found herself in the presence of four law enforcement officers.

Sheriff Gaskin spoke up first, introducing two of his deputies whom Mary had met previously when she'd been at the Jenkins's house. The fourth man was a detective from the State Police, whom she'd never previously met, although she'd heard others talk about him.

She was wary of the detective from the first. He made her feel uneasy. It was as if he could see right through her and read her innermost thoughts while the expression on his face never changed.

Mary wanted to shut the door and tell the men to come back later when her husband was home, but instead she found herself inviting them in. The sheriff asked about her boys, and she called them in from the back yard. She felt a small sense of relief in the company of her children before she became even more apprehensive than before when the up-to-then silent detective asked Frank if he could show him his room. Frank shot his mother a look of panic before composing himself and disappearing into the back of the house with the detective and one of the deputies.

While Frank and the two officers were in the back, Sheriff Gaskin and Deputy Bryce asked her and Jack about what they saw the day that Elizabeth went missing. She tried to tell them that she'd already answered all of their questions before, but the men ignored her pleas and kept asking anyway. Jack, as silent as he could be, responded only when asked direct questions and, even then, only giving one word answers whenever possible. All of this made Mary nervous, and she talked when she was nervous. What was taking so long with Frank in the back, she wondered.

Frank walked toward the back of the house with the detective and the deputy and showed the men his room. It was small, but neat and clean, with posters of airplanes and a Yankees baseball pennant on the wall. He knew the men weren't interested in his room or his decorations, and he sat on the bed, waiting for the interrogation to begin.

"Frank, I'm Detective Stallworth from the Alabama State Police. You know why we're here and I don't want you to be afraid. We just want you to tell us what you saw on the day Elizabeth Jenkins disappeared," Robert said.

"I already told y'all everything I know," pleaded the boy.

The detective stared at the boy silently for a moment before replying, "We both know that isn't true. If you're going to lie to me, this isn't going to go well for either of us. Makes me think you have something to hide."

"I'm not lying!" Frank exclaimed. "I told you guys everything."

"Everything? Frank, we both know better than that," Robert told him calmly. "We already know you were hiding out behind the empty house across the road before the girl disappeared. That's trespassing. That's a crime. We could arrest you right now if we wanted to."

The detective let his words sink in for a moment, and he could see the boy start to squirm. He continued before the child had a chance to panic, "We're not here to arrest you, son. We just want to know what you saw."

"I didn't see anything. I don't know what you're talking about."

"Of course, if you continue to bullshit us, we might have to take you in. We can file charges and throw you in a cell. I'm sure you might start remembering then."

Frank began to cry. He just wanted the men to go away, but he knew they wouldn't.

"I don't know anything about Elizabeth. I had nothing to do with it."

"I know you didn't," Robert said, surprising both Frank and Deputy Willis.

"Then what do you want from me?" Frank asked.

"We need to know everything that happened that day – everything you saw. It might not seem important or relevant to you, but it could be the difference between bringing that little girl home safe to her parents and digging up her rotting corpse from an unmarked grave. Do you want that on your conscience?"

Frank sat in silence, shaking his head while tears ran down his cheeks.

"Then tell us what you saw."

Frank choked back his tears and swallowed hard. He began his story of that fateful day. He told them how he went to the back of the empty house by himself while his brother was out on the street creating a diversion. He explained that he'd looked around to see if any of the windows had been left open or unlocked, but was startled by someone entering the house. He told the officers he got frightened and hid beneath the window in the bushes and waited until the coast was clear before high-tailing it out of there before anyone could catch him. When he got to the part where he left the property without seeing anything, the detective stopped him.

"Now, hold on there. You expect me to believe that you never saw who it was that came into that room?"

"No, sir. I ducked fast before I could be seen and hid myself. Then, like I said, I got out of there before I could get caught," Frank said with as much sincerity as he could muster.

The detective and the deputy looked at each other before returning their gaze to the boy. Robert nodded to Deputy Willis, and he began reciting his well-rehearsed lines to the young man.

"You have the right to remain silent. If you give up that right, anything you say can and will ..."

Frank began to cry.

"Please, don't do this! I swear I'm telling you the truth."

"There's no way that you didn't look in that window, Frank," Robert said bluntly.

"No way in hell," Deputy Willis added.

The boy sat on his bed, sobbing.

"I know this is difficult for you, but you need to tell us what you saw," Robert continued. "Who was it that came into the room?"

"It was Mr. Barney, the real estate man," answered Frank reluctantly.

The men looked at each other, then back at the boy.

"Who was with him?" asked the detective.

Frank shook his head, unable to speak through his tears.

"Was it the little girl? Was it Elizabeth?"

The boy shook his head to indicate that is wasn't.

Deputy Willis's eyes widened in surprise; Robert's gaze remained steady. He already knew the answer to his questions, but he needed to hear them from the boy directly. He understood that Frank needed to finally speak the truth aloud, if only for his own benefit.

"Then tell us who it was," Robert said gently.

"It was my mom!" Frank cried out before pushing his face down into his pillow and bawling uncontrollably.

Deputy Willis's mouth dropped as he heard the unexpected outburst. This wasn't going to be good for anyone, he thought. Poor, poor child. Robert squatted down beside the bed and patted the sobbing child's back, whispering soothing words to the heartbroken boy. He assured him that the secret was safe with them. It had nothing to do with why they were there. It was no one else's business, he told Frank. No one else ever needed to know about it.

His words helped the child regain his composure, and, once he settled down and wiped the tears from his face, the three of them returned to the living room.

When Mary saw the forlorn look on her youngest child's face, she got angry. The boy wouldn't look at her, but the deputy eyed her in a way that she didn't care for. She looked at the detective to try to gauge his thoughts, but the man was as poker-faced as always.

It was then that the detective asked about Jack's whereabouts on the day in question. Jack remained aloof, replying that he'd been in the tree house out back working on a rope-ladder. At this point, Sheriff

Gaskin was about to end all of the questioning and wait until Jake came home. He could see that Jack was going to be no help at all, and he was anxious to know what had transpired in the back room with Frank. Much to his chagrin, Robert started to pursue the subject of the rope with Jack. Not wanting to miss anything, Clifford insisted that the child show them the tree house and the alleged rope-ladder in question. Without hesitation, Jack led the sheriff and detective outside.

Once inside the small tree house, Jack showed them the work in progress. The ladder was comprised of two long strands of rope with several pieces of wood tied between them for rungs. There was still a good ways to go until the ladder was finished, but the design was sound and the work commendable. Clifford complimented the boy on his fine work, to which Jack just shrugged. He wasn't falling for flattery, nor was he telling these clowns anything. Robert took a different tact.

"Where'd you get the rope?" asked the detective.

"Here and there," answered Jack.

"Here and where?" Robert continued.

The boy just shrugged.

"Excuse me? Here and where exactly?" Robert prodded.

"Can't remember – exactly."

"You better change your tone real fast, you little shit," Sheriff Gaskin chimed in. "We're here on serious business, and you'd better start taking this serious."

Jack looked at the big man with a feigned look of innocence. Clifford wanted to slap that look off of his face, but held himself in check, deferring to the detective for the moment.

"Where's Elizabeth?" Robert asked coldly.

"How should I know?"

This was really getting to be too much, thought Robert. He looked at Gaskin and could see that he was thinking the same thing. Fuck this little shit. If the boy wanted to act tough and play hardball, that was fine with him.

"You were seen with her that day. You were the last person to be seen with her that day. You were playing with rope you stole," Robert replied. "It's not looking good for you, Jack."

"I don't know what you're talking about," said the boy. "Don't I get a lawyer or something?"

"You are a minor, you don't get shit," Clifford chimed in.

"Do you need a lawyer, Jack?" Robert asked.

Jack didn't like the way this was going. He was trying as hard as he could to be tough, but now he was beginning to think he was making a terrible mistake.

"I don't have to answer any of your questions," he stated defiantly.

"It would be much better for you if you did," Clifford replied.

"Why don't you can the attitude and answer our questions? We're not going to go away," Robert added. "You know something, and we know you know something. You don't want to tell us, we have to assume you have something to hide."

"Kidnapping and murder is serious business, kid. You sure you don't have anything to tell us?" Clifford asked.

"I already told you, I don't know anything. I had nothing to do with it. I'm just a kid!"

"You're looking pretty capable of bad things from where I stand," Clifford told the boy.

"I'd have to agree with the Sheriff on that one, Jack. You look like suspect number one so far," added the detective.

"I didn't do it! You guys are crazy," Jack yelled.

The two men remained silent, preferring to stare down the now terrified child.

Jack was losing his bravado. Suddenly, he found himself trying to convince the officers of his innocence.

"I had nothing to do with it. You have to know that. Okay, okay, I saw her riding her bike that day, but that was all. I ducked behind the Maguire place to try and find some more rope in their garage. After that, I ran around the back till I got home so no one would see me. I admit it, I stole the rope, but I had nothing to do with Elizabeth missing."

"So, no one saw you, then?" Robert asked.

"No, of course not. I didn't want anyone to see me; I was stealing rope."

"Well, being such an accomplished thief didn't really work to your benefit this time, did it Jack?" Clifford remarked.

"Just to get all of this straight, kid. You were the last person to be seen with a missing child; you stole some rope; no one saw you at that time or for some time after; you don't want to answer our questions;

and you want a lawyer," Robert stated. "I think you're right. You do need a lawyer."

"No, that's not what I'm saying. You guys are twisting my words. I told you everything I know. What do you want from me?"

"Don't worry, Jack. We'll be in touch. You'll tell us what we want, when we want, make no mistake about that," said Clifford.

They left the close quarters of the tree house and made their way back to the house. Jack went back inside, while the men stayed outside to converse for a moment. Robert told Clifford about Frank's admission, much to the surprise and disapproval of the sheriff. It explained a lot, although it didn't help them in their investigation. In fact, they both agreed, it could actually hamper things knowing how jealous Mary's husband could be. Clifford thought that maybe Jake's suspicions hadn't been so out of line, knowing what he now knew about the man's wife.

The sheriff and detective entered the living room at the same time that Jake Bickman arrived home. Jake was not in a good mood at the sight of four policemen in his living room, interrogating his family without his presence, and he let them all know it in short order. He demanded they leave immediately under the threat of legal action from a non-existent lawyer he had no intention of hiring. After all of the crap his elder son had already dished out, these threats weren't in the least effective.

Clifford took the bull by the horns and flipped the situation on the angry man.

"Okay, Jake, we'll leave right away, just as you say. Of course, I'll have to send a couple of officers down to the body shop to ask around about your whereabouts. I'm sure they'll be happy to know that one of their employees is a person of interest in the abduction of an eight-year-old girl. When word gets around, you might find it difficult to wash the stink off, even if you're later exonerated."

"You bastards! I had nothing to do with it, and you know it," Jake exclaimed.

"Do we know it, Jake?" the sheriff continued. "All I know is that you don't want us anywhere around you or your family. You don't want to cooperate with the investigation. You don't want to help us in any way to find that little girl. Most people would think that a family man with children of his own would be more concerned about a child being abducted on his own block and do everything he could to help out. But then again, you're not most people, are you, Jake?"

"What are you trying to say, Gaskin? I had nothing to do with it. I have nothing to hide. I just don't appreciate you trying to blame me and mine for a crime just 'cause your men can't find out who done it."

"We're not interested in blaming anyone. We just want to find Elizabeth Jenkins and whoever it was that took her," Robert stated. "You and yours were all in the proximity of the abduction when it took place, so naturally you're all potential witnesses – and suspects. It's only you and your family's objections and hesitancy that make you look guilty."

"If you don't have anything to hide, stop acting like you do," Clifford added.

"I ain't acting any way," answered Jake. "I was at work, which y'all can check without accusing me of anything. My boys are just boys, and you've already asked them about what they know. My wife was at home, inside and alone, all day."

"Inside and alone, huh, Jake?" Clifford blurted out before thinking.

Robert winced at the outburst. Idiot! What the hell is he doing?

"What's that supposed to mean, Sheriff?" asked Jake.

"Nothing, Jake," Clifford tried to backtrack.

"No, you got something to say, you say it," Jake replied.

"The Sheriff doesn't have anything to say, Jake. Your wife is not a suspect. Let's just stick to why we're here, gentlemen," Robert said, trying to change the subject.

"Gaskin can speak for himself, Detective. Now, just what were you implying, fat man?" Jake insisted.

Clifford was willing to take a bit of grief for his faux pas, but having this drunken wife-beater berate him over his over-sized gut wasn't included. He squared off with the angry red-neck and took a deep breath.

"I wasn't implying anything, Jake. I got something to say, I'm gonna say it. You want me to back it up? I'll be more than happy to drop you right in front of your wife and kids, right here, right now."

"Enough, gentlemen, enough," said Robert. "Let's stick to the subject. Jake, we'll find out soon enough exactly when you left work last Tuesday and exactly how long it takes you to get home. We already know that your wife and your two boys were in the vicinity when the abduction took place. They're potential witnesses and that's why we have to ask them what they might've seen that day. We intend to continue to ask them about it as many times as we deem necessary to find out everything we can about who and what happened out here. I don't care if you, or your family, like it or not. We'll do what we have to do. We're doing it for Elizabeth Jenkins. We're doing it for her parents, just as we'd do it for you and yours."

"I understand that, Detective, but my family weren't the only ones around that day. I'm sure you didn't treat the Petersons the same way you're treating us. What about old man Johnson and his weirdo son down the block? Ain't you interested in them? They're a suspicious bunch, if you ask me. Weren't them colored garbage men on the block then? You guys sure them niggers didn't get a hold of that white girl? Who else was down here?"

"That real estate guy was over across the street, Daddy," Jack chimed in. The officers had Jack worried. He was convinced that they were going to pin the whole thing on him. His father's suggestions about other suspects could only help his case at this point.

"Was he, now?" Jake replied. He glanced at his wife suspiciously at the unexpected news, but Mary just stared at her feet as if unaware of the unpleasant activities around her.

"We're following up on all leads, Mr. Bickman," Deputy Willis said, "including those you just mentioned. We haven't eliminated anyone yet."

"If y'all got anything else to ask, you'd better ask it now or get out," Jake said in disgust, "We got things to do."

"I think that'll be all," Robert replied.

"For now," added the sheriff.

The officers left the Bickman house, showing themselves out and drove away without another word. The cat's out of the bag now, thought Robert. Stupid fucking sheriff and his big mouth.

Clifford, embarrassed by his unprofessional outburst, hoped that Jake didn't beat his wife to a pulp later that night. Still, he reckoned, the woman shouldn't have been two-timing her husband in the first place, loser though he may be. Mrs. Bickman knew what kind of a jealous monster she was married to, and if she wanted to risk a beating by spreading her legs for another man, then she understood that the consequences were going to be severe. Sheriff Gaskin wasn't about to take any of the blame if and when his men answered the call about the inevitable spousal abuse in progress. He was only there to serve and protect. Clifford was the sheriff, not a judge. Judgment would have to come from someone or someplace else as far as he was concerned.

*

June 22, 1959

After the incident at the Johnson place, Robert met with the sheriff at the county station. Gaskin made him wait for almost forty-five minutes in the front lobby before having Mabel show him to the back office. Robert was sure that it was payback for questioning a witness without first placing a courtesy call to the sheriff.

He didn't care if Sheriff Gaskin liked it or not; he wasn't here to make friends. Of course, he reckoned, he wasn't here to make enemies either, and a little diplomacy might smooth things along in the investigation. In light of this, he made no mention of the time-wasting delay when he entered Gaskin's office.

"Good to see you again, Sheriff," Robert said as the two men shook hands.

"Detective," Clifford replied curtly. "I'm glad you could stop by today. It's lucky you even caught me here. Things have been pretty hectic with the Jenkins investigation and all."

"I'm sure they have been. As you know, I've been assigned to work on this for the State Police, and I think it's imperative that we work together."

Clifford nodded. He knew what the detective wanted, but that didn't mean he had to like it.

"Since the disappearance of the child happened in your jurisdiction and with people that you know, it's only logical that most of the legwork be coordinated through your office and with your personnel," Robert stated. "For the most part, our office will assist with additional manpower and resources as needed and at your discretion; the main caveat in the equation, of course, being me."

"What about you, Detective?"

"I'm the one in charge of the investigation as of now."

"Oh, you are, are you?"

"Yes, sir, I am. To make this perfectly clear, I have no intention of hamstringing you here. I'm sure you're more than capable of carrying out your official duties, and I've better things to do than get in your way. At the same time, I intend on taking a hands-on approach, so we'll need to coordinate our actions."

"Wait a minute, Detective," Clifford interrupted. "This incident occurred in Peterson County – under my direct jurisdiction. As sheriff, I'm responsible to the citizens of this county, and that makes me in charge of any investigation. You can go back to wherever it is that you came from and I'll call you if I need anything. Understand?"

"It's you who doesn't understand, Sheriff. The disappearance may have occurred in your county, but it has also occurred in the state of Alabama, which makes it directly under my jurisdiction. This isn't some domestic dispute or public drunkenness incident," Robert stated, "This is likely a kidnapping and homicide. The FBI has already been sniffing around, and, as soon as there's any evidence to suggest a federal investigation, we're all going to be fetching coffee for the suits from Washington. Neither of us wants that."

The detective paused for a moment to let his last point sink in before continuing.

"The best chance we have of solving this case is with the two of us doing what we do best and checking the egos at the door. The only reason you aren't talking with a federal agent right now is because my captain has convinced them that the best chance to solve this is with the two of us working on it while keeping them in the loop."

"Well, I just don't see how we're gonna manage all of this coordination, Detective. I have enough to do right now without having to jump through hoops every time I make a move."

"We'll keep this simple, then. We'll have a daily briefing, by phone, if necessary, to plan out that day's activities. We'll meet up together when the need arises, otherwise we'll work independently of one another. You can contact Chris Sherman at the state office if there are any resources you require. I believe you already have the number."

"We have the number, Detective. So, if I'm to understand you correctly, you expect me to call you every day and ask permission to do my job?"

"That's not what I said and you know it, Sheriff. There's no reason to get snippy with me. We're on the same team."

"So, now we're a team?" Clifford couldn't resist.

Robert was getting annoyed. He was used to the local authorities getting all worked up whenever he got involved in an investigation, but this was too much.

"Enough, Sheriff. I have better things to do than sit here and listen to you whine. We can do this the easy way or the hard way, but we're going to do it my way."

"We'll see about that, Detective," Gaskin added as he stood up. "I believe you know the way out."

Robert left without another word. Dumbass hick, he thought. He knew where this was going and would expect a call from Captain Warner within the hour.

The detective was glad now that he'd gotten involved in the investigation. He was convinced whatever happened to that little girl would never be discovered if that yokel sheriff was leading the search. Thomas and Gladys Jenkins were counting on him. He truly believed that he was the best and only hope Elizabeth Jenkins had left.

Chapter Fifteen

In the days that followed Elizabeth's disappearance, Thomas lived in a daze, unable to sleep or concentrate. He stayed home from work for the first week, though soon returned to resume his managerial duties. Everyone at the bank was sympathetic and allowed him to take as much time as he felt he needed.

What he needed was something – anything – that might help take his mind off of his missing child.

Thomas tried to concentrate on work, but he was not up to the task. As a consequence, his work suffered. His co-workers quietly picked up the slack, relieving him of most of his duties and even double-checking his work. Thomas was unaware of the added burden on his fellow employees. His mind was elsewhere.

The grieving father searched the faces of every child he passed, occasionally seeing his little girl for a brief moment before realizing yet again that she remained lost. He drove a different route to and from work every day in a vain effort to spot his missing daughter. Thomas's heart sank at every mistaken sighting; the hole in his heart becoming deeper and deeper with every passing day.

With every phone call, his ears pricked up; with every visit from the police, he longed to hear the news that Elizabeth had been found. Disappointment and despair became his closest friends, although he kept them hidden from Gladys. He had to be strong for his distraught wife. He felt he'd already let her down beyond repair.

He was the man of the house. It was his job to be the protector of his family. He'd failed miserably at the task and couldn't forgive himself for it. He wept every night in silence, being careful to keep his tears out of view of his fragile wife.

Gladys was unable to function at all. Her demeanor fluctuated between unresponsiveness and hysteria. She stayed at home all day, unwilling to leave even for brief moments in the hope that her daughter might return. She didn't want Elizabeth to come home to an empty house, only to leave again. When Thomas was asleep, she'd sometimes wander up and down the block in a daze, searching for their lost little girl.

Gladys blamed her husband for calling her that day and distracting her, but she blamed his mother even more. If only the woman wouldn't have called at that precise moment and insisted on going on and on about some meaningless gossip, Gladys would have been outside watching over her daughter like she should've been.

Mostly, Gladys blamed herself. She failed her daughter when the child needed her the most. She was an unfit mother. She couldn't look her husband in the eyes. She failed him as well. She'd been unable to watch over their only child. She was a horrible wife. Thomas had done so much for her and Elizabeth. His little girl was the apple of his eye, and she had disappeared under Gladys's supervision. She wanted to curl up in a ball and die.

Sheriff Gaskin and his deputies kept a constant vigil at their house for several days following Elizabeth's disappearance. After that, they came around at least once a day for a few weeks. By the second month, the Jenkins were lucky to hear from the police once a week.

She'd been hopeful when the sheriff and his men initially came around, but her husband hadn't been as optimistic. Thomas became increasingly angry at the lack of progress on the case. He told that fat sheriff how useless he was.

When the detective from the State Police got involved, they'd hoped that progress might be made since the man seemed competent. However, within ten minutes, the distraught parents had no use for the man.

His manner conveyed an unspoken belief that Elizabeth would not be found alive, and they didn't want to even think about that. Thomas called the man's superior, some captain or another, who apologized for the detective's behavior and assured him that he would have a word with the detective. When Thomas demanded that someone else handle the investigation, the captain assured him that

Detective Stallworth was the best detective that he had. Thomas's boss put a call into the FBI, but was informed that they were already keeping up with the investigation and were confident that anything that could be done was already being done.

As their initial shock wore off, the Jenkins became increasingly involved in the investigation, or at least they tried to be. They'd brainstorm among themselves, friends, and family members to try and come up with leads. At almost every turn, the sheriff or the detective disclosed some of the details of their investigation that would prove the potential leads false.

They asked the sheriff about the possibility that the men on the garbage truck might've been involved. Sheriff Gaskin informed them that Deputy Willis and Detective Jackson had questioned the two men, and they'd been cleared of any suspicion. The sheriff said he questioned the driver of the truck himself, and even sent Deputy Willis to the landfill to search for any evidence, but nothing was ever found.

The chance that the men were involved in the girl's abduction was slim, a fact that even the Jenkins were forced to concede once they understood how much effort the sheriff and his men had gone to in following up on the lead.

The couple asked about the mailman, although he was an unlikely suspect, but the sheriff and his deputy had done their homework with him as well. He was cleared of any possibility of involvement. The parents asked about the real estate agent, Mr. Spencer, and there, things got more difficult.

Sheriff Gaskin questioned the agent on at least a half a dozen occasions to try and find any discrepancy in the man's statement. He thought he was on to something early on, and reluctantly involved the detective with the hopes of nailing the suspect sooner rather than later.

Mr. Spencer had been evasive in their earliest attempts at questioning him, only confessing his indiscretions with the Bickman woman once pressured into it. Due to the fact that the man moved independently around town in his professional capacity, it was difficult for him to establish a solid alibi.

Sheriff Gaskin had put a tail on him and ordered around-the-clock surveillance for the first ten days or so, but came up with nothing. He couldn't be totally eliminated from the possible suspect list, but his likely participation in the crime appeared to be progressively more remote.

The authorities wouldn't divulge the details of their investigation of Barney Spencer to the Jenkins, although they tried to assure the couple that he wasn't likely involved. Both Thomas and Gladys had known the real estate agent for a number of years, and couldn't reconcile their image of the man with such a horrible crime, but the feeling they got that the authorities were less than transparent about their investigation of the man fueled their suspicions.

The grieving couple agreed that Barney was an unlikely suspect, although the slight possibility of doubt left them troubled and soured their association with the man.

There were only two possibilities in the abduction of their child, the Jenkins reasoned. One was that a stranger happened along that fateful day and snatched her up in broad daylight. The other possibility was that one of their neighbors was somehow involved.

The prospect that a stranger was responsible was the worst case scenario. It could prove impossible to ever find the culprit, and Elizabeth's whereabouts might remain unknown forever. The authorities had contemplated this unpleasant possibility, and allocated a number of resources to it.

Deputy Stevens was delegated the task of coordinating any information regarding similar crimes or suspects in neighboring counties. His efforts were enhanced by the State Police and the FBI, who compiled similar lists on statewide and nationwide levels, respectively. All leads were followed without delay, but nothing promising had developed thus far.

The unlikely possibility that one of their neighbors was implicated in Elizabeth's abduction was unsettling to everyone who lived on Johnson Road. A thorough search had been conducted on the afternoon and evening of the disappearance by the authorities and local concerned citizens, but no sign of the girl was ever found.

Even though dozens of people resided on the short block, very few of them were known to be in the vicinity at the time of the disappearance. Of the few that were there, most had solid alibis that eliminated the probability of their involvement.

Gladys and Thomas discussed their concerns regarding their neighbors with the authorities. The sheriff had pretty much ruled out the Petersons.

Cheryl and the kids had been accounted for, and, as far as anyone could tell, George hadn't left his office before six in the evening. Purvis Johnson had been seen by Gladys only a short time before her little girl disappeared and also right afterwards when Mrs. Jenkins went looking for Elizabeth. It was Purvis, in fact, who suggested calling the police and had helped to organize the initial search for the girl.

Purvis's son, Jimmy, was also seen right before the girl went missing, but was seen at home soon afterwards in the presence of his father. There was some speculation about the boy, and the Jenkins knew that Jimmy was still on the authorities' radar. Both Gladys and Thomas doubted that the mild-mannered boy was capable of such a horrendous act, much less able to carry it out in such a short amount of time without getting caught.

Gladys was not as sure about the Bickman boys. She told the deputies about Frank Bickman's presence that day behind the empty house next door and of his distressed appearance when she spotted him later on. Frank's unsettling demeanor happened to coincide with the girl's disappearance, something she found hard to dismiss.

She couldn't understand why the authorities disregarded her concerns, especially since they offered no explanation. She told Sheriff Gaskin in great detail about her misgivings about the boys on the subject of the family's missing dog, but the officer seemed disinterested in the matter.

Thomas listened to his wife's theories about the two boys and admitted that their possible involvement sounded plausible. He found it hard to see the youngsters as anything more than unruly kids, but he'd always harbored a bad feeling about the eldest of the two.

He addressed the issue with the authorities numerous times to no avail. He was outraged that, although Jack Bickman was seen by several witnesses approaching his daughter before her abduction, nothing was ever done about it. The sheriff assured him that they'd questioned the boy extensively and that it was highly improbable that the teenager would've been able to kidnap the girl and hide her away in such a short amount of time without anyone seeing him. Thomas wasn't as easily convinced.

It was hard for the Jenkins to live across from the Bickmans now. It was even harder to see the two Bickman children playing in the street seemingly without a care in the world. Their little girl was gone, vanished forever, and it didn't seem right that the two monstrous delinquents went about their lives carefree.

Thomas was outraged whenever he saw the eldest boy. It was all he could do not to confront the child directly. Gladys hated the Bickmans. She was completely convinced of Jack's guilt and the family's complicity in covering up the crime.

Jack felt the anger and suspicion directed toward him by Elizabeth's parents. He knew the police thought he was guilty and were working diligently to put him behind bars for life. The boy began to think that everyone he came in contact with suspected him of wrongdoing. He could feel everyone's eyes on him, examining his every move.

Jack didn't know how to act 'normal', with the situation being what it was. Every clumsy action he took made him feel more awkward and invited further scrutiny. He became increasingly paranoid and anxious, which resulted in an escalation of his already belligerent attitude.

His heightened volatility resulted in a falling-out with his brother, Frank, who'd become withdrawn over the past couple of months since the girl's disappearance. Jack felt ever more isolated, with no one to confide in. He recognized that others felt uneasy in his presence, and he grew uncomfortable with himself.

Detective Stallworth and Sheriff Gaskin had questioned the boy in his tree house shortly after Elizabeth's abduction. Neither of them considered him a likely suspect. The boy had acted like such a smart-ass though that the two men had come down hard on him. Both men agreed that since Jack couldn't be totally eliminated from the suspect list and, since the Jenkins demanded that they consider him a viable suspect, they would keep the pressure on.

The officers occasionally questioned the boy about the crime, even to the point of harassment. Outwardly, Jack played it cool, pretending not to give any concern to the authorities' intimidation, but inwardly he felt a rising tension. His outward appearance of defiance added to the speculation about his guilt. This increased the Jenkins's fury and only served to make Jack's life miserable. He was on a bad rollercoaster that just went up and down, round and round, getting worse with every turn, but he found himself unable to stop it.

Without any proof and little new to go on, the investigation ground to a halt. The sheriff and his men continued to re-examine the evidence they'd accumulated, although they had their share of other incidents to deal with throughout the county. Clifford would sporadically drive out to Johnson Road to check in with the girl's parents. These infrequent visits were uncomfortable for everyone involved.

Unfortunately for the sheriff, Detective Stallworth refused to go away. Robert demanded the same level of intensity in the investigation six months after the girl's disappearance as he had in the first few weeks. He called Gaskin's office every morning and still demanded the weekly reports despite the lack of progress.

The Jenkins initially cared little for the detective's undiplomatic approach, but came to respect his tenacity. Robert personally gave the couple periodic updates, whether or not any new developments occurred, paying no notice to the times they lashed out at him in frustration.

Everyone else appeared to gradually go on with their lives in the wake of the tragedy. This was something that Thomas and Gladys Jenkins found impossible to do. Knowing that Detective Stallworth would never let it go gave the grieving parents a small amount of solace.

They were not alone. Elizabeth would not be forgotten. As far as Detective Stallworth was concerned, whoever took their little girl had better keep looking over their shoulder, he was coming for them.

*

Fall, 1959

The tense meeting between Sheriff Gaskin and Detective Stallworth resulted in a call from Captain Warner, just as Robert had predicted. The three of them had a little 'clarification' meeting and, after that, things progressed a little more smoothly. Gaskin and Stallworth both preferred the absence of the other, but things were what they were.

Clifford resented the detective's involvement, but he had to reluctantly admit that the man had abilities. Stallworth's attention to details could be irritating, but his thoroughness was comforting to the sheriff.

Clifford considered himself more of a 'big picture' guy. The sheriff couldn't trust his own men to be as meticulous as the detective. They didn't have the experience or training, so knowing that the detective was overseeing the numerous details in his methodical way gave Clifford the freedom to pursue things the way he wanted. If only he wasn't required to submit those stupid reports.

When the two men had questioned the eldest Bickman boy, Clifford realized that maybe they'd be able to work together more effectively than he'd hoped. It was unfortunate that his stupid comment regarding Mary's infidelity made him look bad.

He was sure that Stallworth already considered him a bumbling hick and an incompetent law enforcement officer, and his idiotic remark hadn't helped him gain any respect with the man. Clifford understood too well that for the investigation to be successful, everyone was going to have to trust one another.

Trust required respect. As yet, he conceded, he'd done little to earn any. To make matters worse, the reports he was forced to submit weren't helping.

Gaskin knew that his strongest asset was his knowledge of the people involved and the relationships he'd developed over the years. The detective was an outsider and, although he was highly skilled with direct interrogation, he didn't get many results with the casual questioning of witnesses.

There were witnesses up and down Johnson Road, thought Clifford, even if they didn't know what they knew. It was up to him to pry it out of them, with or without their consent.

When Elizabeth was reported missing, Clifford was one of the first officers at the scene. Once at the location, he'd surveyed the area and made a mental inventory of the surroundings and people there.

It was obvious to him where his best chance of getting information existed – that weird house facing the wrong way up at the end of the block. What better place to start on Johnson Road than at the Johnsons?

Sheriff Gaskin had known Purvis for a long time. Clifford was only a deputy when they'd first met. When he ran for sheriff, the old man had allowed him to post a billboard on the busy highway, for which Clifford remained eternally grateful.

Purvis had been more or less a hermit in the early years, and Clifford one of the few men that periodically visited with him. He remembered the surprising news when the old man had gotten married, and had been the one who'd delivered the bad news about Sue's affair and untimely departure.

Over the years, he'd visited with the old man and sat on his front porch, shooting the breeze about anything and everything, both important and trivial. Clifford knew the old man was fairly lazy, seemingly taking up permanent residence in his rocking chair on his porch while ignoring the squalor in which he lived. The amount of time that he wasted away on his front porch meant that, whatever happened on Johnson Road, Purvis Johnson was the most likely one to know about it.

The biggest obstacle for Clifford to get past with the old man was his apparent lack of cognizant ability. The sheriff didn't like to call anyone stupid, although, in his opinion, Purvis was as close as they came to being a simpleton.

It took a great deal of patience and a fair amount of effort to make sense out of the old man's ramblings, which made any direct questioning problematic. Luckily for Clifford, he'd gotten to know the old man reasonably well, and they'd established a rapport, maybe even a decent amount of trust.

He knew that Purvis was skittish and uncomfortable around people for any length of time. When Detective Stallworth popped in on the old man uninvited, the morning after the girl's disappearance, Gaskin almost lost it. Having to follow up with an unofficial search of the property and interrogation of the man's boy didn't help. The damage was done. It took some time after that before Clifford was able to sit and talk with Purvis again without feeling unwelcome.

Once the old man did begin to talk, however, he was a treasure trove of information. He knew almost everything about everybody on the block.

Everyone liked Purvis; even George Peterson had a difficult time staying at odds with the old man, although he did give his utmost effort to the cause. Purvis may have been stupid and lazy, but he was kind and helpful to his neighbors. He knew a lot about the comings and goings on the street, as the vantage point of his front porch assured, but he refrained from gossip and innuendo.

Unfortunately for the missing child, Purvis hadn't witnessed the abduction. He conceded that, even though he'd been absent from his front porch for only a brief spell while he prepared dinner, it was long enough for the girl to vanish. The old man couldn't recall seeing any vehicles on the street that day, other than the ones they already knew about.

He later reluctantly admitted to Clifford that he was wary of the eldest Bickman boy and his possible involvement, but offered that he found it highly improbable that Jack had anything to do with the child's abduction.

Purvis informed Clifford that, although he had thought a great deal about it, he had no good notion of what happened to the girl. The old man found that troubling, and couldn't understand how things like this could happen – especially here on Johnson Road. He agreed with the sheriff that it must've been a chance encounter with some unwelcome visitor who'd been preying on the unsuspecting citizens of the quiet neighborhood.

Purvis was no stranger to the wickedness in the world. The horrific memories of the trenches cemented his understanding of the amount of maliciousness human beings were capable of.

He soberly confided to the sheriff that the little girl's abduction within twenty yards of his front porch was one of the most frightening things that he'd ever encountered and, considering the trauma he'd experienced during the war, this was no small thing.

Chapter Sixteen

Almost eight months after Elizabeth Jenkins disappeared, another set of sirens erupted the relative tranquility of a lazy weekday morning on Johnson Road. By ten-fifteen, the men were off to work and most of the children were safe at school. The only inhabitants left at home were housewives tending to the endless stream of chores their families required, old man Johnson, who was both retired and lazy, and little Georgie Peterson.

Georgie had been kept home from school again because of yet another bout of intestinal illness. This time, the boy had been suffering for a week before he started to recover. Cheryl had expected to send the child back to school that morning until she went to his room to wake him. She was shocked and surprised by his appearance. Georgie had felt much better the night before. Concerned, she kept him home from school another day and called Dr. Garrett's office to make an appointment for later that afternoon.

After packing Agatha's lunch and seeing her off to school, Cheryl said goodbye to her husband and went back upstairs to check on Georgie. As soon as she opened the door to his room, she felt something was wrong. Georgie was pale and cold, his breathing labored. She ran to his side and asked him how he was feeling, but the child was unresponsive. Panicked, the distraught mother called for an ambulance.

It took only ten minutes before she heard the piercing sounds of the sirens in the front of her house, but it seemed like a lifetime to Cheryl. The paramedics examined the boy before putting him on a stretcher and hurrying him out the door to the waiting ambulance. By the time they rushed outside, some of the neighbors were beginning to gather, curious and concerned about the unexpected happenings on the quiet street.

Coming quickly to the distraught mother's side, Purvis assured her everything would be okay and that he'd look after Agatha when she got home from school. Cheryl thanked him and swiftly got into the back of the ambulance with her child before they sped off toward the Emergency Department at Riverside Memorial Hospital.

When Agatha got off the school bus with Jimmy, Deputy Bryce was waiting with Purvis on the front steps of the Peterson house. The presence of the police officer and Jimmy's father waiting for their arrival sent Agatha into a panic. Jimmy and Purvis helped to calm the girl down as the deputy explained that her younger brother had been taken to the emergency room. No further news on the boy's condition was available, and Deputy Bryce offered to drive Agatha to the hospital where her mother and father were already waiting. She got into the passenger seat of his patrol car and the two drove off.

By the time Agatha arrived, her brother had been admitted to the Intensive Care Unit in critical condition. She was reunited with her parents at Georgie's bedside. The sight of her brother's condition caused her to panic once again. After a few moments, Agatha and her father walked to a near-by waiting room. Her mother stayed behind, refusing to leave her youngest child's side.

The day's events proved overwhelming for Agatha, and she quietly wept in her father's arms. The vision of her brother with lines and tubes attached to him, the cacophony of noises and alarms up and down the hall, and the sudden realization of the fragility of life itself was too much for the young girl to bear. George comforted his daughter as best he could, while choking back his own tears for the sake of his family.

When the old man and his weird son showed up, George was actually happy to see them. He'd been growing wary of the poor boy next door and his infatuation with Agatha, and had been trying to discourage any friendship between the two, but, under the present circumstances, he was grateful for their presence.

George had suppressed his animosity toward the old man over the years, seeing that Purvis had helped out so much in the care of his son. He recognized that his neighbor had become attached to the boy, and he knew that little Georgie took pleasure in the old man's visits. The sickly child had spent much of his life confined to his room and visitors were rare, which meant company was greatly appreciated.

George was disappointed that members of his own family, the venerable Petersons of Peterson County, were absent. He'd expended much of his energy over the years extolling the virtues of his heritage and surname, yet, when he needed them the most, they were nowhere to be found. No, George had to reluctantly admit to himself, it was the lowly hillbilly clan that lived in the run-down shack next door that was there for him and his family in their time of need.

Once he'd updated Purvis and Jimmy on Georgie's condition, they agreed to stay with Agatha in the waiting room while George returned to his child's side. When he arrived back in the room, he saw that the boy's condition had stabilized, although his wife appeared even more distraught than before.

The physicians and nurses were asking her questions about the sick child and about the events leading up to his admission to the hospital. Inexplicably, she became angry and uncooperative. George interrupted the questioning, stating that this was probably not the best time for their inquiries. It had been a long day and his wife was both physically and emotionally exhausted. He offered to step out into the hall and help answer any questions that he could, so they left the mother at her child's side and led George into a small office down the hall to follow up with the questioning.

He answered their questions to the best of his ability, although it became apparent to everyone, including him, that it was Cheryl who'd taken care of the boy over the years without much help from him.

He was ashamed to admit that he didn't know much about the child's condition or the myriad of treatments and medications that the child had been prescribed during his illnesses. George considered suggesting that they ask his neighbor, Purvis, because the ignorant old redneck probably could answer all of their questions, but he thought the better of that. He was shamed enough for one day.

He recommended that they call Dr. Garrett's office since he'd been the boy's physician for several years and would more than likely know the answers to all of their questions. The staff at Riverside Memorial had already contacted the doctor and he was on his way at that very moment with the child's medical records.

Dr. Garrett had been concerned about the boy's recurrent bouts of illness for quite some time, and, as he pored through Georgie's chart, he was reminded of how many different medications and courses of treatment he'd recommended. The problem was that Dr. Garrett couldn't determine any one cause to explain what was wrong with the child.

There seemed to be a pattern to the boy's sickness. Georgie would be lethargic and nauseated for a week or so, followed by a day or two of intense stomach pains and cramps. Afterwards, he would regain his appetite and strength and, in a couple of weeks, felt fine again.

These symptoms repeated themselves every four to five months. None of the tests that the doctor had ordered could determine a definitive cause. Dr. Garrett was forced to admit that it might not have been the same cause every time. The child's unhealthy condition over the years made him susceptible to every little bug that came around. Even if there was a main cause for the majority of his ailments, there was still the very real possibility that other viruses or bugs had also been infecting the fragile youth from time to time due to his compromised immune system.

Now, the boy was in the hospital fighting for his life. The physicians and staff at Riverside Memorial Hospital worked tirelessly around the clock to keep the boy alive and try to determine the root cause of his illness. At every turn, they encountered a dead end. Hours turned to days; days turned to weeks. This time, there was no recovery. The child's health showed no improvement.

Cheryl was beside herself with grief. When the boy had been born, it was his father that caused all of the problems with the hospital staff. This time, it was his mother. She kept a twenty-four hour vigil at her child's side. None of the doctors or nurses could approach the boy without her input and interference. She instructed the staff on the proper care of her son, ignoring their displeasure when she criticized their techniques or methods. She demanded that everyone do everything when, how, and where she wanted it done.

Cheryl micro-managed every aspect of the young patient's care, refusing some medications while demanding others that were not remotely indicated. The Ethics Committee at the hospital got involved, although they tread lightly when the woman's husband started to threaten a lawsuit.

The situation came to a head one day when the hospital staff informed the child's parents of their plans to transfer the boy to a long-term acute care facility. Convinced that their child would no longer receive the kind of attention that he got in the Intensive Care Unit of the hospital, the Petersons argued with the physicians and administrators to no avail. In desperation, it was George that took the issue one step further, and, against the wishes of his wife, he called the sheriff.

Sheriff Gaskin didn't want to get involved. He sent Deputy Bryce in an effort to address the problem without having to officially do anything. His strategy didn't work, and the exasperated deputy implored Clifford to handle things himself before a melee occurred in the middle of the hospital. Reluctantly, he made his way over to Riverside Memorial Hospital to see what he could do.

When Clifford arrived at the child's bedside, all parties involved had quieted down, although both sides remained entrenched in their demands. It was a delicate situation, fraught with potential legal pitfalls, so Gaskin was careful. He reviewed the case from the time the child had been admitted in order to get a better understanding of what he was dealing with.

Clifford saw how messy things had become. To the dismay of the parents, none of the doctors were able to determine what the child's problem was, and they were now running out of options as to what to do with the patient. The boy's parents were in denial about their son's poor prognosis, and they had become increasingly demanding in an effort to regain some kind of control in their lives.

When Clifford asked about all of the tests that the physicians had ordered, they assured him that they had run them all. The sheriff noticed a subtle frown on one of the nurses during this explanation, and, for some reason, this stuck with him. During a break from his inquiries, he tracked down the nurse and found a quiet and discreet place in which to ask her a few questions.

Janet Smith had been a Registered Nurse for almost forty years. She'd worked in almost every department in a number of the hospitals in the region and, in time, had acquired a great deal of experience and knowledge. Sheriff Gaskin respected the doctors and the work they did, but he also knew that if anyone knew their patients, it was the nurses who spent the greater part of the day at their bedside. He asked her what her impressions were of the boy's illness and the treatment he'd received.

At first, Mrs. Smith gave him the usual 'ask the doctors' response she'd practiced over the course of her career. When Clifford assured her that anything she said would stay between the two of them, the nurse spoke up.

"You know, all of the doctors will tell you they've run every test, but don't believe it," the nurse stated.

"Really?" asked Gaskin, "What tests didn't they run?"

"They didn't do toxicology tests on admit. By now, it probably wouldn't make a difference anyhow."

"Toxicology?" the sheriff asked in surprise. "You think the boy was poisoned?"

"I don't want to blame anyone without any proof, but my guess is it's a real possibility. Certainly would explain a lot."

"How so?"

"You see the way that mother interferes with every effort to get close to the boy? She dotes on the child, like she's mother of the year, but she panics every time one of us runs some kind of test, or we try to ask questions about the boy's condition leading up to his being brought to the hospital."

"Yeah, so?"

"You ever hear of a condition called Munchausen's-by-proxy, Sheriff?"

"Yeah," Clifford said, scanning his memory. "Well, kind of. I mean, no."

"I'm not surprised. It's a new term for an old disorder. I suggest you look it up. Like I said, I don't want to accuse anyone of anything, much less something like this, but you asked."

"That I did. I don't suppose you could give me a hint?"

"Have you ever heard of someone faking an illness just for attention?"

"You think the kid's faking?"

"No, I wish that were the case. It's the mother here that's been looking for attention."

"I'm not following you."

"My guess is that the only attention that woman gets is for taking care of her sick child. If you ask me, she's the one who's sick."

The wheels spun in Clifford's head. As the horrifying realization of what the woman was saying took form, his stomach wrenched with the thought.

"Thank you, nurse. You've been a big help."

Nurse Smith turned to go, in a hurry to get back to her numerous duties that were piling up. Clifford nodded and watched as the nurse disappeared around the corner. Fucking great, he thought. That's just perfect. How the hell am I going to get to the bottom of this shit? If there is no proof that a crime has even been committed, and likely not to ever be proof, then how can justice be served?

Clifford thought about the situation for awhile and could come up with only one solution. He needed a confession. Not likely, he thought. George would never stand for his wife being grilled on the subject, and it didn't appear probable that Cheryl was going to talk voluntarily. He filed the unwelcome information away in the back of his mind and got on with the unpleasant task at hand.

After a long discussion with the parties involved, an agreement was reached that the hospital would continue with the child's treatment for another week, and, at that time, they'd all sit down and discuss the situation further. Everyone knew they were dodging the issue, but since it was the only thing they could settle on, it would have to do.

Clifford was pleased with the delay. This would give him some time to pursue the matter with discretion. He wasn't exactly sure how he was going to proceed, but he had a good idea who he was going to discuss it with.

Sheriff Gaskin and Detective Stallworth were never able to put aside their animosity toward one another completely, although they did manage to tame it down some. Clifford came to admire and respect Robert's tenacity and skill, even if he would never admit it aloud. Detective Stallworth admitted to himself that Clifford could be useful in spite of the man's haphazard methods.

Gaskin still hated having to report to the detective every week, regardless of having nothing to report. He figured this time he might as well let the detective do some work for him.

It was easy to summon Stallworth, thought Clifford. All he had to do was to do nothing. He was already behind on his weekly reports, so he figured he'd just let it ride a while longer. Sure enough, the next day the detective was calling the station house looking for him. He instructed Mabel to give Stallworth the runaround until further notice – an order she relished performing considering the amount of additional work the detective had inadvertently caused her. Two days later, Detective Stallworth showed up, unannounced.

Robert sat in silence as Clifford laid it all out for him. When the big man asked for his help, he didn't know what to say. He knew how much the sheriff resented him being involved in the investigation of Elizabeth Jenkins's disappearance, so why in hell was he asking him to be involved in yet another difficult case? On the other hand, he recognized how problematic the situation was.

They had one shot at getting the woman to say something incriminating, or they'd both have to watch her get away with it. There was also the unpleasant possibility that they could be wrong. If they pursued their course of action with too much gusto, they would have to live with the fact that they accused and bullied a grieving mother over the unfortunate illness of her son.

Robert told the sheriff he'd be happy to help in any way he could, even if he silently wished that Gaskin had never involved him.

The meeting at the hospital was scheduled for the next Thursday afternoon, but by then, it was deemed unnecessary. George Peterson, Jr. passed away on Sunday evening, with his family by his side.

Agatha and George wept quietly next to their little boy. Cheryl was inconsolable, wailing loudly until hospital security arrived. Even the hospital staff, most of them desensitized to the death of patients, outwardly mourned the untimely death of the poor, sickly child.

An anonymous call from an unidentified hospital employee informed the Sheriff's Department of the youngest Peterson's death. By the next morning, Sheriff Gaskin and Detective Stallworth were discussing their next move over a cup of coffee in the parking lot of the Olde Towne Diner.

They both agreed that their window of opportunity was brief and that they'd have to work quickly. The funeral would most likely be set for Thursday or Friday and, once the boy was laid to rest, it would be difficult to pursue their best line of attack without being hampered by endless legal hurdles. If deemed necessary to prove their case, they both conceded that an exhumation of the child's corpse would be all but impossible to obtain.

Tuesday morning at ten-thirty, the two men met on Johnson Road and approached the front door of the big house near the end of the block. They'd reckoned that this would be the best time to find the woman alone, or, at least, without her husband by her side. They were right. Cheryl Peterson was alone, with the exception of the old man who lived next door.

Purvis answered the door. He led the officers into the kitchen where Cheryl was sitting. The grieving woman was surprised at the sight of the two visitors and, to Purvis, she looked slightly panicked. Over Cheryl's objections, the old man excused himself and quickly left, feigning imaginary chores to attend to.

She wanted to ask them to leave, but she couldn't find the courage to over-ride their insistence for the need to talk with her. She told them she wanted to call her husband first, but the sheriff convinced her that it was unnecessary since they were in a hurry and wouldn't be there long. She felt trapped in the kitchen of her own house by the men, but she complied with their request all the same.

"We're sorry to disturb you, ma'am," Clifford began. "And we're sorry for your loss. Georgie was a good boy and he'll be missed by everyone."

The detective nodded in agreement as Cheryl stared blankly into space. Feeling her knees beginning to buckle, she sat at the table and cast her eyes downward. She gazed at the placemat in front of her, its cheerful, flowery imprint out of place with the despair that hung thick in the air that surrounded her.

The policemen remained standing, towering over her. Cheryl found their close proximity in the small confines of her kitchen intimidating, causing her anxiety to increase beyond her ability to control it.

"There seems to be a problem with one of the lab tests run on your boy," Gaskin said, "and we were hoping you could shed some light on it."

Cheryl's eyes got bigger as she responded, "Tests? What do you mean, tests?"

"Please allow me to explain," Detective Stallworth chimed in for the first time. "There were some indications in your boy's condition that warranted some blood and tissue samples be submitted to an out-of-state laboratory. It took some time to get the results back, and now that we have them, they raise some questions as to the cause of Georgie's illness."

"My boy is dead!" exclaimed Cheryl. "What difference does it make now?"

She began to cry, pressing a tissue to her eyes and lowering her head into her hands. Clifford and Robert glanced briefly at each other before the detective continued.

"It makes a big difference, Mrs. Peterson. Your boy had a lethal level of arsenic in his system."

Cheryl's head popped up immediately.

"Arsenic? Are, are you telling me he was poisoned?"

"Yes, ma'am," Clifford responded. "That's what we're saying."

"But who, who would have done something like that?"

The men remained silent, neither one taking their eyes off of the woman in front of them. After an uncomfortable moment passed, Cheryl could see where they were going.

"You don't suspect me?" she cried out. "How dare you! You come into my house uninvited, days after my son dies, and you have the nerve to accuse me of murdering him! Monsters! Get out of my house!"

Neither man budged.

"You can stop with all of the theatrics, Mrs. Peterson. We already know what happened," Detective Stallworth calmly stated.

"You don't know anything!" screamed Cheryl. "Everyone knows how much I cared for my son. I took care of him time and time again. He's always been sickly, and it was me who nursed him back every time. Just ask anyone. Ask Purvis. He'll tell you. I've given my life to taking care of my Georgie. Now you're accusing me of killing him? You guys are insane!"

"Insane is an interesting choice of words, Mrs. Peterson," Robert replied.

"So now you're saying I'm insane?"

"There's a condition, Mrs. Peterson," Robert continued. "It's where a parent makes one of their children ill so that they can get attention by tending to the sick child. Most of the time, it's the mother. It's a form of mental illness. You already stated that you were the one who took care of the boy. He was under your direct care and supervision when he got sick."

"This is crazy," Cheryl responded.

"Crazy is not the best word to use, Mrs. Peterson," said Clifford. "The truth is that you need help. We want to see that you get that help."

"Help?! You want to help me by calling me a murderer? What kind of help is that? You want to lock me up for life, or put me in the electric chair, and you call that helping me?"

"We don't want to do any of those things, ma'am," Sheriff Gaskin replied. "It's like we said, we want to help you. We know you've been poisoning the child for months – maybe even years. How are you going to explain that? Do you want to sit in front of a jury and take your chances with that story? What's your daughter going to think? What's your husband going to say?"

Cheryl lost all hope at the thought of George's reaction when he got the news. She'd tried so hard for so long just to have him notice her for all of the things she'd done for him. Once he learned the awful truth, she knew he'd despise her forever. And poor little Agatha; she may never get to see her little girl again.

"Mrs. Peterson," Robert said, "we don't want to see you go to jail. It's not what your son would've wanted. We know it's not your fault, but we also know that most people will never understand. Just tell us the truth. Tell us everything. We'll make sure that you can go to some place where they can help you, not to prison, not to death row."

Cheryl put her head down and nodded. It was all over and she knew it. She wished she could die and spare herself and her family the pain and shame of what she'd done.

"I swear I didn't kill him," she sobbed. "You have to believe me. I admit that I put just a little into his soup every once in awhile, but just a little. I was real careful. I never wanted to hurt him. Please believe me!"

Sheriff Gaskin and Detective Stallworth nodded to reassure the woman. Each felt sick inside at the thought of the boy being slowly poisoned to death for years by his own mother, but they kept it to themselves.

"I don't understand," Cheryl continued. "He was getting better. I didn't give him anything for days before he fell sick again. I swear!"

Cheryl broke into tears, unable to continue.

"We believe you, Mrs. Peterson," said Robert. "It probably just built up in his system over time until it was too much for the boy. We know you didn't mean to kill him."

When the two men first got together to discuss the affair, both pretended to know more than they did. Each of them separately looked up the repulsive mental condition in a medical encyclopedia to try to understand what they were dealing with. They had used the knowledge they'd gained from reading those books to trap the woman into a confession. There were no toxicology results. It was all a ruse to get her to talk. Now, they stood in the Peterson's kitchen as the dead child's mother confessed to poisoning her only son. Finally, they began to fully appreciate the meaning of the words they had read.

Cheryl Peterson mourned the death of her child as much as any mother could, despite the fact that she'd been poisoning the boy for years. The men saw that she was telling the truth when she said that she never wanted to hurt or kill the child, as absurd as that claim sounded under the circumstances.

She was as ill as her child had been. It was her brain that was infected, instead of her intestinal tract. All the same, she was a danger to those around her. In particular, she was a danger to the ones she loved. It was true enough that she didn't really belong in prison, but she clearly needed to be locked up.

The sheriff called it in and had Deputy Bryce take her down to the station to book her. He thanked Detective Stallworth for all of his help, who, in turn, offered to call up the district attorney and give him a head's up.

They were both sincere in their promise to try and help the woman. With as little publicity as they could manage, they steered the case through the system quietly.

The courts allowed Cheryl Peterson to plead out the case in exchange for her commitment to the Harrisburg Women's Institute for the Mentally Ill, where she lived for almost thirty years. Once committed to the Institute, she never saw her husband or daughter again.

*

May, 1960

Robert read through the reports in front of him trying to find things that weren't there. He had pages of notes scribbled here and there that he was cross-matching with the reports, but he was running out of loose ends.

It had been almost a year since the girl disappeared, and they hadn't had any new leads for quite some time. Robert had promised the Jenkins that he would find them justice, only to let them down. He let himself down as well. Maybe the sheriff had been right all along. Maybe it had been some random kidnapping by some deviant just passing through, and they'd never discover the truth. Still, something was weighing on his mind about the reports, and he was bound and determined to figure out what it was.

The detective came upon a note he'd written to himself in the pile of crumpled up pages on his desk. On the page was written the words, *Creek Search Report*, followed by a big question mark that was circled. Robert didn't remember writing the note and had no idea what it meant, and that bugged him. He rifled through the reports from Gaskin, but found no mention of anything useful in regard to any *Creek Search Report*. Not to be easily deterred, he searched until he found the official state police record of the area search in the hours and days following Elizabeth's abduction.

There wasn't much in the record that was helpful. It contained a list of all of the participants of the search, most of them being the local and state authorities and a few of the neighbors. There was a crude map of the area and a timeline of events. Robert could see that the search had been pretty exhaustive, considering the downpour that ensued in the days following the crime. No sign of the girl was ever found as far as he could determine. He was about to give up when he noticed one odd item that stood out from the rest.

Buried amongst the details of the report, he noted that some bones had been discovered in the mud along the creek bed at the bottom of the ravine behind Johnson Road. These were quickly determined to be animal bones that had been there for some time and hadn't been mentioned publicly so as not to upset the missing girl's parents. It wasn't completely out of the ordinary for something like that to be found in such a place, he thought, although it did warrant further scrutiny in light of the lack of leads thus far.

Stallworth pored through more of the documents on his desk until he found what he was looking for. An official form from the pathology lab confirmed the bones belonged to a small- to medium-sized dog. This discovery sparked a vague memory in Robert, and he sat in silence for awhile trying to brush away the cobwebs in his mind until he could remember why it sounded familiar.

The particular item he was searching for eluded him at first, so the detective randomly leafed through the various documents until he spotted it in a folder of miscellaneous forms. He remembered finding the crumpled up poster on one of the telephone poles almost a mile from Johnson Road. The poster showed a picture of a lost beagle that belonged to no other than the Jenkins. He re-read all of the reports that Sheriff Gaskin had sent him over the last year, yet could find no mention of the lost dog anywhere.

"God damned sheriff!"

Chapter Seventeen

In the year that had passed since Elizabeth Jenkins disappeared, Purvis noticed a change in the boy. Jimmy was always a quiet child and, even Purvis had to admit, a little odd. Once the old man started watching him more closely, he could sense that his son might be stranger than even he had previously thought.

Purvis realized that there could be many explanations for this change. First of all, the boy was going through puberty. He remembered that he'd also been a little awkward when he was the boy's age. Secondly, he knew that the abduction of the little girl was traumatic to the sensitive teenager. The fact that the police had questioned Jimmy on several occasions was sure to make him a little paranoid.

To make things worse, the authorities had searched the house, the garage where Jimmy spent most of his time, and by the ravine behind their property. Although nothing incriminating was ever discovered, the boy was never officially eliminated as a suspect.

Being aware of the suspicions cast upon him exacerbated Jimmy's self-consciousness, a condition that was already difficult to deal with for a shy, awkward boy. He felt the eyes of the world upon him, and any attempt to act normal made him appear less normal to others. Purvis understood that, by keeping a closer eye on him, he could be altering the boy's behavior, and he attempted to be more discreet about it, although this was easier said than done.

The third thing Purvis considered might add to Jimmy's social withdrawal was a cooling in his friendship with Agatha Peterson. The girl still liked him, but they were forbidden by her father from socializing with each other. Ever since her brother had died and her mother had suffered a mental breakdown, George Peterson turned into an over-protective tyrant who watched his daughter's every move.

The elder Peterson was so eager to eradicate Jimmy Johnson from Agatha's life that he even went as far as to set up dates for her with other eligible boys from the area. Agatha wanted to explain the circumstances to Jimmy, but was prevented from having any contact with him, with the exception of a brief word or two when they passed each other at school.

They were never alone, and the circumstances never appropriate for explanations. All Jimmy saw was that the girl he was smitten with was barely speaking to him and was now dating other boys – a situation that was devastating to the young man.

Jimmy had lost his only friend, just when he needed her the most. In turn, Agatha was kept from her best friend, just as her life had been turned upside down by the loss of her sibling and mother.

"Jimmy!" called Purvis from the front of the house.

"Yes sir?" the boy shouted from the garage out back.

Jimmy had been working on the old car. He'd pieced the rusted jalopy together from spare parts and was beginning to have some success. No one, including his father, ever thought the rust-bucket would run again, but he was determined to prove them wrong.

"I'm running out for awhile to pick up a few things," Purvis told the boy, who had stuck his head out of the garage to see what his father wanted. "Don't forget to bring in the trash cans."

"Yes sir," Jimmy answered before getting back to work on the broken-down vehicle.

He heard his father start up the truck and drive away. Everyone within a half-mile radius probably heard it too, thought Jimmy. The muffler had long since rusted away, and, between the awful noise and noxious fumes that the truck produced, there was little doubt the old man had left.

After awhile, he decided to take a break. He'd gotten as far as he was going to get with the repairs for the moment, so he stepped out of the garage to get some air. Things were quiet on the block, but he began to feel as though something was wrong. He had the uneasy sensation that he was being watched.

Jimmy lived with those feelings for quite some time now. Ever since the little girl vanished, he had the feeling that his father was watching him. Anytime he tried to ask the old man if there was something wrong, Purvis denied it and played dumb. This was a skill that he knew his old man possessed in spades. Purvis would back off for awhile, although the effort his father made in order to not observe him only confirmed to Jimmy that he was being watched in the first place.

The truth was that Purvis had been examining the boy. Something told the old man that Jimmy had witnessed something the day that Elizabeth turned up missing, but was keeping it quiet. He could never prove it, and any attempt to pry it out of the boy proved futile.

The more he tipped his hand about his suspicions, the deeper Jimmy buried it inside. The boy had always been exceptional at keeping things to himself, so Purvis could see he was on the losing end of the battle. In the end, the old man kept his doubts secret, his mouth closed, and his eyes open.

Jimmy strolled around the property while keeping an eye out in the attempt to determine from where his uneasy sensation was originating. He wandered around the front yard, along the side, and toward the back.

Once he got to the edge of the ravine, he paused. For a brief moment, chills ran down his spine, and he shuddered. Whatever was wrong, it was coming from below.

Purvis never allowed the boy to play out back in the woods down by the creek. The slope was steep in places and the paths slippery, so his concerns were not without merit.

When the girl had gone missing, Jimmy remembered the police and neighborhood men attempting to search down there. The old man tried to help, but the endless rain made the going rough. Jimmy spent most of his time trying to keep his father from falling and breaking his neck.

The hunt was difficult for the other men as well, each came back up covered in bruises, scratches, and mud. To their credit, the police searched extensively despite the difficulty, but nothing useful was ever found.

Jimmy couldn't put his finger on it, but there was something not quite right down the embankment. He scanned the area, although nothing looked out of place. He listened intently, yet couldn't hear a sound. That's it, he thought. It's too quiet. Normally, one would have heard the birds chirping, insects buzzing, or any of the multitudes of sounds that emanated from the overgrown wilderness. Not today, Jimmy realized. It was deadly silent.

He could feel the hairs on the back of his neck stand up. He walked slowly and deliberately around the perimeter of the ravine, with his eyes peeled.

The cautious boy looked down one of the small deer trails that cut through the underbrush and saw a footprint going down into the woods about ten yards down. It had rained two days ago and the ground remained moist in spots, so he figured whoever made the print was still down there. The boy cautiously followed the prints down the embankment before he stopped himself.

This could be a trap, Jimmy thought. Ever since he'd exacted revenge on the Bickman brothers, he knew they would stop at nothing for an opportunity for payback.

His old man was gone for the moment, and if they somehow lured him down into the woods alone, he could find himself in real trouble. There were two of them and only one of him, and there'd be no one to come to his aid if he needed it. Jimmy quietly backed out of the woods and walked back to his house.

He paced for a few minutes, trying to decide what to do. He considered bringing out his home-made cattle prod, or some other weapon, and heading down the trail, but knew this time the element of surprise would be against him. If whatever weapon he chose were somehow wrestled from his grasp, it would be used against him with extreme prejudice. There was also the chance that they'd have a weapon of their own – a thought that made Jimmy shudder.

The boy knew that he could just ignore the footprint altogether and go about his day, but in his heart he knew that he wasn't going to. He remembered the feeling of shame after being bullied by Jack and Frank way back when, and he hated the very idea of cowardice. The ravine was behind his house, and no one, not even him, was allowed back there. Jimmy was damned if was going to stand by and ignore the intrusion – damned if was going to be ruled by fear.

His thoughts were interrupted by the sound of the garbage truck working its way down the block. He went out by the curb after the men had left to drag the metal cans back up to the side of the house.

As he watched the truck disappear around the corner onto Riverside Highway, he saw Frank Bickman down at the end of the block, retrieving his own family's silver garbage cans, and he breathed a sigh of relief. If it was a Bickman down by shit creek, deemed Jimmy, it was only one of them.

He stopped by the garage and picked up a metal pipe, just in case, and then stealthily crept down into the woods behind his house. He followed the footprints as best he could, quietly tracking the trespasser with caution.

Taking only a few steps at a time, he paused frequently to look around as he crouched behind the foliage to remain hidden. Every few minutes, he would slowly transverse another ten or fifteen yards before stopping again.

Half-way down the slope, Jimmy lost all sight of the footprints. He searched for any available trails his quarry might have taken, but could see no signs of any activity. Worried that he'd somehow taken a wrong turn, he considered forgetting the entire endeavor and returning home, but he put his thoughts of defeat aside and crept further down the embankment.

The boy paused again and rested in the shade of a sycamore tree. This is stupid, he thought. There's nobody down here. He shook his head and exhaled a sigh of both relief and frustration. It was then that he saw a vision that made him freeze in terror.

Hanging from an old oak, twenty yards in front of him, was Jack Bickman. Jack's eyes were staring right at him. Terrified, Jimmy dropped the metal pipe and scrambled up the embankment.

By the time he got to the top, he was scratched and torn from the overgrown brush and covered with mud. He ran to his house, but his father had not yet returned, so he sprinted to the Peterson's house and banged on the front door.

The door swung open and there stood Agatha, staring at him, an expression of shock and concern on her face. Jimmy was out of breath and trying desperately to tell her something, but was hindered by his ferocious panting.

"Jimmy," Agatha asked him, "what's wrong?"

"It's...Jack..." Jimmy blurted out, between his heavy breaths. "Call...call... the...call...the..."

The commotion had gotten the attention of George Peterson, who'd arrived home from work minutes before. He marched up to the front door and swung it open all of the way, pushing Agatha to the side so he could see what all of the fuss was about. At the very sight of the unwelcome visitor, he began his tirade.

"I thought I told you not to come around here anymore!" he yelled at the boy.

"Please...please...call...the...call the..." Jimmy tried to spit out the words in vain.

"Good God, boy, you are getting mud all over my front porch," George continued. "I don't know what this is about, but you'd better..."

"Call the police!" the panicked boy finally blurted out.

"The police?" Agatha inquired. "What's wrong, Jimmy?"

"It's Jack," Jimmy tried to explain. "He's..."

"He's what?" interrupted George. "Now you listen to me. We aren't interested in any of your hillbilly problems over here. You can take it elsewhere."

George pushed Agatha behind him and tried to shut the door, but Jimmy threw up his hands and blocked him.

"He's down the ravine," Jimmy pleaded. "Please. Call the police!"

Agatha broke free from her father and pushed open the door.

"What's wrong, Jimmy," she asked. "What's wrong with Jack?"

"Why should we call the police?" George interjected. "If you are having problems with the neighborhood bully, you need to handle them yourself. Don't come crying to us."

"You don't understand," Jimmy replied.

"What's wrong with Jack?" Agatha asked again, beginning to get scared by Jimmy's panicked demeanor.

"Yeah, what's wrong with Jack?" George repeated his daughter's question, with no small amount of sarcasm.

"He's…he's dead," Jimmy answered.

"Oh my God!" Agatha exclaimed as she clasped her hand to her mouth in horror.

"Dead?" asked George in shock. "What do you mean, he's dead?"

Jimmy couldn't find the words to explain everything that he'd seen. He pointed toward the back of his house and repeated his plea.

"Call the police. He's down the ravine."

Agatha disappeared into the house to call the sheriff's office while her father stood awkwardly by, not knowing what to do. Jimmy staggered down off the porch in a daze and onto the Peterson's front yard.

He snapped back to his senses at the sound of Purvis's rundown Chevy, barreling down the street. His father slowed at the sight of his boy covered in mud out in front of the big house next to his. Purvis caught a glimpse of George Peterson at the door and knew this was going to be bad.

The old man pulled his truck up onto his front lawn where he always parked it, got out, and walked over to meet his boy, who was running over to him.

"Dad!" Jimmy said. "Down by the ravine."

He pointed to the area behind their house. Purvis's heart sank. This couldn't be good.

"What is it, boy?" the old man asked calmly.

"It's Jack," Jimmy replied, his eyes meeting his father's gaze.

"What's wrong with Jack?"

"He's dead."

"Show me," was all Purvis said as the two of them headed toward the ravine.

Jimmy led the way, with Purvis close behind. Following them was George Peterson, who'd managed to regain his composure somewhat.

Minutes later, Sheriff Gaskin's squad car pulled up to the Peterson house with the siren on and lights flashing, breaking the tranquility that had, up to that point, enveloped Johnson Road. Agatha met him as he got out of his car and the two of them proceeded to follow the path down the ravine behind the Johnson house.

They could see the others further down the path in front of them, and they carefully made their way down the embankment. By the time Agatha and the sheriff caught up to George, they could see the full horror of the situation.

Jack was now lying on the ground, between Jimmy and Purvis, who had the boy cradled in his arms. The old man had cut Jack's lifeless body down from the tree where he'd been hanging and pulled the offending rope from around the child's neck, discarding it on the damp earth beside them. Sheriff Gaskin gently pushed Jimmy aside and knelt down next to Purvis and the dead Bickman boy.

Jack's skin was pale and cold and his body was beginning to stiffen, confirming his death hours earlier and eliminating any chance of revival. The poor child's tongue was hanging out of his mouth in an absurdly grotesque manner and his lifeless eyes bulged out of their dark sockets.

Agatha looked away in revulsion and buried her face into her father's waiting arms. George felt nauseated and tears welled up in his eyes. He never cared for the Bickman boy or his family, and empathy wasn't his strongest characteristic, but the death of the boy brought back painful memories of the recent passing of his own son, memories he'd worked hard to suppress.

Jimmy stood motionless, looking down on his deceased nemesis, not able to turn away. His earlier panic was resolved. He now found himself almost completely unaffected by the dreadful scene. The boy understood that he should be distraught, or at least saddened, by the terrible event. He tried to illicit some emotion from the depths of his soul, but found the effort fruitless.

When the sheriff and his father glanced his way for a brief moment, he almost panicked. He was the one who had discovered the body, so he recognized that he'd be questioned all over again by the authorities. The boy's odd behavior was going to make him look guilty, yet any attempt to fake emotions he didn't possess might backfire.

Jimmy looked away, staring down the ravine at the polluted creek at the bottom. He wanted so much to cry, not for the dead boy or his family, but because he knew that he couldn't.

*

June, 1960

The detective was on his case. Stallworth had been calling the office repeatedly over the last couple of days, leaving one message after another. The sheriff ignored them all. He figured the man was only pestering him once again about the reports, and Clifford reckoned he had better things to do.

Peterson County was mostly rural, encompassing a fair amount of area, but with a sparse population. From Clifford's perspective, there may not be an overabundance of people, but the ones that lived there complained an awful lot. His deputies were always hopping, trying to respond to the myriad of calls the department received around the clock. Even he was forced to deal with many of the trivial complaints they received in order to keep up with the workload. The detective simply didn't understand that the Sheriff's Department could not dedicate endless man-hours to a cold case, regardless of the severity of the crime.

The latest objection to come from Stallworth regarding the reports was the sheriff's failure to emphasize the Jenkins's missing dog's remains that had been found by shit creek. Clifford had cringed when he got wind of the detective's discovery of his omission. He recalled trying to remember the exact circumstances about the mutt's disappearance at the time, without much success. He had left it off the official report rather than call attention to his lack of memory. Now that the detective was clamoring for details, it all came back to him.

The Jenkins's pet beagle had gotten out of their back yard and run off. The family searched the neighborhood and had even put some signs up around the area in the hopes of finding the missing dog, but to no avail. Clifford remembered seeing the posters on a couple of telephone poles along Riverside Highway, but he'd paid no heed. His department was busy dealing with human beings. They certainly didn't have time to search for lost pets.

After Elizabeth was abducted, Gladys Jenkins brought up the disappearance of their dog. She was convinced that the two Bickman boys were responsible. Mrs. Jenkins also insisted that the boys were the most likely suspects in Elizabeth's abduction, particularly the eldest one.

Sheriff Gaskin informed the family that everyone was a suspect and would be investigated thoroughly, although he didn't think it was likely the culprit or culprits were so young. He told her that it would have been difficult, if not impossible, for the boys to hide the girl and her bicycle, or whisk them away from the area without proper transportation. As far as he could determine, neither boy was able to drive or had access to a vehicle at the time. The immediate area had been exhaustively searched, but no sign of the girl had ever been found.

Gladys never completely let go of her suspicion of the boys. Clifford appeased her by leaning hard on Jack. He never thought the boy was guilty, but Jack's smart-ass attitude warranted a little intimidation as far as the sheriff was concerned. He figured he might as

301

well kill two birds with one stone. Besides, the boy needed to learn to respect authority or he was headed for trouble when he got older, thought Clifford.

The moment he spotted the child hanging from the tree he regretted his decision to harass the boy. The little shit hid it so well, always seeming unmoved by anything the sheriff or his men threw at him. If he'd known just how far they had pushed the boy, he might've reined it in some. Now, it was too late. Clifford would carry the guilt and regret over the loss of another child for the rest of his days.

He remembered when they found the dog's bones at the bottom of the ravine. They'd been searching for any clues in the disappearance of Elizabeth, but came up empty. Rain had been pouring down for days, making things difficult for his men.

Clifford hadn't thought for a moment that the skeletal remains had anything to do with the girl. She'd only been missing for a couple of days, nowhere near enough time for her body to decompose to that level if she'd been killed. It didn't take long to determine that the bones belonged to the missing dog, once the collar and tag were discovered.

He instructed his men to keep the news from the Jenkins. The family was already distraught over their daughter's disappearance. At the time, it was too early in the investigation to even suggest that Elizabeth might be dead, and he figured that the last thing the grieving parents needed to see were the skeletal remains of their lost pet being dug up from the mud by the creek.

He never seriously considered the family's missing pet and the abduction of the child to be related in any way. It seemed quite a stretch to him, especially since there wasn't a sliver of evidence to back it up. He also knew it was highly unlikely that they'd be able to prove it, even if the two were somehow linked. Although Gladys suspected the involvement of the Bickman boys when the family's dog got out, she was the first to admit that her suspicions were based purely on intuition.

The sheriff recognized that he'd eventually have to face the detective and spar with him over the matter. He couldn't put the man off forever. Anyone who had the opportunity to work with Detective Stallworth knew the man was relentless. Even so, he didn't care what Robert had to say about the matter. He'd made his decision, and he stood by it.

Maybe he wasn't as meticulous as he could've been when filling out those stupid reports, he supposed. He didn't care about those fucking reports. They weren't going to help them find the missing child. Of that, the he was sure of.

Chapter Eighteen

Barney Spencer remained a prime suspect in the days and weeks immediately following Elizabeth Jenkins's disappearance. Sheriff Gaskin considered him a 'person of interest' and the most likely candidate to be guilty of the horrific crime. Barney proclaimed his innocence to anyone who would listen. The trouble was, as he grimly discovered in the aftermath, very few people wanted to hear it.

There were many things stacked against him when it came to establishing an alibi. For one, he'd been in the area at the time of the abduction and alone in his vehicle. His job afforded him a substantial amount of leeway with his time and location during the workday, so it was difficult to say where he was or would be at almost any given moment.

Mr. Spencer had no witnesses or alibis who could speak on his behalf to clear his name. The fact that he'd lied to the authorities when they initially interrogated him about his whereabouts didn't help.

Barney wanted to keep his affair with Mary Bickman a secret. He told the sheriff and his men about his visit to the empty house on Johnson Road, and he tried to be as helpful as he could. He didn't see where his indiscretions with the married woman across the street had anything to do with the child's disappearance, and he elected to keep that out of his testimony.

The real estate agent related to the police everything else he saw that day, which wasn't much. Unfortunately, that damn detective from the state police had already somehow found out about his dalliance with the Bickman woman and had given Barney the rope to hang himself.

By the time he admitted the affair, he'd already been caught in a lie. Why would they believe him now? The sheriff and his men branded Barney a liar, and they repeatedly pressed him to finally "tell the truth."

Sheriff Gaskin had him followed for days after the girl's abduction. The authorities had questioned his co-workers and many of his clients. They'd impounded his vehicle for two weeks, leaving him without any reliable transportation in the interim. In the end, there was no evidence and no proof of any wrongdoing on his part, so he remained free from incarceration. That was the only good thing he could claim in the year and a half that followed.

The house on Johnson Road was unlikely to be sold now. Even some of the other properties he was certain he was going to sell suddenly received no interest. People were giving him uncomfortable glances and whispering about him behind his back.

Sellers and buyers he'd taken years to connect with would no longer acknowledge his presence. It was no secret throughout Peterson County that he was suspected of the horrific crime of child abduction, murder, and who knows what else. Within two months, the real estate company he'd worked at for more than a decade officially cut ties with him. Barney Spencer was financially ruined.

To make matters worse, word of his adulterous affair made its way around town. His wife moved in with her mother down in the Florida panhandle and took the kids with her. Barney became a social pariah throughout the county. Even the few people who wouldn't go as far as to accuse him of the child's abduction weren't about to defend his scandalous behavior with his client's wife. To top it all off, he knew that Jake Bickman was out to get him.

Jake was a dumb, drunken redneck to be sure; but he was also big, mean, and violent. Barney kept a lookout at all times for the jealous husband lest he be caught off-guard at some unfortunate moment. Everyone in town reckoned he had a beating coming to him, and Barney rightly presumed that no help would be coming his way if he got jumped by the dangerous redneck.

He was broke, scared, and lonely. He missed his job and his place in the community. He missed his wife and kids. He also missed Mary Bickman, and he was afraid of what her husband was now going to do to her because of what he'd done.

Mary had only entered into their affair after Barney had pursued her relentlessly. He'd made promises to her that he'd never intended to keep. He'd took advantage of her unhappy relationship with her jealous and abusive husband to satisfy his own carnal desires. Now, she was trapped in her home with the drunken monster, while the real estate agent ran and hid like a coward. He was ashamed of himself and his lack of courage, honor, and integrity.

When the news of Jack's apparent suicide spread throughout the community, Barney was heartbroken. He wanted to go to Mary and comfort her. He wanted so badly to tell her how sorry he was for everything, but he knew he couldn't. He cried for his ex-lover and for her dead son that night. He also cried for himself, for his loneliness and despair. He knew what he had to do.

The next day, Barney Spencer packed up what few belongings he had left, loaded them into his car, filled up the tank with gas, and headed south to Florida. He saw Peterson County out of his rear-view mirror for the last time as he drove away on a dusty afternoon. When Barney saw his wife and children again, he took them into his arms and begged for forgiveness, vowing to do anything he could from then on to set things right.

***

The third time the police sirens interrupted the serenity of a lazy afternoon on Johnson Road was the one that ripped out what was left of Mary Bickman's heart. She was preparing the family's evening meal when the piercing sounds shattered the quiet afternoon. She instinctively searched for the boys and spotted Frank coming around the house from the back yard.

"Where's your brother?" she anxiously asked.

Frank shrugged and glanced at his mother. Just then, they both turned to look at the police car coming to a stop down by the Peterson place at the end of the block. They could see the sheriff getting out and talking with Agatha Peterson for a brief moment before the pair turned and hurried into the woods behind the Johnson place.

Frank started to jog down the block to see what was going on, but his mother called out to him.

"Frank! Don't you be going down there. Mind your own business."

Frank hesitated for a moment, looking over his shoulder at his mother. He could feel something was wrong in the pit of his stomach.

"But Jack?" was all he could manage to say before turning and running down the block.

Mary's stomach turned. The last thing she needed now was more trouble from the boys. Jack was getting increasingly defiant and disrespectful lately, and she dreaded the thought that he'd finally done something that would result in his arrest by the police. She nervously wiped her hands on her apron as she apprehensively followed Frank down the street toward the commotion.

She made it all the way down to the Peterson place, by this time accompanied by a few curious neighbors, when she saw some figures emerge from the wooded ravine behind Purvis Johnson's house. Mary couldn't understand what her eyes were seeing.

She spotted Jimmy walking silently alone, as if in shock. George and Agatha Peterson were a few steps ahead of him, embracing each other as they pushed through the brush. Mary watched as Frank fell to his knees and began to shriek in agony. Her mind shut out all the sounds around her. All she could hear was a loud ringing as she stared at the horrible vision coming her way.

Purvis was walking beside Sheriff Gaskin, who carried something heavy in his arms. Mary stared at her eldest son's lifeless body cradled in Clifford's arms without comprehension. She told herself that it wasn't her son that she was seeing, that it was some kind of cruel hallucination. Her soul erupted in anguish when she could hide the appalling truth from herself no longer.

Mary ran to her son, moaning incomprehensively, tears gushing from her eyes. Purvis caught her in his arms and steadied the hysterical woman as her knees gave out. The sheriff lowered the boy's body to the ground with care, and Mary cradled the lifeless body of her first born son in her arms. The grotesque expression on Jack's dead face overwhelmed the grieving mother, and she threw herself on top of his body, wailing uncontrollably. By this time, Deputy Bryce had arrived and he assisted Purvis in helping her up, while Sheriff Gaskin tended to the deceased boy's remains.

The aftermath of Jack's death proved tragic for the remaining Bickmans. Shock overtook the family in the immediate days that followed the boy's fatality. The day they laid his body to rest was cold and windy, with a light drizzle falling all afternoon. Hardly anyone spoke. The few voices that could be heard only conveyed empty whispers of little comfort. After Jack's body was lowered into the earth and his plain wooden casket shoveled over with the dark, moist dirt, the family turned on itself in anguish and remorse.

Jake began a drinking binge that had no end. Already a cruel man when drunk, the unexpected loss of his eldest son only served to make the grieving father more malicious. Jake attacked whoever came near him with brutal abandonment, lashing out in his torment. The closest targets were his wife and only remaining child. The effects of his nasty assaults took their toll on the two, who were already overwhelmed with their own painful suffering and loss.

Frank withdrew further and further into himself, refusing to speak for weeks at a time. He dearly missed his brother and only friend, and he felt guilty over the rift they both had created in their relationship in the last year. Frank felt betrayed by his mother and hated his father's unrelenting cruelty. Now, the lonely child felt abandoned by life itself. He told himself that he stuck around to protect his mother, but he knew in his heart that this was a lie. The truth was that he was too much of a coward to stand up to his abusive father. He increasingly felt worthless and alone.

One night, when his father was passed out and his mother lay weeping quietly in the other room, after yet another beating from her husband, Frank left the house for good. He packed up a few of his belongings and threw them in Jack's old duffle bag, then silently let himself out of the kitchen door into the cool night air. He quietly crept around to the front of the house and down the block toward the highway. He paused to look back one more time.

The boy remembered the times growing up on Johnson Road. The good times shared with his brother, and the bad times that grew to be too many. He sighed and a small cloud of mist ascended from his warm breath before dissipating into the darkness. Turning away from his home, his family, and his childhood forever, he walked down the highway toward an uncertain future.

It was three days before Jake and Mary reported their child missing to Sheriff Gaskin's office. Afraid of yet another abduction in the area, Clifford wasted no time starting an investigation. Once the family had been interviewed and it was discovered that Frank had taken some of his belongings with him, everyone agreed that the boy had run off.

He'd stolen some cash from his father's wallet on the way out, so Clifford figured Frank had no plans to return anytime soon. He couldn't really blame the kid. His life must have been hell, living under the same roof as Jake Bickman.

When Detective Stallworth found out about the boy's disappearance, it got his immediate attention. It was rare for Robert to concur with Sheriff Gaskin's initial assessment of almost any incident, although, this time, he reluctantly had to agree. He understood why the boy struck out on his own, even at the tender age of sixteen.

Either Frank would surface at some distant relative's house, be apprehended for some minor offence in a neighboring community, or make a life of his own far, far away from the horrors of his childhood. Robert hoped for the latter. Frank Bickman deserved a fresh start and a fair shake in the world.

Once Frank was gone, the only thing Mary had left was her drunken, abusive husband. Jack was dead, Barney and Frank had abandoned her, and now she was truly alone. Trapped and cornered, Mary began to assert herself. This proved to be a very bad idea.

Jake had lost both of his children. One had killed himself and the other had stolen from him and run off. The only thing Jake had left was his unfaithful and worthless slut of a wife.

She had humiliated him with her infidelity, making him a laughingstock in the entire county. She was never a good mother to his children, and now they were gone. Now, after all that she'd done to him, she had the nerve to stand up to him and call him names. Loser, drunkard, bully – she used them all.

Even after he slapped the look of defiance off her face, she repeatedly came at him again. Looking him right in the eye, she laughed and challenged his authority. He punished her severely, but she refused to learn her lesson. He'd had enough.

No one on Johnson Road initially noticed the Bickman couple's absence. Their house sat unattended in darkness, not a sound emanating from within for days. Jake's car remained in the driveway, unmoved. Newspapers piled up behind it. Two metal garbage cans stood empty by the curb, their glossy, silver exteriors glimmering in the bright Alabama sun.

It wasn't until one hot night in June, when Gladys Jenkins woke to the sound of several loud cracks, that anyone noticed the lack of activity at the Bickman place. Evening thunderstorms are common in the summer months in Alabama, so, upon hearing no further disturbances, Gladys turned over and went back to sleep, paying no attention to the growing feeling inside of her that something was wrong.

The next morning, she mentioned the oddness of the thunder's din and her misgivings about it to her husband. They looked out at the Bickman house across the street and both agreed that there was something not quite right about it.

Thomas shared their concerns with Purvis. The old man asked Jimmy if he'd noticed anything, and Jimmy asked Agatha. Finally, Purvis suggested that someone call Sheriff Gaskin's office, so Thomas called it in.

Deputy Bryce contacted the body shop where Jake worked, but they reported that he hadn't shown up since the previous week. The manager stated that ever since Jack's death, Jake's life had taken a downward spiral and his absence from work wasn't unusual. The deputy relayed the information to Gaskin, who agreed that it was probably best if they dropped in on the Bickmans post haste.

The rancid smell hit the officers as soon as they pried open the door. No one had answered their repeated knocks, so eventually the men had to do what they had to do.

Clifford and Sean were the first two in, and they found the couple in the bedroom. Jake and Mary Bickman were dead and had been for awhile, judging by the condition of their bodies.

Mary's eyes stared blankly at the wall where her missing children's pictures hung. A gunshot wound to the middle of her chest left a bloody hole where her broken heart once beat. Jake's eyes were closed, his body slumped over in an unnatural position and a good portion of his brain matter pasted to the wall behind him. On the dirty carpet between the two sat a thirty-eight caliber handgun, its metal now as cold as the lifeless bodies beside it.

It didn't take much investigation on the part of the Sheriff's Office or the County Coroner to determine what had occurred. 'Murder/suicide' it said on the official report, in the papers, and on the lips of everyone in Peterson County. The funerals were swift and private, and the memory of the Bickmans faded with the inescapable progression of time.

When Detective Stallworth received the news, the only thoughts he had were of Frank. Thank God the boy had left when he still had the chance. Robert hoped the boy stayed wherever he had run off to. There was nothing left for him on Johnson Road.

*

Summer, 1960

When Robert received the news of Jack's death, his heart sank. Although the detective hadn't completely eliminated the boy from the suspect list, he'd long considered the possibility of Jack's involvement unlikely. Unfortunately for the boy, Jack had been spotted in the area at the time of the abduction and his exact actions and whereabouts could never be verified, thus making him, at least, a possible suspect.

Jack Bickman had already acquired a bad reputation for mischief in the neighborhood. Robert had dug into the boy's past and discovered several complaints about the boy and his brother. There were the usual juvenile delinquent accusations of vandalism, involving toilet paper, eggs, or mail boxes, which could never be proven. Along with these, a report of a spray painting incident at the Peterson house during construction resulted in the involvement of the sheriff's office.

Unofficially, rumors abounded over allegations of bullying and intimidation regarding the other children on the street and at school. In addition, Robert knew about Gladys Jenkins's suspicions about her missing dog. This accusation was one the detective considered valid once he learned about the discovery of the pet's remains down the ravine at the end of the block.

In the end, despite his personal dislike of the eldest Bickman boy, Robert believed that the boy wasn't involved in Elizabeth's abduction. It was a long-shot that Jack could've managed to drag the girl away, kill her, and then hide the body in such a short time without being noticed. It was even more unlikely that the boy even had it in him to commit such an atrocious act. Juvenile delinquency and childish vandalism were one thing; murder was something else altogether.

Over time, he began to back off of the boy as a likely suspect when discussing the case with Elizabeth's parents. He understood that the two had fixated on the Bickman brothers and were reluctant to let that go, but he tried to convince them of the unlikelihood of the boys' guilt. He reasoned that, by now, some kind of evidence would've been found if Jack had committed the crime. As it stood, no sign of Elizabeth or her bicycle were ever discovered on or near Johnson Road.

When Jack's body was found hanging from the thick branch of an oak tree down by the ravine, speculation over the child's motive for suicide brought it all back. It had been almost a year to the day that Elizabeth had disappeared when the boy hung himself –which was too much of a coincidence as far as Gladys was concerned. She was convinced that Jack was overcome with guilt over her daughter's abduction and killed himself because of it.

Unfortunately for Gladys, she found no comfort in Jack's death. If he'd been responsible, any information he possessed had died with him. If he'd been innocent, the guilty party was still out there.

Robert knew all about those feelings of guilt – to a degree. He felt responsible for the lack of progress in his attempt to find out what happened to Elizabeth

Jenkins. He felt the sting of shame over the intimidation he'd poured upon Jack Bickman and the result it appeared to have had on the adolescent. He felt remorse over Jack's younger brother's decline at home during the past year and the boy's sudden departure in the middle of the night. He felt guilt over their handling of the Bickmans overall, and of Mary's murder and Jake's suicide that was the end result.

There was something about Jack's death that bugged him. He tried to put it aside, knowing that his suspicious nature and overzealous attention to detail could sometimes lead him astray. Still, he'd wished that the idiot sheriff had done a better job at the crime scene.

As it was, all he knew was that Jimmy Johnson found Jack Bickman hanging from a tree half-way down the ravine; Purvis Johnson had cut the boy's body down; and Sheriff Gaskin had carried the deceased up to the road. No further examination of evidence or questioning of witnesses was ever conducted.

The official cause of death was suicide – cut and dried, case closed. Robert thought about it and knew the sheriff was probably right, and he decided to let it go.

Detective Stallworth put his notes down and walked away from the pile of reports on his desk. He stared at the pictures on the bulletin board on the wall of his office. His eyes scanned the pages tacked up before him until he found himself staring at one photo in particular.

It was a photograph of Johnson Road, taken from the entrance off Riverside Highway, before most of the houses were constructed. The street sign was bent and twisted, overgrown with weeds and spider webs. Past that, was a barely visible, narrow dirt road running between overgrown trees, stretching into the green darkness. A dilapidated little shack appeared partially hidden in the brush toward the back.

Robert sighed. All of those families had moved there in the hopes of building a bright future for themselves and their children. All of those children, he thought. Elizabeth Jenkins, George Peterson, Jr., Jack and Frank Bickman – they were all gone now. Detective Stallworth looked back at the stack of papers on his desk, then turned back to the photo in front of him. The answers he searched for wouldn't be found in the reports on his desk, he conceded. If they were to be found at all, he would find them on Johnson Road.

Chapter Nineteen

When Thomas Jenkins turned the corner onto Johnson Road on his way home that evening, what was left of his heart dropped into the pit of his stomach. Police cars lined the streets yet again, their colorful, bubble gum lights flashing red and blue in the waning hours of daylight. Two cars were parked in front of the Bickman's house across the street from his, and four more were at the end of the block near the Johnson place.

Thomas pulled into his driveway and walked to his front door. His eyes scanned the neighborhood in a vain attempt to find out what was happening. Gladys met him at the door and motioned him inside before speaking.

"What's going on?" he asked.

"Jack Bickman hung himself today."

Thomas was speechless. His thoughts raced at the implications. Gladys understood her husband's response. She'd shared the same reaction just hours ago when she got the news. She walked with Thomas to the kitchen, and they both sat down at the table before she continued.

"Purvis's boy found him down the ravine, hanging from a tree. The sheriff came right out, but it was too late. Jack was already gone."

"Do they know why he did it?"

Gladys knew what he was thinking; the same thoughts had been clouding her mind all afternoon.

"Not yet. No word on whether or not he left a note."

It seemed too much of a coincidence that the boy had killed himself almost a year to the day that their precious little girl had been taken from them. The couple considered Jack a prime suspect in Elizabeth's abduction. Either he was responsible, they thought, or he knew something he wasn't sharing.

The police had been trying to soften the couple's resolve about the boy's guilt over the last year, although with only minimal effect. Jack's extreme and tragic actions were obviously fueled by a considerable burden in the boy's psyche. Guilt was one explanation that could have precipitated such an event. The timing of the child's apparent suicide substantiated the Jenkins's theories. Unfortunately for the couple, the loss of yet another child so close to home only served to exacerbate their bereavement over their beautiful Elizabeth.

It had been a tough year for the Jenkins. They found little comfort in each other's company, and none alone. The initial shock of their child's disappearance had given way over time to an emptiness that could not be filled. They held on for so long to the hope that Elizabeth would be found alive and well, only gradually giving in to the realization that the chances were becoming increasingly remote.

Over time, they'd individually wished that, if indeed, the child was gone, at least her remains would be found, although neither of them dared to speak the words aloud. Closure became impossible without the firm knowledge of their daughter's whereabouts. It was the not knowing that ate away at their souls, their lives, and their relationship.

Anger began to fill the ever-increasing void in their existence. The couple was angry at the authorities for their inability to find their missing child. They were angry at their neighbors for not being attentive enough and allowing the crime to occur right under their noses. The Jenkins were angry at the world for continuing on without Elizabeth being in it. Most of all, they were angry at the white-trash family across the road, whom they blamed for everything wrong in the world.

Thomas's belief that the Bickmans were involved in Elizabeth's disappearance was somewhat tenuous. He secretly found himself reluctantly clinging to the theory because his wife was so invested in the idea.

Gladys was convinced Jack was involved. She hated the entire Bickman family, hated seeing them carelessly going on with their lives right in front of her, day after day. Now that Jack had killed himself, she thought she would feel vindication, feel satisfaction. Instead, doubts began to chip away at her resolve.

The sight of Mary seeing her first-born son's lifeless body struck at the core of Gladys's motherly instincts. The poor woman had to witness the grotesque vision of Jack's disfigured appearance after his strangulation, a vision that would surely haunt her for the rest of her days. Suicide is such an unfathomable and offensive act of violence. It is an act selfish by nature, with the intent to injure, beyond repair, the people who have loved you the most. When perpetrated by someone so young, the senseless and violent act offends exponentially.

No note was ever found. No indication of what drove the youth to such extreme measures was ever discovered. Gladys and Thomas understood just how much the unanswered questions wounded your very being. They understood how strongly they fasten themselves to your heart and persistently pierced your soul. Within hours of getting the news about Jack, the couple's anger toward the Bickman family across the street transformed from hatred and anger into sympathy and sorrow.

Neither of them felt any resolution after the passing of Jack Bickman. Gladys's certainty of the boy's involvement turned to doubt. Thomas almost abandoned the theory altogether. All they could do in the end was watch as the Bickman's lives imploded. They watched as Jake grew increasingly abusive and as Mary grew progressively unstable. Even Frank appeared dramatically changed after the passing of his brother, usually keeping to himself without any interactions with those around him.

The Jenkins saw themselves reflected in their neighbor's plight and realized how their own lives were falling apart. When Frank ran away from home, their hearts were broken over the boy leaving, and they hoped he would find peace and happiness at last. They prayed for his safety and worried about his welfare. Once again, the couple shared in a parent's loss of a child.

On that awful day, when the authorities found the lifeless bodies of Jake and Mary Bickman, they cried. The Bickmans had suffered the insufferable and were unable to recover. The Jenkins decided that they would not follow suit.

If as one, Gladys and Thomas Jenkins simultaneously woke up from the nightmare their lives had become. The couple had grown apart. They no longer shared the same room at night. No more. Thomas had started a routine of working overtime and missing dinner most nights during the week. No more. The two of them had stopped talking to each other for so long that they were practically strangers. They re-introduced themselves to one another. They fell in love once again.

Three years after Elizabeth disappeared, they put her favorite stuffed tiger in an antique wooden chest and buried it in Memory Gardens Cemetery, erecting a headstone in memoriam. The inscription on the chalk-gray marble read:

ELIZABETH MARY JENKINS
September 24, 1951 – June 16, 1959
Our angel in our hearts forever,
until we meet again.

The couple placed a bouquet of yellow roses, Elizabeth's favorites, on the freshly cut grass and said goodbye to their little girl. Purvis Johnson was the only neighbor they invited to the ceremony that day, and he stood at a distance, in his best and only suit, to give them privacy in their intimate moment. Afterward, the couple thanked him for his kindness and said farewell. Thomas shook the old man's hand and Gladys hugged him one more time before they drove away on that hot, summer afternoon. Their house had been sold. The Jenkins had packed. Their lives were waiting to start over someplace else. Purvis waved goodbye and the couple waved back as their car rounded the corner onto Riverside Highway.

Gladys suddenly flinched in her seat, catching her husband's attention.

"You okay, honey?" he asked.

"Yeah, it's just the baby kicking again," she answered. "I think it's a boy this time."

Thomas smiled and put his arm around his lovely wife, pulling her closer to him on the front seat as they headed off to the much happier future that lay ahead of them, far away from Johnson Road.

JOHNSON ROAD

*

Winter, 1962

Sheriff Gaskin was glad the election was over. Even though he had run unopposed, he hated the fact that his job hung on the approval of ungrateful, ignorant hicks that were never satisfied.

It amazed him just how much money it took to hold office even in the poor, rural community of Peterson County. He found it even more unbelievable how many asses he was required to kiss to have access to that money, especially this time around.

He had bent over backwards to satisfy Harriet Smith with her abatement issue, yet still found himself having to beg for donations. The old bat took it for granted that her money would grant her favors whether she spent it or not, and, as much as he hated to admit it, the bitch was right.

Elizabeth Jenkins was abducted three and a half years ago, and the failure to make headway in the investigation had hung over his department ever since. No one cared that the State Police were unable to solve the crime, even after assigning their best detective to investigate, nor did anyone mind that even the FBI had failed to provide any useful assistance.

In the end, the child went missing in Peterson County, and Sheriff Clifford Gaskin was the sheriff of Peterson County. It was his sole responsibility to protect the citizens under his jurisdiction and to provide justice where appropriate. He had failed miserably on both counts.

The sheriff was forced to address the issue of the missing girl repeatedly on the campaign trail and was sick of it. It was difficult, both personally and professionally, for him to watch the investigation grow cold without any clue as to the girl's fate or the identity of the perpetrator.

He felt somewhat vindicated that his theory that a random stranger happened upon the girl and whisked her away ended up the most plausible scenario. The majority of the citizens in the community could never envision one of their own being capable of such an unspeakable offense, so Clifford's assertion was both comforting and the most widely accepted.

Once the election was over, the sheriff thought he'd be able to relax a little and put it behind him. The girl's parents moved out of state and the Bickmans had been laid to rest and rarely spoken of anymore. If it weren't for George Peterson's incessant complaining about the Johnson boy, he might've been able to avoid Johnson Road altogether.

Unfortunately, it was not meant to be. Ever since George's son passed away and his wife was sent upstate to the loony bin, he became extremely possessive and overprotective of his daughter, Agatha. The poor fool never seemed to comprehend his actions only further pushed his daughter toward the strange boy that lived next door.

Over time, the sheriff grew wary of Purvis's son. Although he could never quite place it, something just didn't seem right with the boy. Jimmy was nineteen years old now – not really a boy, but not yet a man. He was, however, just as odd as he'd ever been.

The sheriff remembered when the child's mother ran off with some electrician, leaving both Purvis and Jimmy to fend for themselves in that tiny, dilapidated shack at the end of the road. Clifford had tried to be sympathetic to the boy, considering the hardships he'd endured, but found himself feeling uneasy nonetheless. The fact that the boy was the last person to be seen with Elizabeth Jenkins wasn't lost on the lawman, either.

Clifford made several calls on Purvis to inquire about Jimmy over the years, but they never proved fruitful. The old man had shown himself to be a valuable help when it came to the trials and tribulations of his neighbors, but became increasingly uncooperative over matters involving his own boy.

Sheriff Gaskin always held the notion that the relationship between the two was somewhat indifferent, yet the old man got defensive at the very mention of Jimmy's involvement in anything. It was this behavior that fueled Clifford's suspicions. The trouble now was how he should follow up on his hunch.

Clifford considered Purvis to be fairly stupid and obstinate at times. He could be easily outsmarted, the sheriff believed; however, the idiot couldn't be intimidated. Clifford knew one misstep or wrong word to Purvis and the conversation was over – goodbye, too bad, so sad.

Sheriff Gaskin felt that the old man was covering up something he knew about his boy, something bad. It was up to the sheriff to get the truth, and, difficult or not, he intended to do just that.

Chapter Twenty

"Sheriff, George Peterson here. I've been calling your office all day and I'm tired of getting the runaround."

George was furious. He'd been trying desperately to keep his daughter away from the Johnson boy, but she'd defied him at every turn. He forbade her to talk to Jimmy, but he lived next door. He had no way of forcing Agatha to comply with his rules, and he was frustrated by the situation.

"I demand that something be done," growled the irate father into the telephone. "My daughter is a good girl and needs to be protected from that weirdo."

"Uh huh," Sheriff Gaskin mumbled back, allowing George to continue his tirade.

"You know she's been sneaking around behind my back to see him, despite everything I've done to try to keep them apart. He's no good for her. You mark my words, nothing good is going to come from this. That boy is trouble."

"Go on."

George sensed that the sheriff was merely placating him, but needed to vent nonetheless. Things between him and Agatha had been spiraling down for years now, and no matter what he tried, he was unable to correct things. He was hurt and desperate, but most of all, he was angry.

After the child's mother was sent upstate to the asylum, George attempted to bond with his daughter. They were the only two people left in the big house, and all they had was each other, or so he liked to think. Unfortunately, the distance he'd created between himself and everyone else, even his own family, was hard to reverse.

He had no friends – merely acquaintances – a sad truth that extended even to his immediate family. Just because he wished he and Agatha would grow closer, didn't make it so. George didn't like it when he couldn't get his own way, and he didn't give up easily.

In the days following Georgie's passing, he felt that things were getting better between the two of them. Then, he learned the awful truth about Cheryl.

He was never able to understand how his own wife could betray him the way she had, or how a mother could harm her own child. He'd done everything for that woman, he believed, and she repaid him by murdering his only son. He'd befriended her in high school when no one else would. He'd rescued her from poverty and had married her, giving her the prestigious surname of Peterson in the process. He'd had the biggest house on the block built for her to live in and gave her two beautiful children. All of this proved to be for naught, he thought bitterly. In the end, she'd tried to destroy everything he'd worked so hard to build.

The woman turned out to be a monster. She was an ungrateful bitch, thought George, and her daughter was starting to become just like her.

"I'm calling for your help, Sheriff, and I want something done," George continued. "I know the two of them have been running around behind my back for awhile now, but it's got to stop. She didn't show up at school today. It's not like her to skip school. She should be home right now, and she isn't. I know that boy is involved."

"I see," replied the sheriff.

George understood it when his daughter became angry with him after her mother was sent away. She believed that somehow he should've been able to do something to prevent her brother's death. She blamed him for not being supportive of her mother when she needed him, as if somehow he could've prevented her breakdown.

He knew that she thought he'd played a part and should share in some of the guilt. This idea was ludicrous to George. How could he have had anything at all to do with the terrible events that had transpired? No, it was Cheryl's sickness that caused the trouble. The fault was hers alone.

He hoped that once she got over the initial shock of losing her mother and sibling, Agatha would warm up to him. It seemed to him that things were getting better between them until the Johnson boy started coming around again. Just as it appeared his daughter might confide in her own father, she turned her attention to the neighborhood Romeo. When he tried to intervene, he was painted as the bad guy.

George initially tried to be nice about the situation and only mildly suggested that Agatha find other friends. When she resisted his advice, he went as far as trying to introduce her to other eligible boys in the community. He hoped that she might tire of the poverty-stricken redneck next door in favor of more promising suitors. None of his interventions were successful. Instead, they only pushed his daughter farther away from him and toward the oddball Johnson boy.

After the Bickman boy killed himself and the panicked Jimmy came banging at their door, all hope was lost. From that day on, the two adolescents were inseparable. What was only a friendship at first, turned into love, a painful fact that even he couldn't deny.

He couldn't bear to see his only daughter make the same mistake he'd made – marry someone beneath her. He had paid a heavy price for his blunder, and he swore he would do everything in his power to keep her from making the same mistake.

"There's something very strange about that boy. You know it, I know it. Hell, everyone knows it!" George ranted to the sheriff. "If it weren't for respect for his old man, I would take matters into my own hands. That boy is trouble, mind you, and it's only a matter of time before something bad is going to happen, or should I say, something else bad."

The irate father waited to hear the sheriff's response, but was greeted with silence. He could hear the shuffling of papers through the phone and felt his anger rising. Damn stupid, good-for-nothing, fat-ass sheriff was ignoring him. How dare he! This was George Peterson he was talking to, not some drunken redneck. He breathed heavily into the phone, breaking the silence and waking the distracted man on the other end of the receiver.

"I see," the sheriff replied. "Is that all?"

"Is that all? Have you even been listening to me? This is an outrage!"

The sheriff responded, letting George know how busy his department was and telling him that the Sheriff's Department was going to get right on it. The lawman was blowing smoke up his ass, he knew, telling him how he was going to send one of his incompetent minions over to investigate.

George wasn't happy about having to deal with some underling deputy, but figured this was as good as he was going to get at the moment. Maybe the deputy would at least listen to what he had to say, instead of ignoring him altogether, like the fat, useless sheriff had just done.

"When is your deputy coming? I don't have all day."

Gaskin offered to connect him with some dispatcher to schedule the deputy's arrival. George couldn't resist taking one more dig at the incompetent jackass before being passed down the chain of command.

"Don't make the mistake of ignoring this, Sheriff. My family has been running things in this county since before you were born. Don't make me remind you that your job depends on results."

He stayed on the phone for a few minutes before a woman came on the other end and informed him that one of the deputies would be out to see him shortly. He slammed the phone down without another word and waited, stewing in his anger.

He paced back and forth, pausing once in awhile to peer out of the window, hoping to catch a glimpse of his daughter and that loser who lived next to him.

It was only thirty minutes before he saw one of the police cars pull up to his house, but it was thirty minutes too long as far as he was concerned. He watched through the lace curtains in his front parlor as one of the deputies sauntered up to his front porch and knocked on the door. George waited a good three minutes before making a move. He figured that they'd made him wait, so he'd return the favor. Just as the officer turned to walk back toward his car, he swung open the door.

"It's about time you showed up."

Deputy Willis looked at George with contempt. Composing himself, he addressed the irate father as professionally as he could manage.

"Good afternoon, Mr. Peterson. My name is Deputy Sean Willis."

The deputy reached out his hand to George, but pulled it back after an awkward pause when the man refused to recognize his greeting.

"I understand you have a complaint to file about one of your neighbors," the officer continued, unaffected by the man's rudeness.

"I have more than a complaint, Deputy. My daughter is missing," George replied with disdain.

"Missing?" Sean asked in surprise. "How long has she been gone?"

"I haven't seen her since this morning. Come inside, I don't want to give the neighbors a show."

Deputy Willis followed the man into the large house, and George led him into the kitchen to talk.

"When was the last time you saw your daughter?"

"Agatha. Her name is Agatha, and I saw her this morning before work. I got a call from her school, she never showed up. I rushed home to check up on her, but she's not here."

"I see. Well, with all due respect sir, it's only two-thirty now," the deputy remarked as he glanced at his watch. "I understand your concern, but it's not a long enough time to report someone missing. I'm sure she'll turn up soon."

"It's long enough for me. I know my daughter, and I know something is wrong. She wouldn't have missed school. I've been calling your department for help going on months now, and nothing's been done. Now this. I demand that you find her immediately!"

"What makes you so sure that she's not going to come home soon, Mr. Peterson? Did she say anything, or leave a note?"

"No, no, nothing like that. I just know. I've had a bad feeling all day. I even came home early from work. A father knows. I'm telling you, something is wrong here."

"Do you have any idea where she might be?"

"I don't know where, but I know with who. She's with that Johnson boy. She's always with that Johnson boy. He's a strange one, too. I know something is wrong. I don't trust that kid. There's no telling what he'll do to her."

"Well, did she take anything with her that makes you think she took off for good?"

"I don't know. Not that I know of."

"Is it okay if we look in her room? We might be able to find a clue as to where she went."

George led the deputy upstairs to Agatha's room. The two men looked around briefly to see if the child had packed a few clothes or left anything behind that might give them an idea as to where she might be. George felt uncomfortable in his daughter's room and even more uncomfortable allowing the officer to poke through his daughter's private things.

"Can you tell if anything is missing?" Sean asked the girl's father.

"No. I mean, I'm not sure."

He was ashamed to admit that he didn't have the slightest idea what Agatha had or didn't have. He liked to believe that he was an attentive father, but it was times like these that exposed his selfishness and aloofness. The unwanted attention embarrassed George, and he responded with anger at the deputy.

"None of this matters. I'm telling you, something's wrong here. Why are you looking in the one place we know she's not? We're wasting time."

"Please, Mr. Peterson, I'm only trying to help."

"I told you where to look. Find that Johnson boy, and you'll find my little girl."

"I understand, Mr. Peterson, and I intend to do that. You'll just have to be a little patient."

"Patient? I have to be a little patient? Is that what you told the Jenkins when you couldn't find their missing daughter?"

"Now, wait a minute, Mr. Peterson. I'm here on your behalf, so I'd appreciate it if you didn't speak to me like that. Unless you want me to leave right now and forget the whole thing, I suggest you watch how you talk to me."

George paused for a moment before replying, "I'm sorry, officer. I'm just worried about my little girl."

"Its okay, Mr. Peterson, I understand your situation. I swear to you that we'll do everything we can to find her. I'll report directly to Sheriff Gaskin as soon as I leave here. You'll hear back from us soon, so don't worry. Well, at least try not to worry."

There was nothing left to say, and George followed the deputy out to his car.

"Find my girl, Deputy. I'm begging you. Please take this seriously. She's all I have left."

Sean nodded, then returned to his car and drove off. He knew that George was probably getting all worked up over nothing and that his daughter would more than likely return shortly. Knowing George, Sean figured that he wouldn't even bother to notify the Sheriff's Department, and he'd let them waste time and resources in vain.

The deputy assumed that Sheriff Gaskin would blow off the entire incident as another one of George Peterson's hysterical tantrums. He was probably right, too, thought Sean, but deep down inside, he felt that maybe the worried father was right. Sean had an uneasy feeling about this one, but, unlike the detective he admired so much, he didn't have the experience or expertise to grasp the significance and react accordingly.

As Deputy Willis wrestled with his intuition and attempted to compose a report to present to the sheriff about his visit with Mr. Peterson, Clifford was struggling with his own suspicions about the Johnson boy. The sheriff had recently visited the boy's father yet again to try and pry some information about Jimmy out of him, but had come away with even bigger doubts.

Purvis had become increasingly uncooperative with him, but Clifford had persisted. He felt that he might've gotten somewhere with his questioning had that pesky detective not shown up unexpectedly.

Detective Stallworth's visits had become gradually more infrequent over the years. However, the man never did completely go away. Now, out of the blue, he showed up at the worst possible moment.

Clifford knew that Purvis never cared for the detective in the first place and was only polite to the man out of respect for his position. When Stallworth drove up, just as the sheriff was in the middle of asking the old man about his boy, he was certain that it appeared to Purvis that it was a set-up to try to intimidate him. Clifford was well aware that intimidation was the wrong approach to take with the skittish war veteran, and he cringed at the very sight of the detective that day.

To make matters worse, the detective had stopped by because he'd noticed the missing vehicle. Clifford wondered how he'd missed that. The boy was gone, the car was gone, and now George Peterson was accusing Jimmy of running off with his daughter. Good God, if that girl didn't show up soon, there'll be hell to pay, he thought.

All of this only served to remind him of the Elizabeth Jenkins abduction and his confident assertion that the child had been whisked away by an outsider to a place far, far away. The certainty of his previous convictions had long since eroded as his suspicions about the Johnson boy escalated. Now he could feel it eating away at him that he'd failed to notice something else on his last visit to the Johnson place.

*

April 24, 1963: 3:07 pm

Robert stared at the burly man standing at the curb. The bearded crossing guard reminded him of the sheriff – a memory that stirred up an uneasy feeling that had been slowly brewing inside of him for weeks. His subconscious was trying to tell him something, although the detective couldn't figure out what it was. He desperately tried to jog his memory, searching his thoughts for any clue that might indicate the source of the nagging feeling that'd taken up permanent residence in his stomach. He was unsuccessful thus far, but felt that it was just off his fingertips.

He inched his car forward through the school-zone traffic, pausing at the corner to let the children pass. It was dismissal time at Oakdale Elementary School, and he inadvertently found himself caught up in the bumper-to-bumper traffic that inevitably arose with the sudden influx of activity in Old Town on a weekday afternoon. He glanced again at the crossing guard, thinking that the big man almost had the air of a deviant. The detective wondered if any of the children's parents ever expressed similar concerns about the man's appearance to the sheriff.

Robert found the situation amusing, considering the close resemblance the guard shared with Sheriff Gaskin. He almost felt sorry for the sheriff, knowing how many petty complaints the man must have to deal with on a day-to-day basis.

Thinking about Sheriff Gaskin brought on his acid reflux again. Yes, that was it, thought Robert. Whatever was bothering him had something to do with the sheriff.

The detective tried to remember exactly when and where he was when the bubbling in his stomach had started. When did he see the sheriff last, and what else occurred at that time? Was it something that was in one of the reports that set it off? Perhaps it was something that was missing from one of the reports? When did he last see Gaskin?

He seemed to recall running into the sheriff when he went out to Purvis Johnson's place to see if the old man's boy was around. The sheriff was there when he'd showed up. Apparently Purvis's snobby neighbor, George Peterson, had been complaining that his daughter, Agatha, was seeing the boy against his wishes. Robert might've found the situation amusing if it weren't for the misgivings that he himself secretly harbored about the boy.

Jimmy Johnson always seemed a bit of an odd duck to Robert, and not just because his eyes were two different colors. He'd questioned the boy on numerous occasions when Elizabeth Jenkins disappeared, although there was no indication that he'd had anything to do with it. Nevertheless, something about Jimmy was subtly unsettling. Robert couldn't quite put his finger on it, but he had the impression that there was something disturbing hidden within the quiet lad.

It was difficult to get anything out of Jimmy. He didn't talk much, yet didn't give the outward appearance of being evasive. His father, Purvis, was much easier to talk to. The old man could be obstinate at times and was dumb as a sack of hammers, thought Robert; yet, on occasion, Purvis had some fairly exceptional insights into his neighbor's affairs.

The detective knew that Purvis Johnson was lazy. He preferred to sit on his front porch all day, smoking his camels, and keeping watch over the neighborhood. The old man's vantage point from the end of the block gave him a front row seat on the happenings going on in his neighbor's lives. Unfortunately for the detective and the sheriff, Purvis was much more tight-lipped about his boy's activities.

Robert wondered if the old man shared his misgivings about the boy, but he understood that Purvis would never share any negative feelings about his son. The detective was just as certain that the old man would do whatever he could to make sure no harm would come to the sensitive youth under his care.

Diingg a liing! Ring, ring, ring!!!

His attention was drawn to a little girl on the sidewalk next to his car. She'd just mounted her little pink bicycle and was ringing the bell attached to her handlebar as she took off down the street.

That was it! The bicycle! He could see it plain as day, hanging on the wall in Purvis Johnson's filthy garage. It was dirty and full of cobwebs, but it was a *girl's* bicycle!

Damn it, thought Robert, some detective he was. The damn thing was just hanging there in the open for all to see, yet Gaskin, Purvis, and even he didn't take any notice. Elizabeth Jenkins had disappeared, never to be seen again, and neither had her bicycle – until now.

The crossing guard was waving the cars forward, but Robert ignored him, lost in thought. The drivers behind him blew their horns in annoyance, waking him from his trance. He watched as the little girl rode away on her bike, disappearing from view, and then he stepped on the accelerator. Robert grabbed the radio from the dashboard and called the State Police dispatcher.

"Detective Stallworth here. Ten-twenty: Hidden Springs. Request backup, three to four officers. Ten-forty-nine: Eleven-thirteen Johnson Road, Peterson County. Ten-fifty-four: Tell them to bring some shovels."

Chapter Twenty-One

Clifford sat in his police car along Riverside Highway, hidden from the oncoming traffic. Almost everyone in the vicinity knew he favored the spot near Lil' Ray's, although this didn't keep him from using it. The sheriff didn't give the locals much credit that they'd slow down in an obvious and well-known speed trap. The considerable revenue his department produced over the years confirmed his assessment. The location offered a bonus in that it kept the drunks that frequented the local watering hole on their toes and, hopefully, off the road.

One of the slow-witted employees of the highway bar was standing outside, hosing down the bar mats. Clifford chuckled as he watched the skinny old janitor make a complete mess of the task.

"Moron," the sheriff muttered to himself with amusement.

Moments later, Clifford's attention was drawn to the sight of five state police vehicles cruising past on obvious official business.

"What the fuck?"

Clifford hit the gas, at the same time calling Mabel on the radio. He wanted reinforcements and he wanted them now. Sheriff Gaskin was the authority in Peterson County, and he had every intention of pushing his considerable weight around. How dare the State Police come charging into his jurisdiction without even so much as a courtesy call! Clifford knew who was behind this disrespectful transgression and exactly where they were headed, and he followed close behind.

Purvis Johnson sat in his favorite rocking chair on his front porch, lazily puffing on a cigarette and blowing smoke rings through the cobwebs that draped down from the rickety overhang. He was enjoying the break from his previous labors. The old man had managed to throw some dried brush and rotten limbs into a pile to burn that morning, and that was about as much work as he could motivate himself to do for the entire day.

When the line of white sedans came screeching around the corner from the highway at the end of the block and barreling down the street, he stopped rocking and tossed his cigarette on the porch, stomping it out with the heel of his muddy boot.

"Som' bitch," he muttered to himself.

Purvis hated uninvited company. Hell, he hated company altogether, especially law-enforcement types on official business. He remembered with a certain level of disdain how disrespectful and pushy they'd been when they'd searched for the missing girl. Purvis and Jimmy had cooperated in every way they could, yet, in the end, they were treated like trespassers on their own property. The old man had almost broken his neck when he slipped in the mud and fell halfway down the embankment while looking for the Jenkins girl. If it weren't for Jimmy, he might've been killed.

No thanks came their way for their trouble. No sir. Instead, the sheriff and the detective insinuated that his own son might've been involved. They were a bunch of ungrateful bastards as far as Purvis was concerned.

To add insult to injury, the two men had been coming around again lately, all because Jimmy was dating that spoiled, little, rich girl next door. He'd had enough, and no matter what they were racing down the street to attend to, this time they were going to get an earful.

The convoy of white sedans pulled up to Purvis Johnson's house. Some drove onto his lawn to park, as if he had no rights to his own land at all. It didn't matter to the old man that his yard was in shambles – antique junkers and car parts were thrown around like it was a landfill – or that his rusted, run-down pickup truck was similarly located. It was his lawn to do with as he pleased, not community property to be trampled upon by just anybody. He took in a deep breath and exhaled slowly to steady his anger as he waited for the men to approach.

Detective Stallworth was the first to exit his vehicle and the calmest of the lot. He walked toward the old man in an unhurried and steady gait, his eyes never leaving Purvis's face, his expression stoic and unchanging. Purvis met the man's gaze with fire behind his eyes, unblinking and unintimidated.

"Mr. Johnson," Robert greeted the man.

"Detective."

The men looked at each other for a brief moment, sizing each other up. The other troopers walked up, forming a semi-circle around the old man on the porch. Purvis stood his ground, his expression never wavering.

"Is there something I can do for you?" he asked.

"I'm afraid there is. For one, we'd like to have a talk with your boy. Can you get him for us?"

"Not here. Anything else?"

"Where is he?"

"Not here."

The two men stared each other down, neither giving ground.

"Can we look in your garage for a moment?"

Detective Stallworth glanced over at the rusty, tin garage and saw that the door was wide open. He knew the old car that'd been its previous tenant would be missing. He did a double take and his stomach dropped when he saw no sign of the bicycle that had previously hung against the back wall.

"Nope."

He turned back to the old man.

"Nope? What do you mean – nope? Are you trying to hide something from us, Mr. Johnson?"

Purvis remained silent. Robert stared at the old man, but knew his options were fast becoming limited. He hadn't expected this when he called in the troops and led everyone down to Johnson Road in hot pursuit. Fucking old coot was considerably brighter than he looked. He wasn't about to give up his boy to the authorities, no matter what the disturbed youth might've done, and the detective knew from experience that it was useless to try to get the old man to cooperate when he didn't wish to.

"Purvis," Sheriff Gaskin chimed in. "I don't know what you're trying to pull here, but it's in the best interest of everyone if you'd just cooperate."

Clifford had finally arrived at the gathering. He'd pulled up behind the state authorities, but hung back until three of his deputies arrived. Gaskin didn't want to be the odd man out, with all of the troopers mulling about, and have his position diminished even less than it already had been.

He instantly saw that Purvis was infuriated over the intrusion by the detective and his men, and he knew how stubborn the old man could be. It was highly unlikely that any of them would be successful getting Purvis to cooperate. If anyone could talk sense to him, it would be the sheriff. Clifford saw his opportunity to show up the arrogant state troopers, and he jumped at it.

Purvis glanced over at the sheriff and replied, "Cooperate? Is that what you call it? You trespass on my property, demanding to see my boy, and ransack my home without so much as an explanation, and you want me to cooperate? You can all go to hell."

"No one here has any intention of ransacking your home. We just want to ask Jimmy a couple of questions. I'm sure if you calm down and just allow us to do our jobs, we can clear this up and get on like nothing ever happened."

"Do you think I'm stupid, Sheriff? A parade of cop cars pulls up to my house and a dozen officers surround me and demand to search my property and harass my son, and you think we'll just clear this up and get along in a matter of minutes? Is that your story, dip-shit?"

Clifford wanted to punch the old man in the face. Who the hell did he think he was, calling him a dip-shit? Fuck the ignorant old hick, thought Clifford, throw him to the wolves.

"What happened to the bicycle, Mr. Johnson?" Detective Stallworth asked.

Clifford almost choked. The bicycle! That's it! He remembered seeing it hanging from the wall of the garage the last time he was out there. Damned detective beat him to the punch again. His mind raced as he looked at Purvis and tried to imagine just how much the old man knew about his deviant boy, and just how long he'd been hiding it from them all.

"Bicycle? What bicycle? What the hell are you talking about, Detective?" Purvis asked.

"You know damn well what I'm talking about, Mr. Johnson. There was a child's bicycle hanging up on that garage wall the last time we were out here, a girl's bicycle. Now, it's gone. Where'd it go?" Robert asked.

"I got no idea what the hell you're talking about. I don't 'member seeing no bicycle in that there garage. Damn thing is full of crap as it is. Told my boy to get rid of some of that junk, and I s'pose he did."

Purvis turned back toward Clifford and added, "That Peterson fella sure got you steppin' and fetchin', huh, Sheriff?"

Clifford kept his mouth shut and glared back at the insolent old fool.

"Ever since that girl took a likin' to my boy, y'all gotta harass us. Figures. No justice for a regular fella 'round these parts. Gotta be rich to have rights 'round here."

"This has nothing to do with Jimmy's dating habits, Mr. Johnson," the detective stated. "We have reason to believe that he knows something he hasn't told us about Elizabeth Jenkins's disappearance. The way you're acting, we now have reason to believe you're keeping things from us as well. If you have nothing to hide, then there's no reason for you to not cooperate. This isn't going to go away until we get answers. I'm not going to go away. You want to get rid of us, tell us what we want to know. So, I'm asking you again. May we have a look inside your garage?"

"Sure can – long as you got a warrant. You got a warrant, Detective?"

"We can get one, Mr. Johnson."

"Get one, then. 'Course you can't, 'cause you got no cause to search. If you did, you'd a had one already. Ain't that right, Detective? If you ain't got enough reason to search, you ain't got enough reason to come harassing me and mine. Now get the hell off of my property."

Purvis took a Camel out of his shirt pocket and snapped open his Zippo. He lit the cigarette and took a long drag, staring into the detective's eyes as he blew a cloud of smoke into the man's face. A smirk crept over his face as he stood there, silently waiting for the men to retreat and lick their wounds after their humiliating loss.

The policemen walked back to their cars and huddled, discussing their options. Purvis stood his ground, casually smoking his cigarette, seemingly without a care in the world.

The old man's thoughts were running a mile a minute. He'd been suspicious himself about what exactly young Jimmy knew, and about who he did and didn't tell. He knew that the boy had gotten close to the girl next door, and it was only a matter of time before trouble came knocking.

Purvis hoped that the girl would tire of his son's poverty and poor prospects, yet it never happened. The old man understood that love was one area in which any attempt at manipulation on his part was useless. It would only backfire.

He stayed out of it, and merely kept a watchful eye on the situation. Unfortunately, the idiot rich man next door tried to intervene at every turn. The end result was true love, and the two kids became inseparable.

Now, it appeared that the girl's father assumed that the two had run off together, and panicked, sending the authorities straight to Purvis' doorstep. For his part, the old man would play it cool. If they wanted to get at his boy, they'd have to go through him. He had every intention of making them earn their paychecks in the process.

After a lengthy discussion, the policemen determined that the ravine and area behind the Johnson house was county property, and no warrant was needed to search down there.

It was a long-shot, they all agreed, although at the moment, it was better than nothing. They couldn't just leave with their tails between their legs, after the way the old yokel had berated them. If nothing else, they had to show Purvis who was boss.

Clifford thought the search was foolish. He surmised that nothing would be found down the treacherous slope, and they'd come out empty-handed yet again. The very thought of Purvis sitting on his front porch, laughing at the sight of them covered in mud and despondent over a total lack of progress after expending so much labor in the process, was unbearable.

Unfortunately, he had to agree that they couldn't just leave now without putting him out in some way, so all they had left was to aggravate the old man by digging around behind his property. Besides, Clifford surmised, he knew how uncomfortable the geezer was with all of them hanging around, and he reasoned they might get lucky if the younger Johnson showed up unexpectedly.

The troopers stood around, talking amongst themselves in muted tones, while the sheriff's men followed their lead. Clifford stood to the side, not wanting to be a part of the useless venture, yet not wanting to risk being left out if something came of it.

Robert scrambled down the ravine, poking around through the brush and muttering to himself under his breath. Something was gnawing at his insides as he wandered back and forth amongst the overgrowth and mosquitoes. The detective could feel the hairs on the back of his neck stand up, and a sharp pain developed in his stomach as if the acid was about to burn through the lining and into his abdominal cavity.

He stopped under the big oak tree Jack Bickman's body had been cut down from, a strand of tangled rope still attached to one of the branches overhead, and brushed away the damp earth under his boot, sensing that something was just a tad different in this particular spot. He crouched down to inspect the area closer – a cue for the other troopers to retrieve the shovels.

"Get the shovels. We'll dig here."

"Now, now, Detective. Just what do you expect to find?" the sheriff asked.

As far as Clifford could determine, the spot that the detective picked looked just the same as any other. The odds that they'd actually uncover anything of value seemed remote at best, despite requiring a great deal of effort by everyone involved.

The slope was treacherous, the ground full of stones and roots, and the entire area overgrown with thorn bushes and sharp limbs – not exactly the best spot to dig a hole. The detective's men jumped to follow Robert's hunch, as if success was all but certain.

The trooper's actions caused the sheriff to rethink his position, and he decided to have his deputies join in, just in case they were on to something.

"Don't just stand there, boys, dig in," Clifford instructed Deputies Stevens and Bryce.

The men dug, and the hole grew deeper. Each took his turn at the laborious task, until it seemed as if all they would find was mud and tangled roots and stones. Their certainty in the detective's intuition began to waiver, though Robert's bearing never changed. They continued to dig.

When it appeared that even the detective was ready to throw in the towel, a slight change in the color and consistency of the soil became apparent. White, powdery sand became visible alongside the dark, moist dirt, and everyone there thought the same thing – quicklime.

The men dug with an increased focus until an object emerged from the earth. Setting their shovels aside, the officers brushed the loose dirt away by hand until they uncovered a grisly item. A human skull gazed unseeing into the empty sky, a ghastly smile grinning up at the sober men who looked down into the unmarked grave.

Sheriff Gaskin looked at the detective, and Robert met his gaze. After a brief moment of silence, the men resumed their task. This time they delicately brushed away the soil from the skeletal remains in an attempt not to disturb the evidence.

Detective Stallworth spotted a small glimmer of metal in the dirt next to the rotting bones. He reached down, gently scooping it up in his fingers. He climbed out of the hole and held the item up for closer inspection.

He carefully brushed away the dirt from the delicate silver chain and let it dangle in the sunlight for a moment. Attached to the end was a heart-shaped locket. Clifford stood next to the detective as he gently opened the locket and peered inside. The faded picture of a young boy smiled back at the two men.

"Jimmy," Clifford stated aloud.

They looked at each other with the same realization, just as a loud bang echoed through the air, making them jump. Another explosion erupted, and the men's attention was drawn away from the grave at their feet and toward the noise emanating from above. They saw a dark billow of smoke climbing into the bright blue sky and a red glow issuing from the intense flames at its base. They heard another boom ring out.

"Wasn't anyone watching Purvis?" Stallworth asked incredulously.

The humiliated officers shifted uncomfortably, no one making eye contact while the sound of Purvis's rusty muffler echoed off the neatly lined houses up and down the block as the old man drove his truck down the road. He quickly turned onto Riverside Highway and disappeared from Johnson Road.

By the time the officers scrambled up the embankment, he was gone. The rickety shack facing the wrong direction that stood watch over the neighborhood for so long was engulfed in flames. The nine police cars sitting out front were useless, their tires slashed and radios smashed.

Bewildered neighbors came out of their homes, curious about the unexpected and disastrous events, yet no one saw a thing. No one ever saw anything on Johnson Road, both the detective and sheriff would conclude. No one except for Purvis Johnson – he saw everything.

George Peterson ran frantically up to Clifford, who was busy tending to the chaotic scene. George was looking for Agatha. Had the sheriff seen her? He'd begged the sheriff for months to do something about his girl and the Johnson boy. Had the sheriff seen Jimmy?

Clifford's heart sank, and he looked over to Stallworth. The detective truly felt sorry for Gaskin for the first time. Robert felt ashamed that he'd been at odds with the man all of this time when, at the end of the day, it was the sheriff's people that were affected the most when they'd all failed to protect the innocent.

Yeah, they'd seen Jimmy. They saw his smiling picture in his mother's locket, next to her rotting corpse, buried behind the boy's house. Jimmy was just a boy when the picture was taken, just a boy when the locket and his mother ended up in that hole.

No, they didn't know where Jimmy was, or Agatha, or Elizabeth Jenkins, for that matter. Looking back at the ashes that would be the only reminder of the crooked little shack, the detective wondered if they would ever really know the truth about all of the terrible things that had happened on Johnson Road.

Epilogue
May, 1963

"A sixth body was discovered today in Peterson County, Alabama. No identification has been made, but authorities are working around the clock to identify the remains. The main suspect, one Purvis Johnson, remains at large. Law enforcement authorities have announced an unprecedented manhunt in the search for the missing suspect. He is considered armed and extremely dangerous."

The news station blared the unwelcome news to the mostly empty room at Lil' Ray's. The reception wasn't the best this far away from Birmingham, but it didn't matter to anyone. They all knew the awful story.

Reporters far and wide had descended on their once-quiet little town, until the whole area had turned into a circus. The traffic was bad. You couldn't get a seat at the Olde Towne Diner come lunch time, and Lil' Ray's started to get a crowd at happy hour.

Normally, the increase in business and money that followed would be good news for the poor community, but this was one instance when it was not welcome.

No one could believe that the terrible events had happened there. No one could believe that it happened to them. No one could believe that it was one of their own that committed those terrible crimes.

Theories arose around town involving conspiracies, nefarious plots involving outsiders, and evil doers from afar. Most of the citizens knew that these theories were just wishful thinking, though many chose to believe them anyway.

Body after body had already been dug up from around that house on Johnson Road. Susan Johnson, Harry Lejuine, and an unidentified body were recovered down by the ravine. The charred remains of several more, including Jimmy Johnson and Agatha Peterson had been discovered inside the ashen ruins. Inside of a hidden root cellar, what was left of Elizabeth Jenkins's body was found pad-locked in a deep freezer. The intense heat from the flames cooked the child's body like a Thanksgiving Day turkey. No, it was all too obvious who the evil doer was.

Everyone held their breath, waiting for the day the monster would be caught. The fine, church-going citizens of Peterson County wanted to feel safe again. They wanted justice. They wanted their pound of flesh.

"Damn shame. That old man even killed his own boy," Danny Boy pondered aloud.

"Shit, that weren't his kid no how," replied Bubba. "Sue had him with Jimmy Magee, long before she met Pur..., long before she met that asshole."

The name of Purvis Johnson was no longer allowed to be spoken aloud at Lil' Ray's. Scores of strangers who came into the bar to gawk or ask questions were escorted out after making the mistake of breaking the rule.

"Poor girl, gettin' mixed up with a monster like him. Hope they catch him soon. I would give anything to have five minutes with him in a room alone," Bubba declared.

"They ain't gonna catch that old man," Danny Boy stated. "Hell, they ain't even got a picture of him. Son-of-a-bitch been livin' here for years, and ain't no one knows a thing 'bout where he came from or where he's goin' to. The old man was like a ghost."

"Shut the hell up, you old fool. Why don't you go clean the terlets an' make yourself useful for a change," Bubba barked out.

"We return now to Peterson County, Alabama, where one of the worst serial killers in history has…"

Bubba reached up, slapping the television knob with his large paw, turning off the machine.

"Play something on the jukebox, will ya?" he hollered to no one in particular.

A brief moment drifted by before the needle could be heard landing softly on the spinning vinyl. The record scratched and sputtered a few seconds before the soulful sounds of a steel guitar flooded the room. The occupants of Lil' Ray's sat in silence as the wailing of the electric guitar echoed like a missing child's cries, eternally drifting in the wind, searching for home.

THE END

ACKNOWLEDGMENTS

Thanks goes out to Lisa Herrington, Dawn and Dennis Lavoie, Paul Heingarten, and Lee Auger for reading my rough draft and assisting me with editing, and a special thanks to everyone in the Bayou Writer's Club for motivating me to become a better writer.

I wish to thank my mother, Dr. Louaine L. Spriggs, for her tireless efforts in helping me transform a pile of words into a cohesive story and for her support and encouragement throughout. I also wish to thank my father, Jesse, for everything he has done to allow me to follow my dreams, my brother, Charles, for the outstanding observations and advice, and my sister, Lisa, for access to her vast graphic arts knowledge and help with the cover. A warm thank you for my son, Matthew, for teaching me to never turn my back on my creative side in the face of the mundane reality of everyday life, and my step-daughters, Arielle, for her contagious laugh, and Destiny, for the awesome cover photo.

Most of all, I wish to thank my wife, Jennifer, without whom this novel would never have been written. You were the first person to believe in my ability to put pen to page, even when I wasn't as convinced as you that I'd see it through. I must confess that more than a few of the best ideas in the book came from your delightfully warped mind. I love you with all of my heart.

ABOUT THE AUTHOR

CLAYTON E. SPRIGGS works as a health care professional in Southeast Louisiana. Married with a son and two stepdaughters, he is an active participant in the Bayou Writer's Club and a dedicated member of the Who Dat Nation.

Thank you for reading my book. If you enjoyed it, please take a moment to post a review at your favorite retailer.

Clayton E. Spriggs can be contacted at
cespriggs@pennmillpub.com

www.pennmillpub.com

For updates about Clayton E. Spriggs' projects, new releases, and exclusive VIP promotions sign up on the Penn Mill VIP Mailing List.

EXCERPT

On the following pages we have included an excerpt from *Billy* by Clayton E. Spriggs.

COMING SOON:
BILLY

**Deep in the swamplands of Louisiana,
a monster is born.**

Hidden away in the cypress swamp of the Atchafalaya Basin, a cabin sits on pilings long driven into the murky water, home to a family of Cajuns known as the St. Pierres. A newborn joins their brood, a badly deformed infant who arrives unwelcome and unwanted. He is believed to be sent from the depths of hell itself as punishment for the unspeakable sin from which he sprang.

Soon, the boy grows into the monster they have feared all along. Seizing their opportunity, they drug him and chain him up in the attic until they are able to dispose of their curse once and for all. The only problem now is that they lose access to the dark, cramped space overhead. "No problem," exclaims Poppie St. Pierre. "No reason to ever go up dere again."

When the wrath of Hurricane Katrina comes to Bayou Noir, they are forced to confront the terror that awaits them.

In the aftermath of the great storm, a group of college kids set out to look for survivors, never to be seen again. Detective Nicholas Vizier is hired to locate the missing search party, and he recruits local gator hunters to aid in the search. As their expedition leads them further into the swamp, they find more than they bargained for. They find Billy.

From the opening chapter in the backroom of the cabin on Bayou Noir, to the creepy confines of St. Elizabeth's Institute for the Mentally Ill and the haunted ruins of Lost Bayou Plantation, 'Billy' will send you on a terrifying adventure until the shocking conclusion that will haunt you long after you put the book away. So, turn on the lights and prepare yourself for the horror that will surely come with every turn of the page and find out the answer to the riddle, "Why didn't they go up into the attic?"

Chapter One
Bebette

"**D**on't just stand dere, *couyon*; get some water berling!"

Dorcelia St. Pierre didn't suffer fools, even when the offending party was her husband. She could see her daughter was in agony, and the dimwitted patriarch of the family was doing nothing but getting in the way.

"You watch how you talk to me, woman. I'll not be trifled with in my own house."

The big, ugly oaf shot his wife a dangerous glance that she understood too well. Dorcelia knew her husband was cruel and could be violent when provoked, but she'd had enough. It was beyond repulsive what the sick bastard had done to his own daughter that brought them this shame, but the girl was in a perilous state.

365

"Ooooooohhh! Aaaaaagh!" the child shrieked in agony as she writhed in pain on the sweat-soaked sheets. Her cries echoed off of the bare cypress walls in the confined space of the back bedroom, competing with the clamor of the rainstorm that rumbled against the tin roof overhead.

"You need to go get Doc Besson before sumptin' bad happens," Dorcelia implored her husband in vain.

She knew the old fool wouldn't budge. He'd embarrassed the family with his unspeakable sin, and he'd do everything in his power to distance himself from the crime. Even the life of his only daughter didn't hold weight against his misguided sense of pride and instinct for self-preservation.

"You know 'taint happenin', woman," Poppie belligerently replied. "Da rain be comin' down strong for hours now. No way to get help now even if I were inclined to do so."

Poppie St. Pierre knew his wife well enough to know she was all talk. She stood silently by when he did those regretful things in a drunken, lustful state, and she now shared in the guilt. It was the girl's own mother that forbade any discussion on the matter, as if silence might retroactively undo the transgression or prevent its reoccurrence. She'd been proven wrong on both counts.

"Eeeeeehhh!" the girl screamed between labored breaths.

"Dis be on your head, *capon!*" Dorcelia spat back at her husband as she turned to tend to her afflicted child.

"You shut dat door. *Fait pas une esquandal!* You slow down dat racket," Poppie shouted as he turned his back on the women with righteous indignation. How dare she call him a coward under the roof he provided for her comfort! Damn woman's got a slappin' comin' her way, he thought, as he walked away and unsuccessfully attempted to put his daughter's screams of agony out of his mind.

Dorcelia slammed the wooden door on her husband's back and tended to her daughter's needs. She was no midwife, but she'd had two children of her own. Dorcelia took her daughter's hand, feeling the child's grip squeeze tightly. With her free hand she stroked the sweat from the girl's forehead and tried to soothe her as best as she could.

"Dere, dere, *cher*, shhhhh. It's gonna be alright. Momma's here."

"I'm scared, Momma," the girl cried.

"I know, Lillian. You gonna be fine. Jus' listen to me and do da best you can, and I'll pull you tru dis."

The girl nodded and started to breathe heavily as the torturous clawing in her gut resumed. Dorcelia pried her hand free of her daughter's grip and positioned herself at the foot of the bed in preparation for the imminent arrival of the family's newest member. She could see that her daughter was close now, and Dorcelia found herself as afraid as her daughter. She hid her feelings for the sake of her frightened child and swallowed hard.

"It's almost time, *cher*. You gonna have to push when I tell you and breathe when I tell you. It's gonna hurt sometin' awful, I ain't gonna lie to ya, but you gonna get tru it, I promise."

"Aaaaaaahhhhhh!" Lillian screamed and twisted on the bed as the baby inside of her tried to push itself out of her womb and into the waiting arms of a cruel world.

"Oooooooowwwww!"

"Push! Push!"

"Eeeeeeehhhhhh!"

"Breathe now, child."

Dorcelia could see Lillian was ignoring her instructions. The girl's face was turning red from the exertion as she bore down trying to expel the offending item from her body and the agonizing pain with it.

"Breathe, Lillian, breathe!"

A splatter of blood sprayed into Dorcelia's face, and she recoiled in disgust. Peering down between her daughter's legs she saw the baby's head emerge with force, then its slippery shoulders come out one at a time. Dorcelia took a deep breath and grabbed hold of the newborn to help guide it out.

She almost dropped the child in horror when it suddenly pushed out on its own in a violent fury, ripping a ragged gash in its mother's body, and spraying more blood around the room in its wake. Suppressing the abrupt sensation of nausea, Dorcelia held onto the wriggling baby in her arms and glanced up towards her silent daughter.

"*Oo ye yi!*" Dorcelia cried.

Lillian's face was forever frozen in agony, the last sensation she was to know in her short, sad life. The girl's eyes stared blankly towards the heavens while her limp body lay in a pool of blood on the dirty sheets. Her once ruddy complexion was now a ghostly white, contrasting with the blue lips of her repulsive grin.

Dorcelia's tears ran down her face as she cried in silence, her voice not able to reach the depth of her mourning. The wriggling ball of flesh in her arms broke her trance, and she glanced down at the baby she held. The child was covered in blood and amniotic fluid. Dorcelia grabbed the cleanest piece of cloth near her and began to wipe away the sticky mess and inspect the newborn. She could tell right away something was horribly wrong as she peered down into the baby's face.

"Bbbaaa aaa aaa!" the infant cried, spitting saliva and more blood into Dorcelia's face.

Dorcelia retched with disgust at the sight of the deformed baby in her arms. Its eyes were a reddish color, reminding Dorcelia of the blood that surrounded her. The baby's face was misshapen, and it resembled one of the vile creatures that inhabited the swamp more than it did a human being. His hips and legs were out of place, resembling those of a frog. The webbing around the baby's toes and its thick, discolored skin added to the child's reptilian appearance. She counted six claw-like fingers and toes on the revolting beast's appendages, which the devoutly Catholic woman took as a confirmation of God's condemnation of her husband's unforgivable sin and her own apathy to her only daughter's plight.

"My God, woman!" Poppie exclaimed as he burst through the door. "What is dat terrible noise? You scaring da chirren."

Poppie froze in horror at the unexpected sight before him. His daughter's contorted body lay lifeless on the blood-soaked sheets, and the vision of his wife reluctantly cradling what appeared to be nothing short of a monster in her outstretched arms made him stop short.

"*Qui c'est q'ca?* What is dat?"

"Dis be your doin', *Grand Beede'*. God has sent his judgment for your sin."

"*Oo ye yi*! It be a little monster. A *bebette!*" Poppie exclaimed with shame and horror.

He glanced towards the lifeless body of his daughter stretched out on the bed. "Lillian, what you done to us, *peeshwank?*"

"Don't be blamin' da girl or da baby. It your doin'. You be da only monster here," Dorcelia replied accusingly.

"Bwaaa waaaa bwaaa," the newborn cried.

Poppie was at a loss for words. He looked down at the deformed creature in his wife's arms with disgust before turning away in silence. He knew his wife was right. The creature was a curse from God for his unspeakable sin. He refused to acknowledge that it was merely a baby. If he admitted that to himself, he would be forced to concede it was his child. He was the monster's father. No, he refused to do that. It wasn't a baby at all; it was a curse. It was an unholy creature, a demon child, a little monster. The Cajuns had a name for such a beast – *bebette*.

EXCERPT

On the following pages we have included an excerpt from *The Dissector* by L L. Spriggs.

Another Great Mystery Novel from Penn Mill Publishing. Available in eBook and Paperback at Amazon.

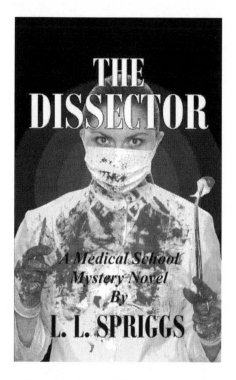

Greed, Lust, Revenge and Murder in a Medical School.

When Dr. Sarah Whitley entered the doors of the medical school, she thought the dream she had worked so hard for had finally come true. She had attained her first position as an Assistant Professor of Anatomy in a prestigious medical school in a uniquely historic city. Instead, what she found was the beginning of a nightmare that would change her life in ways she never imagined.

She had always looked up to the professors who had taught her throughout her education. They were 'all knowing'; they were never wrong; and they were well respected professionals - everything she aspired to be. It didn't take her long to discover that her new faculty colleagues were flawed human beings, driven by greed, ambition, and lust. And they all had one thing in common - fear. Fear of the powerful and ruthless, Dr. Roberts, the Head of the Department of Anatomy.

While all Sarah wanted was to concentrate all her efforts on becoming an effective lecturer and anatomy lab instructor, she inadvertently discovered the secrets hidden behind the closed doors of the offices and research labs of her fellow faculty - from the illicit affair between two scientists, to the sexual predator masquerading under the guise of a well-funded researcher, to the manipulative and double-crossing Department Head.

When compelled by Dr. Roberts to spend more time in the morgue, assisting with the embalming and preparation of the cadavers to be used in the medical school Gross Anatomy course, Sarah sees things that she shouldn't see. But asking questions could be dangerous...

Prologue
MEDICAL SCHOOL PROFESSOR MISSING
WHERE'S THE DOC?

You couldn't miss the headline on the front page of the Times-Picayune newspaper, and the story was featured on all three of the New Orleans television news programs - at least for a couple of days until something juicier came along. Several of the administrators of the Medical College of Louisiana were interviewed, but none of them had anything meaningful to contribute. They did, however, take the opportunity to praise Dr. Roberts for his leadership of the Department of Anatomy and for his years of service to the Medical College.

Gossip ran rampant among both the faculty and students of the medical school, and the rumors about what had happened to Dr. Roberts encompassed all possible scenarios - he was hit in the head and had amnesia; he was working for the CIA and had to go underground; he had run off to Tahiti with a Bourbon Street stripper; he was abducted by aliens. Dr. Lily Roberts, the good doctor's wife, was even more mystified by her husband's disappearance than anyone. She thought they had been close. After all, they had been married for forty-two years. Sure, they had had some rough spots in their marriage, but that was years ago, and they had gotten over that. In fact, they had been talking about his retiring soon so they could spend more time with their children and grandchildren in Ohio.

She had been a little irritated when he hadn't called to tell her he'd arrived safely in Lucerne, Switzerland for the conference he was going to attend. But she had just chalked that up to the time difference and the possibility that he had gotten caught up in greeting colleagues he hadn't seen for years. After two days of no word, however, she called the police.

First, the police contacted the hotel in which Dr. Roberts had been planning to stay, but the hotel had no record of his ever having checked in. They then contacted the airlines and found that his scheduled flight from New Orleans to New York had left on-time, but he hadn't been on it, nor had he been on his connecting flight to Lucerne. Just to make sure that he hadn't changed his plans at the last minute, the police checked all flights leaving New Orleans on the last night he had been seen. They found nothing.

A full scale investigation ensued and the detectives from the New Orleans Police Department made it a point to talk to anyone and everyone associated with the Anatomy Department, from maintenance people to full professors. They found out that the last person to see Dr. Roberts was Mrs. Sanders, his Administrative Assistant. She had left at her usual time, she said, and Dr. Roberts had still been in his office doing some last minute work before catching the airport shuttle for his trip.

After checking with the shuttle service, they found out that the shuttle had indeed picked up several people from that location on the night in question, but the company couldn't find a list of passengers. The shuttle driver didn't remember picking up anyone fitting Roberts' description, but that didn't mean much, he said, because there were quite a few passengers that night and he really couldn't be sure.

The detectives ran Dr. Roberts' credit cards through the system, but none had been used since the day of his disappearance. His bank accounts hadn't been touched. Same for his cell phone records. No calls going out; just a long list of unanswered incoming calls, most from his wife's number.

Despite the early publicity and the efforts of the Police Department, no new clues emerged and the case quickly went cold. The detectives had to move on to more pressing issues, but they assured Dr. Lily that the case would remain open and they'd continue to follow any new leads.

For her part, Dr. Lily Roberts spent most of her days ping-ponging between deep despair, soul-wrenching anger, and unrealistic hopefulness. Where was Yancey?

Dr. Yancey Roberts, it seemed, had vanished into thin air.

Made in the USA
Lexington, KY
09 February 2016